Trekked

Jamie Mayes

Edited by Ruby Boston

ISBN: 978-1-7347159-0-3

DEDICATION

To the little boy who stole my heart- Lee3.
To the man who held my hand- Dewayne.
For my sisters who feel their voices are not heard.

TREKKED

TABLE OF CONTENTS

TREKKED

INTRODUCTION

When I first started writing this book, my mission was to share the stories and struggles of being a black woman not only in America but across the world. As I created the characters of this book, I realized many other people played significant roles in shaping black women's practices, beliefs, and attitudes. Therefore, I had to incorporate those who helped this story about black women come to life. Still, there is no denial- this book *is* about the beauty, power, and prowess of black women. It analyzes the truth about how we are underestimated, undervalued, and overlooked, even though we are the cornerstone of our families, communities, and this world. This story begs two questions: Is resilience our greatest enemy or our most significant strength? Has humility obscured the pain of black women? So often, the physical and emotional neglect of black women seems permissible because we are so resilient. Our humility has frequently caused us to suffer in silence and to be misjudged as difficult and mean. Our stern demeanor is often criticized; however, our constant experience of being first to excel but last to be recognized has grossly impacted our tolerance in relationships and expectations of society.

Though this novel is a fictional depiction, it is a realistic story where I aim to present the juxtapositions of black womanhood, our communities, and the strength of family with the black woman's story being the central element of connectivity and success among all three components. This work is my opportunity to create an inclusive experience for humanity to feel the burden and blessing of being a black woman. As I penned the path of Madyson, one of the main characters, I realized the energy and influence of the black woman has a significant impact on the lives of our children, partners, and community. Therefore, I could not solely focus on the obstacles of the black woman; in doing so, I would undermine the very element of who she is- always caring for others, the lifeline for all humanity, and a warrior whose strength is magnified by each obstacle she conquers. Thus, Madyson becomes interconnected with the community where her misfortune takes place because it is the place where her pain, grief, and struggle become her power, motivation, and victory. For years, Grace has hidden her own pains and troubles by covering her trauma with smiles and pretending she is unbothered. She finally pulls back the burden of her shame and finds restoration in the strength of her daughter and the support of her husband. Leah is finally free to embrace the power that her great-grandmother gifted her and use her passion to propel further into her life's purpose.

Though the men's role may seem secondary in this work, their significance to this story should not be downplayed or misinterpreted. Men and women are the ying and yang of society; they balance right and wrong. Their singular experiences produce collective missions for change. They are the essential element of cultural change when they work together; they can also be the greatest hindrance to progress. The passion for change can exist within women, but the act of change can only occur when women and men work toward it. Therefore, this novel is not solely about black women; it is also about the essential role of men and the influence they have to help change move forward.

Mr. Blackston's support empowers his proactive wife, who is outspoken and comfortable in her skin. Blake's willingness to be open with his sister allows readers to see a more empathetic part of Leah. Brad's recognition of his wife's value is one of the most important reasons their family survives during an experience that could've torn them apart. On the contrary, we can see that men who do not have a moral compass can destroy themselves and weaken their communities.

In addition to celebrating the power and beauty of black women, I hope that this book brings forth the pains that black men and women have experienced. In recognizing the influence of the black woman and the need for her to experience elevation, I hope men and women can work together for the cause of alleviating so much of the pain we have experienced as black people. We must recognize the daily experiences of the black woman and her achievements despite the odds. We can then seek to lessen her strife by advocating for her and her children. I hope that the alleviation of her pain will help us propel forward in purpose and with pride, unapologetically celebrating all that black women have done to give life to this world.

As I wrote this novel, I considered my son, my godchildren, and my students- the torch carriers of the future. We can no longer minimize the cry in their voices and the need for an evolution that gives us equality, fairness, and opportunity. Future leaders must be given leadership and direction instead of criticism and minimalization of their pain. True, they are our ancestors' dream, but we must show them that every step of the journey leads to a more fulfilling life. They cannot be complacent with nor defeated by modern claims of unity and freedom, while so many of our brothers and sisters suffer at the hands of injustice and strife. Young leaders must be willing to become educated about our history, empowered to lead, and energized for a trek that is not easy but is worth the fairness, justice, and equality they deserve.

-Author Jamie Mayes

Trekked

TREKKED

TREKKED

CHAPTER 1

"I know you said you don't need it, but please take this cooler," Karen said as she held up the red and white cooler. It was a traveling cooler Karen had used for over twenty years. Each time the Johnson family traveled, Karen would pack the cooler with snacks and put it on the back seat. It was usually loaded with just the right mix of fruits, chocolate, candy and at least one bag of trail mix for her husband. Now, all of her children were grown, and Karen was trying her best to pass the cooler tradition to her youngest child. Madyson knew her Mom's goal, but she was determined to not take the faded cooler with brown smudges on the corners and a handle that popped loose occasionally.

"Mom, I don't want that Goliath-sized cooler taking up more space in my backseat," Madyson said as she gave a slight glance toward the back seat and then looked back at her mother. Madyson curved corners of her lips into the sweet smile that made her mom melt.

"You have nothing back there!" Karen peeked into the backseat one more time, "Please take it with you. I made your favorites: one with ham, Swiss cheese, and avocado and the other peanut butter with honey- Miss Bees Honey, to be exact. Ben, I even made bologna and cheese for you. I fried the bologna, so the edges are crisp just the way you like them. Please take it." She tried to shove the small cooler through the driver's window.

This was just like Madyson's mother. Karen Johnson was always over prepared, and she had a possible solution for any problem. Karen also believed in saving money. After raising three kids and taking museum and water park trips every summer, it was natural for her to pack a backpack anytime anyone in the family was traveling. Even when Karen's grandchildren came to visit, she was sure to pack snacks for their ride home. But this was not a family trip, and they certainly were not going to any museums or waterparks, so Madyson did not see a need for it. Still, it seemed her mother was nearly pleading for her to take the cooler.

"Let me do this. We will take one sandwich each and one bottle of water. How is that? Our goal is to stop and eat along the way. We want to check out roadside stands and local favorites. Louisiana and Mississippi have some of the best food in the South. Then, we must stop in Georgia to eat at some of those restaurants owned by the stars! How can we do that if you load us up with enough food for breakfast, lunch, and dinner? We can eat the sandwiches now since it's getting close to lunch, and then we will stop later on. How's that?" She decided to meet her mom in the middle. If Madyson took the cooler, her mom would add blankets, first aid kits, extra sets of clothes, and all kinds of things she did not need. They would also be delayed for at least another hour.

Karen reached into the cooler and pulled out the sandwiches and water. "Okay, take these two. Call me every few hours. Washington, D.C. is a long drive from here, and I just want to know that you guys are okay."

Their eyes locked for a minute. Madyson's mother did this every time she took a trip.

Madyson laid her forehead in her hand and shook it from left to right. "Mom, why are you acting like that is not the norm for us? How many times a day do we normally talk? I call you between almost every class," she laughed.

Karen closed the door and leaned on the driver's side window. "I know, but I can't believe you are going so far away alone. I can still change my plans and go with you. Your dad will be okay. He probably wants a break anyway."

"Mom, I'm not alone. Ben and I are taking this trip together. We are young adults; it's time, Mom. Besides, I've taken a few girls' trips, so this is not my first time traveling without you. I know D.C. is the furthest I've gone without you, but it is not as far as it seems, okay?" she said.

Karen Johnson took a deep breath and then looked at her youngest child. She looked at Madyson's hair, which was in small box braids that had been pulled to the top of her head and wrapped into a bun; then, she looked into Madyson's eyes. "Okay, okay. I'm just not prepared for you to become a woman. I need my little girl who is still hanging on my pants leg everywhere I go," she said as if she wished Madyson could return to her childhood.

"Ma, now you know I am always your little girl. It's Daddy who wants me to grow up and get out of his wallet," Madyson laughed. "I'll tell you what- when we get back, you can treat me to a mani-pedi and lunch at my favorite spot, and I will tell you everything about the trip. How's that?"

The twosome fell out laughing. "Aren't you the best

daughter ever?" Karen replied. "But I gladly accept your offer, and I am going to hold you to it as soon as you get back." Karen and Madyson heard a soft rumble and a sudden stop. Karen raised her head and looked over the hood of Madyson's car; Madyson looked out of her passenger window. Ben had just parked his car in front of the last door of the garage. He was getting his suitcase from the trunk. For a minute, he struggled to get the enormous leather suitcase. Ben pulled the brown hunk, and the brown hunk pulled back. He gave it one final jerk, and the bag came up out of the trunk before dragging Ben to the ground. He slammed the trunk shut and looked up to see two sets of eyes staring at him.

"What did I do?" He asked. He began dragging his suitcase to the car. It had no wheels, so it made a loud noise as he got closer.

"I have told him to order new luggage a thousand times. I knew I should've gotten him a new suitcase the other day," Madyson whispered to her mother. To Ben, she said, "Nothing. I was telling Mom not to worry about us."

Ben laughed, "Oh, yeah. Mama Karen, you have known me since I was a little boy. You know I will protect Madyson; look at these muscles." He flexed his arms, which were in decent shape even though he was not very big. There was a noticeable gap in his tee-shirt sleeve, which made his flex seem a little mightier than it needed to be.

"Well, you get the point. She's in good hands," Ben laughed.

Madyson shook her head from side to side. "Anyway, Mom," Madyson continued, "We will be fine. We have cell phones, roadside assistance, a tire changing kit, and sandwiches. Dad checked the tire pressure and the fluids this morning after you reminded him about five times last night. Thanks to you, we are very prepared."

Karen leaned in to kiss her daughter. "What would any of you do without me?" She laughed and then looked over at Ben. "And I know. Your mom and I already had our morning coffee talk. We both know you are the responsible one; it is this one who worries me. Out of all of my children, she gave me the most gray hairs." Karen patted the top of her head.

"Noooo," Madyson chimed in, "being old when you had me gave you gray hairs. Don't blame that on me!" They started laughing.

"Okay, your dad and I will be waiting to hear from you. He tried his best to take a half-day at the plant, but his crew was not meeting the deadline. He wants his last six months on this job to be strong, so he needed to stay. Dad said to tell you he loves you, and he put some extra money in the glove compartment."

"That's my daddy!" Madyson smiled. She started the car, "Okay, Mom, we won't make it to our half-way point before dark if we keep chatting with you. I will call you in two hours. I love you." She blew a kiss.

"I love you, too, Baby Girl. Remember, don't look too much like a tourist, or people will target you. And don't stop in small towns if you don't have to. Everywhere isn't friendly in the South," Karen replied.

"I got it. I got it all, Mom," Madyson said. Madyson put her shades on and turned her head to the side, so her cheek turned upward. Mrs. Johnson leaned in and planted a kiss right under Madyson's cheekbone.

Madyson started the car's engine and swiftly backed her shiny black Honda out of the driveway. Ben already had his headphones on, and he was bobbing to what she assumed was some old school hip-hop or J. Cole. He loved J. Cole. Ben followed him on every social media page, and he had been to three J. Cole concerts. He had even let his hair grow out for a little while, and then he got dreads claiming he was doing it because it was the style. Ben was never a guy of high fashion, and he certainly never did anything because it was the trend.

"He's like the Tupac of our generation," he had told Madyson when he went to his first J. Cole concert. "He's not a rapper; he is a philosopher. He talks about life and culture. It's not about a new dance or selling drugs and any fake street stuff like that. He is trying to get us to understand some things about culture, society, and the struggles of black life. His beats bring you in, but his lyrics speak to your struggle. Listen to him."

Madyson laughed. "Your struggle? Ben, you're from the Height Hills. Your biggest struggle is which pair of Jordan's to wear today," she said.

"That used to be my struggle, college girl. I, well, my parents were putting up $200 a pair to see me in the flyest kicks. I was out here yelling, 'Support black businesses,' but wasn't supporting my own empire. After I spent two hundred dollars on somebody else's gear, I couldn't do it anymore. I took that same two hundred a month and started putting it in a savings account. I've got no regrets about the way I see that money grow. Shit, I want Jordan money, too, and I can't get it if I'm spending it. I'd prefer to invest it in some work boots so I can keep doing these electrical jobs," he said.

Ben had done well for himself despite his parents'

disappointment that he had not gone to a four-year college. When he got his license as an electrician, he started taking contract jobs across the country. When they learned that Ben was making almost as much money as his dad and living nearly free when traveling for work, they saw his profession and their son a little differently. For a while, Ben had an upscale apartment, but he was gone so much that he asked his parents if he could move into the room over the garage and pay rent when he came home so he could save more money. They loved their son and agreed to the deal, insisting that he did not pay rent. They didn't use the room over the garage very often, so they moved his old bed out there and moved his dad's man cave to Ben's old bedroom in the house. Ben insisted on paying his parents, but his checks were rejected. So, he usually just put the money directly on his little brother's college tuition by calling the university.

He was proud of his little brother, and they had a close relationship. When Ben's brother went off to college, Ben made sure he was home to help pack his things and drop him off at the university. Though they were three years apart in age, they got along very well. Ben's brother sometimes traveled with him during the summer and holiday breaks from school.

"My brother got an extra scholarship this semester, so he didn't have a balance. I'm so proud of that dude; staying on top of his grades is really paying off." He had a small grin on his face, which was rare for someone who was always serious. "Can we swing by the ATM, and I will put money in my mom's account?" he asked.

"Why do you insist on paying your parents, especially after they asked you not to? You don't even stay that long?" Madyson said.

Ben replied, "I moved back out of convenience and to save some more money. My parents don't have to let me stay. Besides, I'm a grown man. A man pays even if no one asks him to."

"Still the boy I grew up with," Madyson jokingly said as she used one of her hands to pull her braided hair bun loose. The tiny braids cascaded downward, landing between her back and the driver's seat.

"A man," he said back forcefully. "I know you have enjoyed the playboys on campus, but every male doesn't have to be thirty to grow up. And we don't have to run through a bunch of women to sow our oats before deciding to do what's right. Some of us do the right thing, regardless."

Madyson looked at Ben. "Is this what you are doing the whole trip? Being woke and conscious and a strong black man for twenty hours? I'm just asking for myself because I want to have fun."

Ben rolled his eyes and let a grin ease across his face. Madyson was always his reminder to take it easy and enjoy himself. "Na'll, I promise to relax. I plan to splurge a little bit. I even brought my big wallet."

Madyson grabbed her chest and deeply inhaled as if she was appalled. "You brought the big wallet? Lord, help us! You might spend a hundred dollars at the mall! You might even let me shop at my favorite high-end store in peace since I saved my last four student worker checks for this trip. Maybe you will be twenty-two instead of forty-two this weekend!"

They both started laughing. Ben got her message; he was going to relax during this trip.

"Maybe," he said sarcastically, "I will do the best I can."

"Well, if I see anything I think will look fly on you, I will say that J. Cole or Tupac made it. I'll check the label to see if it came from the Motherland," she laughed.

"At least you know what moves me," Ben joked back.

Ben and Madyson had grown up down the street from each other. They had played together as children, and they knew nearly everything about each other. The most important thing they knew was that they were nothing alike. Madyson had struggled to stay on the honor roll her entire life, while Ben had coasted through his classes and taken honors and advanced courses for college credits. Madyson loved the arts and had been a dancer since she was four years old. She was talented, too. She was on the performance team and traveled with a dance troupe for a few years until she said competing kept her too busy. Madyson kept taking dance classes throughout high school but only a few times a week for fun. Ben was a computer nerd and historian who made a B in eighth grade P.E. because he could not learn to two-step. He enjoyed watching sports but had never played any. Instead, he spent his time reading or gaming with his friends and his little brother.

Madyson thought the world was a melting pot, and she was fully convinced that America belonged to men and women who worked hard. All it took was the dedication to overcome challenges and be successful in a country where freedom was a right. She knew there were some problems in society, but she preferred to surround herself with her diverse group of friends who "saw no color." They only believed in red- the color of blood when it hit the air. When discussions about race and culture came up, Madyson often said, "When love is in the air, it overpowers all hate." Her friends loved art festivals and pop music. They paid little attention to mainstream news, even giving the side-eye to social injustice issues. Their ideal solution was for everyone to look at each other on the inside, no matter how unrealistic the idea was. For Madyson and her friends, it was easier to avoid uncomfortable conversations and dealing with problems that happened right in their own community and school. That was where Ben and Madyson shared the most significant difference. Ben believed that America had disenfranchised every race except for the white race.

He spent his free time reading up on his ancestry and history, telling Madyson that there was so much to learn about the 350 years America leaves out of textbooks. Each year, Ben scored perfectly on the history state exam multiple-choice questions. The one thing that cost him points was his essay response. Instead of providing a textbook response, Ben used that section to write his rebuttal to the questions. His history teachers tried to get him to understand the importance of doing what the state wanted on the written part of the test.

Ben told one teacher, "I cannot be true to a system that is not true to me. I, therefore, choose only to be true to myself and my culture."

He once got defensive when a stranger attempted to compliment him by saying he was "woke." He told the guy that the only one who had been sleeping was America; black people had been unfairly misinformed. This mentality was often the wedge that separated and challenged Madyson and Ben's friendship. Ben's aggressive pro-black attitude was sometimes offensive to her. Though Ben claimed that pro-black did not mean he was anti-white, she felt uncomfortable when he brought up race issues, especially when her friends were around. So, she stopped inviting him to gatherings and social events unless it was a family affair.

It wasn't that she didn't value their friendship; he made it hard for her to be around people who saw the world as she did. She did think Ben was a bit aggressive, but she also knew that he was passionate, and he had a good heart.

Her other friends asked why she still hung out with him, and she never felt comfortable telling the truth, so she said she was kind to him because he needed someone, too. However, the reality was that Ben had always been her protector. All of Madyson's life, he had looked out for her like a brother. During her sophomore year of high school, they went to a house party. The DeLaughter twins, Erin and Aaron, had begged their parents to let them stay home alone while they went out of town for the weekend. Erin and Aaron were seniors, and they convinced their parents that they were technically adults since they were eighteen. Their parents fell for it, and the twins sent one text two-hours after their parents were gone. By ten o'clock that night, the house was filled with nearly every student from the school and several college students. The mansion was a one-story, 6,000 square foot California-style house with a red stucco roof. They had a heated pool and a jacuzzi with towering palm trees hanging over it in the back yard.

Cindy, one of Madyson's best friends, sent the text to her. She swore Madyson would have the night of her life. The DeLaughter twins were known across the city, and everybody wanted to be seen with them. Madyson's parents had a comfortable lifestyle, but the DeLaughter family had generational oil money, which came with popularity and power. A party with the DeLaughter twins sparked Madyson's interest. Cindy's statement proved to have quite some truth; they knew the night would be different as soon as they pulled up in front of the mansion. There were cars down the long driveway and outside of the iron fence. Music blasted from the house, and bright flashing lights were visible from the street. The electric energy could be felt before Madyson and Cindy made it to the front door. Madyson didn't hold back; she followed Cindy's lead. Madyson had always been easy to persuade, so she only needed a little friendly encouragement to take the three-shot challenge.

"I've never drunk before," she told Cindy.

"That's the great part, Madyson! It's going to be even more fun. I promise your party life will go to another level." The sea of cream-colored faces jeered as Madyson contemplated whether to take the shot.

"It's vodka. Don't be scared, Madyson. It's a baby drink for newbies," Cindy coached as the crowd looked on. Cindy was a gorgeous blonde-haired, brown-eyed white girl that the girls envied, and boys loved. Cindy was most popular for being pretty because she could care less about being perceived as anything else. She was nice; she was just shallow. Her parents' money kept her in a nice car and top-of-the-line clothes. Her parents didn't have DeLaughter money, but they were well off.

She and Madyson had become friends in elementary school, long before Cindy knew the value of being pretty or understood that her dad was successful. They had remained friends because they liked so many of the same things, even though Cindy's lifestyle was much faster and a lot freer than Madyson's. Cindy was the opposite of Ben and one of the first people to tell Madyson that he was too "weird" for them.

Madyson looked around the room and saw Ben leaning against the wall with one of his friends. He was watching Madyson intently, and she knew he was trying to decide whether to run over to stop her. He didn't, though; their eyes met briefly, and he turned his head to talk to his friend. Ben didn't even fit in at this party. He didn't drink, pop pills, smoke weed…or party, for that matter.

"Come on, Madyson, don't be scared!" someone suddenly yelled.

"Yeah!" The crowd screamed.

Rock music was blaring, and the dim lights in the house now seemed brighter, almost like spotlights shining on Madyson. She was on stage, and the show was just beginning. Some people were dancing, but most of them were in the kitchen, packed around the giant island, egging Madyson on. They were cheering as if she were a quarterback at a national championship game. Even though Ben's eyes told her she should not do it, the adrenaline of the crowd was more powerful than Ben's cold stare. Madyson closed her eyes and squeezed the shot glass tightly, hoping to erase the sight of Ben's judgmental face. She put the shot cup to her lips and leaned her head back. The crowd went wild. The music got louder, and the group was going crazy. She took a huge swallow and felt a fiery burn as the alcohol crawled down her throat.

Madyson brought her head forward and expected to see Ben leaning against the wall, but he was gone.

Her friends weren't, though; they were cheering her on to take another shot. So, she did. And she didn't stop there. Madyson spent the night taking shots and playing drinking games. Cindy had been drinking with her, but when Cindy's boyfriend interrupted the duo's party, she left. Madyson stumbled about the room, and the crowd was still hyping her up to take another shot. However, it wasn't as much fun without Cindy, so she babysat a mixed drink for a little while and giggled with some girls she had seen at school. Even though they didn't know each other well, they managed to find plenty to giggle about until Madyson became bored and needed to pee. She stumbled across the room, trying to find the bathroom. She got up too quickly and instantly felt the effects of six shots and two cups of a random punch they mixed up in a trashcan. The room started spinning; Madyson's body was tingling, and her legs felt too heavy to pick up. She kept trying to move, but it felt as if bricks were tied to her feet. She leaned against the wall, and it became her safe spot. Just as Madyson gave up on any hopes of trying to move, she felt her body being lifted. She felt a bright light shining in her face. For a moment, she thought she had reached a spiritual realm; maybe God was calling her home. She realized that God probably wasn't wearing cologne, and she wasn't sure if God would be massaging her butt.

"Wherrrreee…" she moaned as her body floated in the arms of the stranger.

"Shhhhh," he said, "I'm taking you down the hall to sleep this off."

"Wheeerrreeee…." Madyson grunted again.

The voice laughed softly. "To the room to lay down. Everything's going to be fine. I guess you had too much fun tonight. Just relax; I've got you."

Madyson could hear other voices, but she was not sure who they were. Her head was too heavy to lift it and see. *Maybe they are disciples,* she thought to herself.

Madyson let her body go limp in the stranger's arms. She had no idea who was holding her, but she was so drunk she could not find the strength to argue. She had no energy in her to fight, and she was sure she would vomit at any minute. Sleep (or unconsciousness-she was not sure) was just starting to settle in when her body suddenly jolted.

"Where the hell are ya'll taking her?" she heard someone ask.

"Man, what are you talking about? To the room to lie down. She's drunk," her savior said.

"You are damned right, and you know she is. So why are *you* and Rico taking her to the room?"

"Man, look, Ben, I'm not here for this tonight. I'm just trying to be a good friend to Madyson. Why don't you and your gangsta crew get out of here before we have a problem?" Madyson's hero said; he sounded angry.

"Hell na'll. We ain't going nowhere until you put Madyson down. *I'll* take her home; we live near each other anyway. I know about your track record, Kade. You find the drunkest one at the party and act like you are trying to help them; then, you knock 'em down. And I guess you brought a little audience to watch or maybe try to participate. Well, it's not happening tonight; we will all beat your ass." Two of Ben's friends had arrived at the party, and they were standing behind him like bodyguards. Everyone knew Ben was not the type to fight, but his friends would not hesitate to handle any situation on his behalf.

"You heard him," one of Ben's friends said, "Put Madyson down."

"Man, look, I'm not repeating myself. I said put her down!" Ben said. Kade huffed and then put Madyson down. She was still horribly drunk and began stumbling. Ben and his friends grabbed her and started walking toward the door. Kade looked at Rico, who had been recording the situation.

Ben turned around and walked toward Rico. He stopped and looked right at the camera, "You put out one video about her, and we will all come for your ass, too."

Rico and Kade looked around for their friends. Though they outnumbered Ben and his duo, the room was now quiet and still. Even the music had stopped playing. Kade looked down the hall; most of the teens from the party watching to see what would happen next. He looked around at his crew again. One of them started looking at his hands and then tucked them into his pocket, never making eye contact with Ben. Everyone had heard the rumors about how Kade raped drunk girls while his friends would stand outside the door to keep an eye out until he finished his work. Kade was filthy and vile, and his friends weren't much different.

Kade's parents eventually knew, too. Not long after the incident with Madyson, one of Kade's friends threatened to turn him in. The claim was that he had a video of Kade bragging about how he had sex with two of the cheerleaders while they were passed out in the bed at a house party on the lake, and Rico had recorded it, too. Suddenly, Kade disappeared and then appeared on Live Chat Express saying his family has been willed some money and decided to start over in a new city.

He was lying by a pool with shades on while the sun was glistening on his tan chest. In the background was a girl in a yellow bikini walking around the side of the pool.

"Get your game up!" he bragged before turning the video off.

If what Kade was doing was part of the game, there were a lot of people losing. That night, Ben made sure Madyson wouldn't be one.

Ben tried his best to cover for her drunkenness, but he could not come up with a viable explanation; Madyson wasn't allowed at house parties in the first place. She was grounded for a month, and her traveling abroad trip was canceled.

"If we can't trust you in the same city, we damned sure can't trust you in another country. It looks as if you will just have to find a job this summer," her father said. He was infuriated and hurt. He had given Madyson nearly everything she wanted; there was hardly anything to which he said no. Her mother was lost for words and didn't talk to Madyson much for almost a week. What hurt Madyson the most was the morning she found her mother quietly crying over her coffee. If they had learned that her irresponsibility had almost cost her virginity, their relationship would have been permanently tarnished. Madyson spent months apologizing to Ben and thanking him for keeping that night a secret. She then knew that regardless of how awkward he seemed around her other friends, she could always count on Ben to look out for her. As Madyson's high school years ended, so did many of her so-called friendships, including her faux friendship with Cindy. Life changed; Madyson changed, but her relationship with Ben remained the same. He was always her friend, loyal and honest, but never judgmental.

With the skies bright and the sun beaming down, the day looked perfect as they turned out of the bank's driveway and headed down the highway. They listened to the radio for a while, opting for an old school R&B station with relationship talk segments between the songs. Madyson looked at Ben endearingly. Madyson and Ben had been jamming and having car karaoke to some oldies when the talk show host, Teddy the Man, came back on. Teddy was the most popular radio host in the area, and he was known for causing a stir in relationships with his questions and topics of the day.

"Hello, lovers and loved ones! We are back, and we are answering the question, 'What color is your love? Black, White, or any color that comes in the box? Caller number one, what do you say?" the show host asked.

"Well, my love is any color that comes in the box. I used to say I'd only date black women, but then I met a white woman who was so sweet, kind, and loving. I just couldn't deny it anymore. Ooh wee, she made me feel so good; I had to let her know how I felt. My family was, well…surprised, but they started calling her white chocolate, and the rest was history. It's been eight beautiful married years!" one caller said.

The host chimed in. "Humph! And they lived happily ever after in the swirl! Isn't that beautiful? Next caller."

It was an older woman. "Well, Teddy, I've dated many races, Asian, Arab, Hispanic-"

"Damn, sis!" he interjected.

"Well, it's a big world we live in, Teddy," she said with a smooth, sensual voice. "In the end, nobody connected with me, related to me, and could ultimately move me like my tall, black, strong brother. I met my king, and it's been love ever since; we just got engaged!"

"Well, well, well. They say black love is a powerful thing," Teddy said. "Let me turn on a throwback love song for all the lovers out there...black, white, yellow, red, orange, green. Good R&B brings together all lovers!"

Madyson looked over at Ben, "I already know how you'd answer that question-"

"No, you think you know," he said.

"You'd date a woman outside your race?" Madyson asked.

"No, I would not." He said, laughing. "But I don't tell other people what to do when it comes to love. I actually chatted with an Asian girl for a while; she loved my hair. Said my skin color drove her wild. But I couldn't get into her. We could only talk about surface stuff like food and hobbies. If we talked about the news, I felt like I had to be careful about what I talked about because we didn't see things the same way. Hell, we didn't live life the same way. I need a queen who could relate to me. Even if she thinks I am too strong-willed, she knows why I'm this way. It's only one type of woman who can get that- she's a woman who looks like me and can feel what I feel. Besides, black women are built like goddesses, and I'm not just talking about the body. The way she thinks. Her attitude and swagger; the way she says something and how she says what she needs to say. The way she commits herself to everybody, even people and things that aren't her problem. If a black woman shows up, she feels she has to fix what's broken. She might feel hurt that she doesn't get full recognition, pay, or appreciation, but that doesn't determine whether she will do the right thing. Shit, I ain't found another like her. I love my queens."

And just like that, Madyson felt 10,000 feet higher- uplifted, empowered- and Ben wasn't even talking about her. But she couldn't let Ben know that; there was only so much leverage and power she was willing to give him. Too much credit, and he'd have his chest puffed out.

Instead, she said, "Sounds like you like a woman who pretends to be your mama."

"Madyson, being my mama and being like my mama are two different things. I don't need another Mama. I can do my own laundry and make myself clean my room. However, my mama is a good wife to my dad. Why wouldn't I want a woman with that quality? Don't you want a man who is like your dad?" he asked.

"No!" Madyson blurted with laughter. "He's cheap, and I don't need that negativity in my life."

They both laughed. "I know you are joking," Ben said. "Man, your dad thinks the world of you and your sister. Besides, your dad's not tight; he's money-wise. Taught me a few things."

"Well, wouldn't you make the ideal son-in-law," she retorted with a snort and chuckle.

"I would've married your sister, but she was too old for me," he said, laughing. He was always quick with his comebacks, and it made Madyson laugh even harder.

They drove for the next hour listening to the radio in silence, interjecting a small talk in between. Eventually, Ben reached into the backseat and found the sandwiches. Ben munched on his sandwich and then asked Madyson if she wanted hers. He polished that one off too. "I'll tell you what," he said with his mouth full, "I don't know what your mom does to these sandwiches, but they taste so good."

"It's called mayonnaise," Madyson joked, but she knew what it was. Her mama did everything with love. She made sure peanut butter touched every corner of the bread and that the bananas were carefully placed in rows. All slices of banana were as close to the same thickness as possible. The bologna was fried with the edges and center evenly browned, and the cheese melted between two slices of good quality bread, not the dollar bread at the bottom of the shelf in the store. In essence, she made everything with love. When food was made with love, it always tasted different. Ben ate both sandwiches, savoring each bite. When her mom called, Madyson could say they enjoyed the sandwiches. Ben enjoyed eating them, and she enjoyed watching them disappear.

After what seemed like a long trek, they crossed the Louisiana line.

"What?" Ben looked up and smiled.

"Nothing," Madyson replied. "I'm just happy I'm taking this road trip with my best friend. We needed this!"

"Yep," he smiled. "Who knows how long it will be before we see each other again. I start my last long-distance job when we get back. And when I finish that at the end of the year, our new business should be up and running. We will be handling electrical jobs all across the region."

"Um, Benjamin, you're pretending like we don't talk every day," she replied.

"Yeah, but it's never the same as seeing each other. Eating lunch on camera is never the same as eating in person," Ben said.

Madyson shook her head in agreement. "True, but there's nothing like you waving your steak or fancy pear-glazed pork chop lunch in my face while I enjoy my nutritious wheat crackers at the nursing school's front desk.

"Hey, young one," Ben said as he rubbed his stomach like an old man and started grinning, "your season is on the way. You will eat as many of those fancy avocado bowls as you like."

"Aw, the perks of being a real grown-up," she laughed. "I keep thinking about how cool it is that you guys are opening your own company. Mom and I drove by the new building site the other day, and it is coming along quickly. My best friend is totally doing it big!"

Ben looked down bashfully. "Oh, really? As much as you complain about nursing, you have done a hella of a job getting through school. You will be graduating from college in December. You already said you don't want to come back here, and the hospital where you did your internship offered you a job. That's another reason this fall-break trip is perfect for us. It's our last chance to be free before we both have grown folks' problems." They laughed.

Madyson turned on her signal, swerved into the lane of oncoming traffic, and passed up a slow-moving car. "That all sounds great, but I don't know if I am ready to be away from my parents. I mean, I could just get a job in town."

Ben put his phone down. "Madyson, it's time to grow up. You can't come back here to live with Mommy and Daddy and let them treat you like a little girl. I know you. You just don't want to take on grown-up responsibilities."

It was hard for Madyson to admit how scared she was to be a grown-up. Even though she did some things for herself, her parents took care of almost everything, including her car note, insurance, and cell phone bill. Madyson's mother even called the university to check the balance on her fee bill each semester, and Karen had the log-in for her financial aid information so she could complete Madyson's paperwork. Madyson only had to schedule her classes and show up to class each semester. All of those responsibilities would soon belong to her, and she just wasn't sure she could handle it all. Madyson used to deny it when her siblings talked about how spoiled she was, but the closer she got to graduation, the more she realized her parents had made her life extremely comfortable.

"I'm not ready yeeeeeet!" She stretched out the word "yet." "I need about two more years, and I will be ready."

Ben laughed. "Yes, you are. You are more ready than you think. Your parents can't keep babying you, and I know it was your mom who put this in your head. Damn, I love her too, but she has everybody spoiled, especially you."

"And what's wrong with that?" she asked.

"Nothing," Ben started, "except you'll never grow up. Your parents are getting old, and the world is hard for a woman, especially a black woman. Your parents babying you could backfire one day. This world does not give a damn about your mama and daddy or you."

"Yeah, yeah. You talk so much noise, but one day you will have a daughter, and I want to see how tough you will be on her."

Ben reached for the car cell phone charger and

plugged it into his phone. "I wouldn't mind a pretty little Angela Davis or Shirley Chisholm."

"A Shirley Chisholm?"

"Not the name, the woman. She was revolutionary and brilliant. I want her to lead and not be afraid to speak her mind either." Ben's voice faded, and Madyson could see the passion in his eyes as he thought about the future.

She laughed and shook her head. "I can see it now- a little natural fro in the classroom telling the teacher that white history isn't American history and that she should educate herself. Little Shirley will be wearing dashikis and making every class project about the black man's brilliance."

"Hopefully, that will no longer be a fight she has to take on. Maybe by then, black history will be incorporated into the educational curriculum across America; we won't be begging to have it as a possible elective. She can focus on leading, not advocating."

Madyson chuckled inside; he had already forgotten about his promise to relax. "I'll tell you one thing for sure, Ben. The woman who marries you must be on top of her business. You did not come to play games," Madyson laughed out loud and rubbed his shoulder.

He smiled. "At least you know." He connected his headphones into his phone and reclined his seat. J. Cole was ministering to him again.

Madyson didn't disturb his rest; she used the time to enjoy the radio and do some thinking. Even though she was one semester behind, it seemed as if the college years had zoomed by too quickly. Madyson thought about the last four years and wondered if she had done enough. She had only attended a few parties. She only joined one organization, and that was the one for nursing majors. Madyson had hoped time would slow down, but it seemed that time was speeding up. Becoming an adult reminded her of all the changes in friendships and relationships. She hardly kept in touch with any of her childhood friends, and she didn't even miss most of them. Her greatest longing was to simply come home to her parents and sleep as much as she could before going back to school.

Nursing school had opened her eyes to the process of aging. Some of the patients she saw came in walking. Some came in on a stretcher; some arrived in a wheelchair. Regardless of how they came in, none of them would ever leave the same. She had seen people at peace with old death and devastated with young death; yet, death still came. Madyson felt her youthfulness was a safe place that kept her shielded from the difficulties of the world. When she wasn't in nursing mode, she could call her mother or even Ben or her sister, and the world of sickness and pain existed no more. Madyson feared that moving away from those who kept her youthful would cause her to grow older much faster than she was ready to.

Madyson looked at the sky. The sun was just starting to go down, but it was still daylight. Madyson looked at the clock. It was after 5:30. She had not called her mom yet, and she knew there would be a lot of hellraising if she didn't call soon. Madyson fumbled around between the cup holder and the stick shift. She exchanged glances between the road and the console, trying to locate her cell phone.

"Damn," she mumbled as she felt her phone brush her fingers and then heard it fall to the floor of the passenger's side.

"Ben," she called. "Ben."

She wasn't sure if he was asleep, but he heard nothing she said. Madyson didn't want to wake him; Ben had come to her house after driving into town from his last job. She knew he was tired. Madyson looked at the road once again and then looked at her phone. It had slid behind her seat on the floor. *I can reach it,* she thought to herself. She turned her head to the side, hoping this would help her reach the phone. She could not get down quite far enough, so she came up to check the road again. Then, she reached down, this time taking her eyes from the pathway to stretch her fingertips to reach the tip of the phone, which had slid even further away. Just as she pushed the phone closer, Madyson felt the car veering across the road and realized she could no longer see where she was going. Madyson jerked her body up and looked around quickly. She had swerved onto the shoulder of the road and was driving in the grass. She turned her wheel sharply, nearly losing control of the small car. After a few more swerves from the shoulder to the edge of the yellow lines, Madyson finally gained control of the vehicle.

"Man!" Ben yelled. The commotion had awakened him. "What happened? You fell asleep or something? Do I need to drive?"

Madyson laughed. "No, no, I was trying to miss a deer, and I just got a little carried away." She was not telling him that she was reaching for her phone. She'd never hear the end of it. Ben believed in safe driving. He was the type that bought a cell phone holder even though his car had Bluetooth capabilities.

"A deer in the daytime? Look, if you are sleepy, I can drive," he said.

"You can drive? I think you are the one who was

snoring a few minutes ago. I got this. Go back to sleep, but can you hand me my phone in the back before you do?"

"Sure, just tap me if you change your mind. Hell, I am trying to make it to my next birthday," Ben picked up her phone and then put his headphones back on.

Madyson let out a small chuckle; Ben never trusted her driving. She looked at her phone and then realized the Bluetooth was connected, and she could have voice dialed her mom from the steering wheel anyway.

She scrolled to her mother's number and clicked on "Mom." The phone started ringing.

"Hey, Baby!" her mother chirped on the other end. "How is it going?"

"It's going okay. According to the GPS, we are leaving Shreveport, and we are heading toward a city called Monroe, so we are making it in good time."

"Yes, I know where Monroe is. We used to go up there to visit some friends years before you were born. You're making good time, and that's a good place to stop for the night. Where's Ben?" Madyson could tell that was more of a demand than a suggestion.

Madyson looked over at him. "Where do you think he is? Fast asleep like Dad would be," Madyson replied.

"Well, is he going to help you drive?" she asked curtly.

Madyson rolled her eyes. She knew her mother would find a way to fuss. "Of course, he is, Mom," she replied. "We agreed that I would drive on the first day, and he will drive on the second. We can both have a full day to enjoy riding and stopping for sites, too. On the way back, we will do the same thing. The good news is Ben has slept nearly the whole way, so I haven't had to stop yet."

"Okay. Well, did you eat your sandwiches?"

"Mom, yeah, we definitely enjoyed them. You know you make the best sandwiches." She didn't dare tell her mom that Ben had eaten them; she and Ben wouldn't hear the end of that for the rest of their trip.

Karen was silent for a minute. "I guess I just shouldn't have packed those. You don't need me babying you anymore."

Madyson sighed and felt a little guilty. Her mother tended to be overly sensitive about getting to do things for any of the children. If they seemed less than energetic about her attempts to be a good mother, her feelings were hurt. "Mom, you know I need you. I just don't want you putting up a fuss behind me. I appreciate the food and everything you do for me. I am always going to be your baby girl."

"Oh, I know. It's just so hard to accept that you are getting ready to graduate from college. Then, you will really be a grown-up. I am just not ready. You are the last of the bunch, and I am about to be an old lady with an empty house. I guess I will need to get some cats."

Madyson and Karen burst out laughing. Even though they laughed, Madyson realized the changes in her life were affecting her mother quite a bit.

"I mean, you have to chill with the drama, Mom. I don't even know what I am going to do when I graduate. Besides, if it means that much to you, you and Dad can take care of me as long as you want."

"Well, that's the tricky part. Your daddy loves his little girl, but he can't wait to get you out of his pockets. He swears you cost more than all of your siblings, even though your big sister did all of those pageants."

"Mom, he says that all of the time."

"The difference is he knew how to give her a limit and tell her no. He still has not figured out how to tell you no, and you know it. He *still* goes on and on about your eighteenth birthday. 'She said she wanted a real-life Mexico experience, so the whole family went to Mexico. The girl damned made me go into my retirement!'"

"But Mom, we got a great deal on group tickets, and my brother and sister paid their own way!" Madyson recalled.

"Girl, you know your dad believes anything above $500 is expensive, even if it's his annual tickets to the football game. Daddy Johnson says he doesn't know why the tickets are so high when the coaches and players make way more money than he does, but he still orders the seats closest to the sidelines," Karen said.

They exchanged "hums" and "sure doeses" for a minute before it was silent. Karen took a deep breath.

"Anyway, I am not going to keep you. It's getting late, Madyson. You guys need to find somewhere to stay in the next two or three hours if you don't stay in Monroe."

"Yeah, we plan to get a room in Jackson, Mississippi. That's only a few hours away," Madyson finally admitted.

"Okay! Well, I will be waiting to hear from you. Ben, wake up!" she shouted. Ben didn't move.

"He has on earbuds, but he's okay, Mom. He had just gotten home not long before we left."

"I love you, Baby Girl," Karen said.

"I love you, too."

"Bye," they chimed at the same time.

The phone line went silent.

Madyson looked at the GPS. They were somewhere in the middle of north Louisiana, and Monroe was about thirty minutes away. They had been on the road for about three hours and had not made any stops since leaving Dallas. Madyson was trying to get to Monroe before making a stop. However, she had to use the restroom, and she was starting to do the pee-pee dance in her seat. She looked at Ben once more; he was sound asleep. Madyson looked at the GPS again. They were covering good mileage as they neared the next city. Her mother had warned her about stopping on back roads and in unfamiliar places. They weren't exactly traveling on the back road; it was still considered a highway. They had decided to take the highway instead of the interstate because they wanted to enjoy the ride and because it was not far from their first destination.

Madyson wanted to make it to the city, but her bladder was giving her location no consideration. She had to go. Up ahead, Madyson saw an old gas station on the side of the road. It was run down, but it was open, and it had fairly new gas pumps. Madyson pulled over and decided not to wake Ben, who was snoring. She could run to the restroom and come back before he even noticed they had stopped. There were one car and two big pick-up trucks in the dirty-gravel parking lot. One of the vehicles proudly displayed a confederate flag in the back of the window. The bumper sticker read, "Fighting terrorism since 1863," and it had a confederate flag beneath it.

Hum, she thought, *What happened in 1863?* Madyson was never a keen history student for this very reason; she was horrible at remembering dates. She would have to google this later or ask Ben, but now, she needed to pee. Madyson left the car running and got out. She did the pee-pee dance to the front door and pulled it open.

At the counter was an old white lady with grayish-blonde, shoulder-length hair. As Madyson got close to the counter, she could see her face a little better. She looked as if she might have been pretty once, but hard work and sadness had ruined her. Wrinkles pushed downward on the sides of her mouth, and "M" shaped wrinkles creased her forehead. Her skin was tan, but not from the bed; it looked more natural and un-fading.

"Whatcha need?" She asked in a backwoods, country-twang voice.

"I need to use your restroom, please. Do you have one?" Madyson asked.

Just then, Madyson heard a noise behind her coming from the back of the store.

"It's broke," a dense, raspy voice said. Madyson could hear the voice breathing before she saw the person. A greasy white man with a dirty ball cap on that said "All American" was coming up the aisle. He had long stringy hair; his t-shirt was dirty, and it showed his slender but pot belly.

"Can't nobody use it," he grumbled.

"Damn it, Randy," the lady barked, "I just told you he fixed that toilet this morning. You just don't listen. You don't run nothing around here, no ways. Probably pissed outside because you wanted to anyway." She rolled her eyes and wiped down the counter with a dirty white towel. She seemed less than pleased to see Randy.

The woman reached for the key, which was hooked to a giant tire. "Go to the back of the building and make sure you close it when you come out."

Madyson turned to go to the restroom. Randy's

face was strawberry red. It was then that Madyson noticed two other men standing in the back of the store staring at her. They all had on hats, and one of the caps was just as torn and dirty as Randy's. The hat on the third guy's head had Confederate flags all over it. The men weren't saying anything, but their eyes sent a message that made Madyson shift her weight from one foot to the other. For the first time, Madyson felt uncomfortable being the only black person in the room. She felt as if she didn't belong.

Madyson kept walking to the door, and the men kept watching her. Just as she was about to head to the restroom, she changed her mind. Even with her back to them, she still felt the men watching her. She could feel their eyes creeping up the back of her shirt and dancing on her neck, which made her hair stand on its ends.

"Never mind. I will stop at the next place. Thank you," Madyson said. She handed the key back to the woman, and briskly walked out of the door. She was so nervous that she began frantically searching her pockets for her keys, forgetting that she had left the car running. She looked up, and the men were now staring out the window.

Madyson got into the car, backed out of the gravel parking lot, and headed down the road. It was starting to get dark. Fluffy clouds had become thin lines across the sky, which glowed with dark orange and purple tint. Low growls came from Ben, who was still fast asleep. Madyson could hear Tupac's "Me Against the World" coming from one of his earbuds, which had fallen onto his shoulder. She had decided to let Ben sleep until they arrived in Monroe. It would be nearly dark then, and she would need him to keep her company on the way to Jackson. She was still shaken from her encounter in the store, but she started to giggle when she heard, "The projects is full of bullets; bodies is droppin'" blaring from Ben's earbuds. Madyson laughed harder when she thought about how whether Ben could relate to the lyrics. He was so "woke" sometimes, she wondered if he had gotten enough sleep. He insisted that times hadn't changed much since the sixties and that black people had to invest in themselves and "call white people out on their bullshit." Those were his exact words. Madyson disagreed, but she learned to be quiet. Arguing with Ben about culture was like pouring gas on a brush fire; it was sure to take off.

The sun had gone down a bit more, but the stop at the gas station had slowed down their progress. They were only a few miles closer to Monroe. A sign said they were about eighteen miles away. Madyson heard a beep and then saw her cell phone flash. "Damn it. I guess I need a new charger," she muttered as she looked at the five percent notification. Now, she would have to stop in Monroe, or her parents would have a fit if they could not reach her. She turned on the radio and began searching for a local radio station. The radio scanned for a few moments and then stopped at a station where a high-energy D.J. was mixing music and cranking up the evening show.

"Yo, yo, you! It's D.J. Flow, and I'm here with you for Dinner Time Dynamite. Don't turn your radio off because I have the party you need to get you home. I know it's been a long day, but it's Friday, and I promise you I'm gettin' your weekend started right!" Hip-hop music started blasting from the radio. It was something Louisiana people called Bounce Music, telling listeners to shake it, twerk it, bounce it, and work it. Madyson began waving her hands and moving her waist to the beat of the music. She loved Louisiana music; it made her want to party and reminded her of the time when some of her friends and she went to New Orleans for the Bayou Classic. Louisiana music was infectious; she felt like it went into her soul and awakened parts of her she didn't know existed- the parts that she had been told only girls at the hood schools could understand. The rapper directed her to shake her booty, so she shook it. He asked for her name, so she screamed it. Then she turned the music up so loud she woke Ben.

"Whoa! What's going on? You know you don't rock with the hood like that," he laughed and murmured in a low voice; his eyes were still closed. He ran his hand across his eyes and opened them slowly.

"Ben, don' make fun of me," she retorted. "I can get down when I need to. I didn't just dance on the dance line, okay?"

"Oh, can you?" He laughed.

"Yes, I can. You must've forgotten. Who came in second place against a New Orleans chick at the Classic?"

Ben laughed. "I'll give you that. For someone who had never been to a black bowl game and had never been to an HBCU, you represented. I guess that was your 'for the culture' moment."

"See, there you go, Ben. Why do I need to be an activist when you do it for me?"

"I know what you want, Madyson, and I'm not giving it to you. I just woke up, and I am not about to give you another black culture lecture this soon. We have about sixteen more hours left for me to do that."

Madyson twisted her face and said with a smirk, "You just woke up? My brotha, I thought you were always woke!" They burst out laughing, and Ben threw up his "power-to-the-people" fist, which made Madyson laugh even harder.

The bounce song ended, and commercials promoting car accident lawyers selling their claims to get people millions for a stubbed big toe came on. Madyson's mind drifted back to her experience at the store. Even though she didn't want to tell Ben what happened, Madyson couldn't stop thinking about how uncomfortable she felt about the eerie experience.

"Ben, the weirdest thing happened when you were asleep. I stopped at a gas station a few miles back- "

"-you stopped?" Ben asked. Madyson hadn't wanted to tell Ben because she knew how he would react. He was no better than her mother regarding how they felt about stopping in unfamiliar towns, especially small ones in the South.

"Yes, you were asleep, and I really had to pee. Well, I still need to, but it's not as bad. Anyway, I had to get the key and go outside to use it. There were some really freaky looking men in the store, and they just kept staring at me. They made me so uncomfortable."

Ben sat up in his seat. "Madyson, the next time wake me up."

"Ben, I just needed to run- "

"I don't care. Wake me up. You can be so careless sometimes. We are out here in the middle of nowhere, and we know nobody except each other. That's not cool. Anything can happen. And, hell yeah, they looked at you strangely. We are out in the middle of the damned woods. I know you haven't been exposed to much, but you should know better than that," Ben chastised.

Ben was right. Her parents would have a fit if they

knew what she did. Her mother had told her at least ten times not to go anywhere alone on this road trip.

"I know, and I am sorry," she said.

"It's all good. I just know your mom and dad would have my ass if anything happened to you," Ben said as he laid his head back on the seat.

"That's true," Madyson laughed.

The D.J. had started another round of music, and they passed a sign that said thirteen miles to Monroe. It was now dark, and occasionally, headlights would dot the highway in front of them. The sky and the roads were clear; Madyson and Ben were in and out of chatter as they coasted the next three miles. As they drove down the highway, they noticed a sign ahead that read "Detour."

"Hum, that's odd. The GPS didn't say anything about a detour," Madyson said.

"Sometimes the GPS is on point. Sometimes I don't know who made the GPS because she is totally off. We might as well use a paper map and call DOTD."

Oh my gosh, it's like riding with my dad, Madyson thought as she laughed to herself. He always complained that computers didn't know as much as humans think they do and that a "good old-fashioned" map is the best thing one can use when traveling. "We are much too close to Monroe to turn around, so let's just follow the detour sign. If we turn around, we definitely won't make it to that downtown jazz spot tonight. I saw it on social media, and it looks pretty cool," she said.

Ben nodded in agreement. They made a right and headed down a small black paved road. Thick bushes and tall trees were on each side. Lush grass lined the side of the highway with some of the long blades leaning sideways. Though it was dark, Madyson could see the reflection of water off the side of the road.

"It's dark as hell back here," Ben said. "Drive slowly. Don't rush because a deer or anything can come out of those woods. Let me check the GPS again." Ben picked up his phone, but there was no signal. "No signal. What about yours?"

Madyson's phone had a very low signal, and her battery was too low to use the GPS.

"Well, keep going," Ben said. "We should get there shortly."

Madyson and Ben had not seen any other cars on the highway, but they continued trudging forward, knowing they had to be closer to than farther away from their stop for the night. Just then, a set of headlights came their way.

"Okay," Madyson said. "Traffic is picking up again. We must be close." She let out a sigh of relief.

A second set of headlights was headed their way. The lights on the vehicle were bright, and it was apparent that it was a truck. There were lights on the top of it and an extra set on the bottom. They had all of them on, and they shone so brightly that they hurt Madyson's eyes.

"Um, could someone turn their lights down?" Madyson said as she flashed her headlights in an attempt to get them to turn theirs down. Instead, they made them brighter, causing Madyson to slow down and swerve, nearly going off the small shoulder of the highway.

"What the hell!" she yelled as she pulled the wheel back to the left to get the car onto the road.

"Just be careful, and let's get out of here now!" Ben said as he looked back at the big truck whose taillights weren't far away.

Madyson pressed down harder on the gas. Another set of lights was headed their way. She was slightly relieved to see another car. This time, the lights were normal, but something was wrong. There was another set of lights. It was another truck, and they were swerving. The first set of lights came into Madyson's lane and then went to the other lane. The second truck did the same thing twice. Madyson couldn't tell whether the trucks were going around each other or were just going back and forth in the same lane. Once again, one of the trucks came into their path, and this time it didn't move.

Adrenaline ran through Madyson's body. The truck was getting closer, and it appeared to be increasing speed as it got closer. She felt as if she had cotton in her mouth, and she could feel her pulse beating in her temples. Ben sat up and leaned in to get a closer look at what was ahead. Something about this was wrong.

"Madyson," Ben said purposely calmly. "Do you remember what kind of car those men were in?"

"Ben, I don't think- "

"What fucking kind of car were they in!" he yelled.

"They were in two trucks and a car!" she yelled back.

"Drive, Madyson! Drive!" Ben screamed.

Madyson put her foot on the gas, driving as fast as she could, but the truck was still in her lane. She couldn't back up, and the road had no shoulder. It went directly into a muddy and water-filled swamp. Even though it was dark, she was able to see the reflection of the water and the woods' outline.

"What am I going to do?" she yelled.

"Swerve!" Ben yelled.

Madyson swung the car into the on-coming traffic

lane. The truck came into that lane.

Ben tried to calm himself to give clear directions. "Don't move, Madyson; just focus. Wait until you get close, and then get back over," he said. "No, no, don't cry; just be calm, okay? We will be alright."

Madyson could see the headlights within a few feet of her car. Just like the other truck, they were bright and almost blinding. Madyson tried to focus her eyes so she could see how close the vehicles were. She had to move at the right moment, or the truck in their lane would crash into them. She checked her rearview mirror. Neither she nor Ben had noticed the set of extra-bright headlights behind them now. The trucks were working together.

"Ben! Look!" Madyson pointed at the rearview.

"What the shi-. Madyson, swerve, but don't stop!" he yelled.

Madyson rechecked the rearview mirror. The truck's lights got closer, making it hard for Madyson to measure how close it was. She guessed it had to be close because the truck in their lane in front of them began blowing its horn. Madyson whipped her wheel to the right; then, she swerved to the left. The small car jerked with every motion, and, for a minute, Madyson was scared she would lose control of it. However, she regained control and sped down the road. She looked in the rearview mirror again, and Ben looked behind them; both trucks were gone.

"Ben, I think we are safe. I don't know where we are, but let's get the hell out."

Ben nodded. "No doubt. Now! We should only be a few mi-."

Just then, the small car was jolted by a strong force. There was a loud crashing sound, and Madyson lost control of the car. She felt an impact on the passenger door behind her. Madyson was screaming, and Ben was yelling, but neither of them could do anything. Bright lights shone on Madyson's face. With a flash of light, Madyson saw something in Ben she had never seen before- fear. His body was coming toward her as the car went airborne toward the woods. Madyson closed her eyes and braced herself for the unexpected.

CHAPTER 2

"Were you able to get everything squared away?" Grace asked as she stuck her head over the side of her employee's cubicle. Bianca was leaning into the computer screen closely and moving the mouse from side to side. Grace looked out the window to see how dark it had gotten.

"Yep. I am finishing the last file now," Bianca replied. "I am determined not to take anything home this weekend. There are a Teleflix movie and a bottle of wine with my name on it, and I don't need any distractions." She closed the document on the computer screen. Bianca began shuffling through a few papers next to her computer and then stuffed them into a manilla folder lying under the stack. She looked around her desk as if moving five documents made it look any less messy.

"Okay! It has been a long day for both of us. I will look over it on Monday. I will empty trash cans and put them by the door for the night cleaning lady," Grace said as she stood up and pushed her chair under the desk.

Bianca smiled, "In other words, you are waiting on me."

Grace smiled back. "You know I'm not leaving anyone in this building, especially when it gets dark so early in the fall."

"I will be finished in five minutes, Boss Lady." Bianca logged off the computer and began straightening her desk. She had considered leaving everything as it was until Monday, but one of Bianca's pet peeves was coming into work with a messy desk. She said it was a sign that it would also be a messy day. So even though it took a few extra minutes, Bianca cleared and organized her desk each evening.

"No rush. And do *not* call me boss lady. You do your role; I do mine. But we all work as a team," Grace laughed.

"But your check is officially fatter than mine!" They both roared in laughter as Grace collected bags of trash; Bianca stood up.

"Imagine that. I can afford dessert after lunch now. Whoever thought," Grace replied.

Grace had a thing about hierarchical positions at work. Unless she needed to flex her power, she didn't believe that anyone employee was more important than the other. She had only been promoted for a year, and many of her employees were once her co-workers and managers. She believed the team worked better when titles weren't the focus of the job.

Grace walked over to the door and waited while Bianca put her jacket on. Then, the two women headed out of the building together. Grace went to the back door of the office and twisted the handle to make sure it was locked. When they were outside the building, she looked around cautiously to make sure they were safe. Anytime she left after dark, Grace tried to take all precautions. Even though their office was in a pretty decent part of town, she never took that for granted.

"I feel so sorry for your daughter because I know you are like this all the time," Bianca laughed.

"And I feel sorry for your mama because I know you are like this all of the time. So free-spirited and not worried, and many times, not cautious, but you mean well," Grace said with a smile. "My daughter has been taught to be careful, but you, my girl, leave the office late and make simple mistakes. You certainly don't pay attention to your surroundings. Do you think I text you when you stay late just to make sure you turned the lights off?" Grace and Bianca made eye contact as they went toward their cars. Grace winked and smiled at Bianca, who smiled in return.

Bianca reminded Grace of herself, a young girl who loved helping families and who had great potential. Like Grace, she came from a single-parent home, but Bianca's life had been a little tougher than Grace's. Bianca had three other siblings, and her mother often struggled to provide for them. If her mom wasn't struggling to find a job with enough hours, she struggled to find a job with enough pay. She grew up in a rough neighborhood, and violence was a regular problem. Despite her challenges, Bianca graduated from high school with honors and earned a scholarship to the local university. She left the West Coast and came to the South, where she decided to stay after she graduated from college and landed a job. Her decision was a good one; life in Monroe was turning out pretty well for her. She had just gotten engaged, and Bianca and her fiancé were planning a small destination wedding over the summer. These were things Grace had learned when she became the supervisor for her team. Bianca was always working hard and proficiently, and she was genuinely nice. When Grace saw potential, she loved it and tried to support it.

"Can't help but love you," Bianca said from the door of her vehicle.

"That's what they say," Grace smiled. "Relax this weekend and enjoy time with that handsome fiancé.

See you Monday!"

Grace started her engine and turned on the radio. She switched the station from the oldies to soft jazz. Her morning commute and her evening drive demanded different atmospheres. The oldies reminded her of family reunions and weekends with her grandmother; it gave her energy for the day. Jazz helped Grace wind down and decompress. Today, she was a bit exhausted after a long week. One of the employees was on maternity leave, and Grace had agreed to help with her caseload. Working on open cases was one thing but closing out cases at the end of each month was tedious. It was a process that Grace didn't have to do often anymore. As the supervisor, she usually reviewed and approved files before they submitted them to the state; however, it had been a while since anyone in the office had birthed a newborn, and rather than overload the employees with additional work, she took part of the load too. Grace reminded herself that the new mom was one of their best employees and that the employee would be off maternity leave in two more weeks. It was worth the sacrifice to keep her from being overwhelmed when she returned.

Grace had recalled the days when her children were small and how much responsibility it had been as a new mom. Even with her supportive husband, there were many days when he worked long hours and when the children just wanted their mama. Times had changed since Grace had given birth; now, her job had a total support program for new moms. They did everything from providing dinner to helping single moms with the baby during their six weeks off.

Grace put her hand behind her head and massaged

her neck. She laid her head on the seat of her Infiniti truck and closed her eyes for a minute. Traffic was bumper to bumper, which was normal on a Friday night. She looked down at her clock. It wasn't as late as she thought, but time was ticking. She looked at the busy four-lane highway once again. Just as she was about to get frustrated, the light changed to green, and her lane cleared. Grace was able to flow through traffic and across the big bridge where traffic was much lighter, and the interstate took her straight toward home, which was nearly twenty minutes away. She didn't mind that part, though. The ride home was her quiet time before dinner and family and taking care of everyone else. Though she wasn't supposed to spend this time thinking about work, she usually did replay the day in her mind.

Grace neared her exit and shifted the vehicle to the right to get off the interstate. Grace's truck maneuvered down the dark highway, occasionally hitting a bump in the road. Headlights shone in her direction; she flicked her lights a time or two to remind opposing drivers to beam down. "Pretty sure that's Mrs. Ricks with those unnecessary bright lights," she mumbled. Grace had driven this highway so many times she was used to the same people driving the same route.

Grace was halfway home and had been trying to figure out what she would cook for dinner. Her family had abandoned going out or ordering out on Fridays long ago. Restaurants were always overly packed and were not worth the wait. The packed lines meant rushed food and sending food back was an even bigger nightmare. If she ordered food to go, it was either cold or not ready. If it wasn't fixed right, she had to drive to town to take it back. There were only a few restaurants from the neighboring town that delivered out to the country. When there wasn't a home game or some other event at her kids' school, Friday was the perfect night to whip up a quick dinner. When there was a game, it was a good night for leftovers.

To Grace's left was a road that had been closed for nearly three years. There was a bridge about seven miles down the road. It had gone out during a terrible rainstorm; the town could not afford to fix it, and the state said they would not. As a result, they didn't finish the road's extension, which meant it was a dead end. The detour sign was so old; it had been replaced months earlier. Tonight, it had been moved to the side of the road, and it was pointed in the wrong direction. No one went down that road; there were no houses back there. Grace slowed down and peered down the road, interested in seeing why the sign had been moved. Maybe they were finally working on the bridge. She saw a single set of taillights facing her but nothing else. The lights were so far away that they looked like three tiny dots. She could tell it was a pick-up truck. *Maybe it's hunters,* she thought to herself as she kept driving toward home. During hunting season, they sometimes drove down that road to get deeper into the woods. Grace turned the radio back to the oldies station and got into the swooning voice of the Friday Night Lovers' mix. By the end of the third song, she turned onto the gravel driveway that led to her house.

Lights lined the walkway up to the porch. They dotted the landscaped lawn, flashing just enough light to see the green shrubbery, plants, and herbs that decorated the front yard. The automatic porch light was on, and the garage door began opening as the sensor responded to Grace's sensor pad. Grace pulled her pearl white SUV into the garage.

Despite feeling exhausted when she left work, Grace's energy had suddenly come back. Something about coming home to her family always made her feel good. Brad would be getting off work soon, and the kids would be coming from school practices and activities. Grace opened the door and took one foot at a time out of the car. She grabbed her bags and went into the house. The smell of cinnamon apple delightfully met her senses as she opened the front door. Grace had caught a sale at her favorite store, and now *This Ought to be a Sin-a-min Apple Pie* candles, plug-ins, and melts were throughout the house. Truthfully, Grace hated the name, but she loved the smell. They reminded her of her grandmother's holiday apple pies because they were Grace's favorite. Grace missed Big Mama. She had dutifully raised Grace after her mother died when Grace was six years old. Big Mama swore Grace was the sweetest girl she'd ever known. Though Grace wasn't a perfect child, she knew Big Mama was all she had; therefore, she tried to do what Big Mama expected- make good grades, be obedient, and work hard. Big Mama made life plain and simple, "Love what loves you. Get rid of what doesn't. Your joy is all you have in this life; preserve it." The depth of those words grew as Grace got older, and they meant more to her now than she ever thought they would. Even though life was good, some days were still hard without Big Mama. She had been Grace's best friend.

Grace took the ground turkey out of the freezer and then began searching the pantries for the night's meal. A quick turkey stroganoff was a great starter; she grabbed the box of mix from the pantry. She opened both doors of the refrigerator and spotted the lettuce, cucumbers, and tomatoes. Grace always kept garlic bread on hand, so she knew there was a box in the freezer. Grace searched the lower cabinet next to the stove for a large skillet for the stroganoff. Then she flipped through the cupboards to find the pink salad bowl, the light blue colander, and the clear mixing bowl.

"I'll tell you. Leah just puts stuff anywhere," she mumbled. "In the cup cabinet. Wow."

She placed the salad bowl on the counter and checked the dishwasher for the colander. It was there. Grace found the Louisiana seasoning and garlic salt in the top cabinet. She tore open the ground turkey and put it into the bowl. She added dashes of seasoning and began mixing it with her fingers. As she worked her way around the kitchen, Grace's mind drifted back to the times before life changed.

Grace had completed her studies at a university about thirty miles from home, the same one where Bianca had gotten a scholarship. She lived on campus but did not indulge in college life. Though her grandmother did not try to hold her back from living, she did ask Grace to remember how hard she had worked to get her a better lifestyle. "Before I had the privilege of workin' at that factory, I spent many a'years scrubbin' white folks' floors and mendin' their clothes and tendin' to their children. You ain't never got to know what that's like, Gracie. Take advantage of what God's given you and get you an education. Can't nobody take that from you," she said. Grace never forgot those words, and she took them with her. She wanted to make Big Mama proud. Her grades were stellar. She hung out at campus activities but rarely partied and didn't drink. It paid off in a significant way when she decided to go back for her graduate degree, and an old professor contacted her about a scholarship opportunity. Brad had gone to a school in the opposite direction; his parents thought putting distance between him and Grace could bring the couple to an end. He attended the local university and lived at home until his junior year when he got an apartment. Difficulties with his parents made him decide that it was best to get an apartment. He dated a blonde-haired, blue-eyed girl named Stephanie, who was president of one of the most exclusive white sororities on campus. It was well-known that her parents had plenty of money, and no one was sure exactly how the two linked up. Stephanie's family was filthy rich, and everyone knew it. Their relationship gained Brad a lot of connections and new friends. Many knew of Brad's family, but they belonged to the hard workers who were financially stable, not the high class, filthy rich community. Brad's relationship placed him among social ranks to which he was not accustomed. Still, none of this could remove the absence he felt for Grace. Their love was natural; it was pure. He often found himself daydreaming about Grace when he was out with Stephanie. He was thankful that he caught Stephanie cheating on him; it was his escape from a relationship that had become more about publicity than love.

Grace had done some casual dating in college, but she hadn't been able to find a man who made her feel as Brad did. Even if they were nice guys with great potential, it just wasn't the same. Despite being in love with Brad, Grace had no intention of going back, figuring she would eventually get over him. She accepted her sadness over their break-up as a natural feeling, one she couldn't shake.

"Grace, are you gonna take me back?" he asked one day while they were in a casual conversation on the phone. Brad had called claiming that he just wanted to check on her and Big Mama because it was close to the holidays.

"So, now that you've caught her cheating, you want to run back over here to me. Is that how it is?" she asked.

Brad took a deep breath. "You broke up with me!"

"Yeah, Brad, it's kind of hard competing with your racist parents and rich white women falling all over you on that campus!" Grace yelled back.

"I never cheated on you, Grace, and you know I don't uphold my parents' hate. It's embarrassing!" Of all the things that hurt his feelings, bringing up something he could not control was the most painful. "I love you, Grace Michelle. I never stopped loving you, and you know it. I know things haven't been easy for us, but that has never changed how I feel about you. I've been asking you to take me back for a long time and-"

"-I wasn't taking you back while you were dating someone else-"

"I didn't think you'd ever take me back, Grace. What was I supposed to do?"

There was silence on the line.

Brad stammered. "I can't change my parents. I can't change them. I tried to change them, and they tried to change me. But I promise you, Grace, I only love you. I will never let them mistreat you, and I will always protect you. I had to do something to try to move on because you wouldn't even answer my calls. It didn't work, though. I will do anything to keep a smile on your face; I'll buy-"

"I don't need things. I need love," she butted in.

"Gotdamit, you've got it, Grace. Why won't you just receive it from me?"

"I want four bedrooms and two bathrooms. I want a kitchen big enough to drive my car into because I'm in this for the long haul, Brad," Grace said.

After earning his degree in business, Brad decided to open a small architectural design and construction company with the mission to give Grace just that. He had done a rather good job of making Grace happy, much to his parents' demise, but he had not created the lifestyle all on his own. Grace's Big Mama had gifted them twenty acres of land when they got married. She gave them the other thirty acres when she passed away. Brad started by putting a double-wide trailer on it, asking Grace to give him time to build their dream home. But destiny would show them greater favor than they imagined.

Brad bought some land a few miles from their double-wide trailer and built the company. He started with two employees, and he hired the rest of his men through a temp agency. Brad slowly built his team of employees by permanently hiring the men who proved they were excellent and skillful workers. Brad was good at his job, and he had established a strong reputation with his university, so they gave him one of his first contracts. It would lead Brad to become one of the most demanded architects and general contractors in the Southern region. He was so well-known, he bought a small plane and learned to fly so he could get to meetings that were more than an hour away and be back home with his family for dinner most of the time.

His achievements had earned him a reputation where he didn't have to meet with prospective clients most of the time; they hired him off the strength of his name and his work. His meetings could be conducted online, whether they were the first-time meet and greets or project progression meetings.

His success earned his family a home bigger that was more ornate than the modest one Grace once imagined. The house was still relatively modest in size, but it was made of stone, and inside were four bedrooms and three and a half bathrooms. Their master bedroom suite had a sitting area with luxurious handmade rugs and quilts. Their bathroom had top-of-the-line amenities with heated floors and heated toilet seats. When Brad offered Grace something larger, she blurted out, "Who's going to do the housework? I don't need a home where I can't scream at our kids from the other end." Brad laughed, but he knew Grace was serious. He gave her the most beautiful, cozy, quaint home he could and then bought a beach home on the coast of Alabama. They wanted the vacation home far enough for them to forget their busy life but close enough to get there if they decided to go on the spur of the moment.

Brad asked Grace to quit her job and stay at home, but Grace said Big Mama had not saved up money for her college degree to sit at home and cater to a man all day. Of all the things he loved about Grace, her raw truth was something he loved most. Still, he refused to give up his hope that she would retire early so she could be at home.

It only took a few minutes for Grace to pull together dinner. This family favorite was also her favorite for those two reasons. The stroganoff was simmering on low heat on the stove. The salad, along with salad dressing, croutons and diced slices of freshly cooked bacon was on the center of the table. Four bottles of water had been placed in the freezer, and a bottle of wine sat on the counter. It was still cold from being stored in the refrigerated wine rack. Grace had just enough time to enjoy a glass in peace before everyone got home. She filled her crystal wine glass a little past halfway and signaled the radio, "Play Marvin Gaye's 'I Want You.'"

Even though this song was a little older than Grace, it was one Big Mama used to play when she was cooking up dinner on Friday nights, and her lady friends would come over for cards and gossip. Grace never forgot how excited she felt. Big Mama usually made Frito pies, nachos, or country roast beef sandwiches with gravy, and the women would bring the chips, salsa, or some other side and the drinks. Grace sat on a stool at the bar watching Big Mama sing and dance as she got the food ready for her lady friends. Even though Grace didn't get to sit at the table with the grown women, she did get a big plate of whatever they ate, and Big Mama would let her watch television as late as she wanted. Grace would eavesdrop now and then so she could hear the women talk about church gossip, their husbands, and their children. Grace took one more swirl and let her hips swing from side to side, just like Big Mama used to.

She loved moments like this; as much as Grace adored her husband and children, between parenting and being a wife, she had to snatch a few moments of quiet time when she could. Two active children and a busy husband meant Grace came last even when she put herself first. But they were worth it. Just as the song went off and she polished off the last sip of wine, the door opened and in walked her son Blake.

"Hey, Blake," she smiled.

"Hey, Mom," he replied as he walked over to kiss her on the cheek.

"Oh, my goodness, no game tonight, but you still smell like the locker room. Shower quickly, please!" Grace waved her hand in front of her nose.

"Yeah, we still had practice. I got to start with varsity today, and Coach said he is ready for me to *start* in the next game!" Blake laughed.

"Your coach is pretty excited about how well you've been playing, but I checked those grades today. You are dancing dangerously close to a C. I suggest you tighten up in class, or the only time you'll be spending after school is in tutoring," Grace fussed.

"You will be happy to know I already requested early morning tutoring for two weeks. I can't risk not getting in the National Honor Society this year," he replied.

Just then they heard footsteps coming down the hall. "And who cares about getting into National Honor Society anyway. It is just a bunch of geeks who think they are the cream of the crop. Half of them are smoking weed in the bathroom and drinking at Daniel's farm on the weekend," said Leah, Grace's oldest child.

"Lady Optimism, how nice of you to join us. I guess you are finished giggling on the phone with your boyfriend," Blake retorted.

Leah reached into the refrigerator and grabbed a soda. "Call me Lady Realism. Everybody knows the National Honor Society got caught drinking at the conference last year and almost got the club suspended from the school for three years. Daniel's mom was at the school raising sand and making all kinds of threats; in the end, she had to make a big donation to keep everyone out of trouble and keep their names in the clear. Well, of course, we know it was really to keep Daniel's name clear. I am so glad I rejected the invitation," Leah said as she headed back down the hall to her room.

Blake frowned at his sister for a moment and then turned his attention back to Grace. "Don't listen to her, Mom. Imagine how it would look if a division one school saw my grades and my school activities. I'd get into anywhere!" Blake shrieked in excitement.

"I know son, and I know you are not one of those kids. Focus on improving that chemistry grade, and I know you will get it. Now, a more important question-who is going to take you to early morning tutoring since you can make your own plans?" Grace asked matter-of-factly.

"You'll be glad to know I asked Dad. I told him about the grade and how you would have my backside if I didn't bring it up. He said I just have to be up and ready when he leaves for work!"

Grace arched her eyebrows. "It seems the men are taking care of business. I have no complaints," she replied. "Let's focus less on this stuff and more on this delicious dinner. It's one of the few free Friday nights we get during the fall. Leah, I think your dad is pulling up!" she yelled. "Get off the phone with that boy and go wash your hands!"

Grace began placing the stroganoff and dishes on the table. Blake grabbed the waters from the refrigerator and put them on the table in front of each chair.

Brad entered the hallway from the garage and made his way to the kitchen. He walked up behind his wife, who was leaning over to place dinner plates in front of four seats at the table. Brad put his hands around Grace's waist and gave her a gentle squeeze before running his hand down her thigh and between her legs for a quick massage.

"Well, well, somebody is ready for a free Friday night," Grace laughed as she stood up and leaned into her husband's arms.

"Closed a good deal, got out of the office on time, and my wife is bent over showing me that ass when I walk in the door. What could make me happier?" Brad said with a smile on his face.

Grace turned around and put her nose to her husband's. "Wash up, let's eat dinner, and the kids can entertain themselves in their rooms or something tonight." She kissed Brad on the lips.

"Man, can't ya'll save that stuff for when we are asleep. I am so grossed out!" Leah said as she came into the kitchen. She took a seat at the table, and Blake sat next to her.

The teens immediately dived into the food, piling the stroganoff and salad onto their plates. Blake had the spoon for the bowl of stroganoff in one hand, and he was already shoving food into his mouth with the other.

"My goodness, Blake. You don't have to eat like an animal," Leah said. "Mom, it's like feeding three football players; I swear."

"Well, I'm just balancing out all the bacon and salad you took," he replied. Leah reached over and pretended to stab him with her fork.

"Hey!" he yelled.

"All right, you two! Blake is a growing boy; he's just hungry," Grace smiled.

"And don't leave Leah out. She's a growing girl!" he laughed.

Leah gave him a snarky side-eye and then reached across the table. "Hey, it's no shame in my game!" They all started laughing.

"I cooked plenty," Grace said. "There is more on the stove." Before she could finish her sentence, Blake was at the stove digging in the pot.

They were quiet for a few minutes, enjoying each other's presence and the hot meal. Blake and Brad mumbled about sports while Grace and Leah talked about her activities at school.

"I want us to do something different with the theme for the Christmas semi-formal. I mean every year we do the same red, green, and white. Those are not the staple colors for Christmas, and our decorations are out of style; we need a change. Our sponsor was not happy with my suggestion, but I'm not giving up," Leah stated adamantly.

Grace sipped her water. "Leah, can you go with the flow for once?" she asked.

"Mom, I mean no disrespect, but could you *not* go with the flow for a change?" she responded.

Grace looked at her curtly. Her father butted in, "Now, Leah, don't get out of hand."

"Dad, seriously. I mean no disrespect, but Mom opposes everything I suggest, especially if it's outside the norm or 'tradition,'" Leah said using air quotes.

"And you oppose everything that's already in place," her mother said.

Leah took a deep breath and looked at her brother, who pretended to be more interested in his salad than he needed to be. "This is the same school that brags about having student leaders, but they never actually let students lead. Changing the colors for the formal is a minimal change, but it could be so cool for us. That's all I'm saying." Leah jumped up and grabbed her cellphone, which was across the room charging. "I know we have a 'no cell phones at dinner' rule, but I just want to show you some of the ideas I have. Look. This dark purple, lilac, silver, and white are beautiful," she said as she showed the pictures to her parents and brother.

Grace shook her head. "I can't deny, it's beautiful."

"Even I have to admit it's pretty cool," Blake said.

"The old decorations are worn out, so we have to get new ones anyway. We have the money in our account; plus, they make a killing on ticket sales," Leah insisted.

"I'm convinced. Have you tried this approach with your sponsor?" Brad asked.

"I've tried every approach. The sponsor doesn't even have a reason other than 'that's the way we've always done it.' Which is tired and played out," Leah said as she headed to put her phone back on the counter. "I have one more thing up my sleeve, though. I'm going to run a poll on social media and see what my classmates would vote for. I'm going to put up four options instead of two. I will bring the results back to her and see if I can convince her again."

"Not giving up is the key. I like it, and I say go for it," Brad said. He was a businessman, so discussions like this impressed him, especially when one of his children had it.

Grace didn't look up from her plate, but she did state, "If she doesn't agree with you this time, drop it, okay?"

"Sure, Mom," Leah said in a mannequin-like response. It wasn't what she wanted to say, but she didn't want to engage in an argument that was too common and too frequent between her and her mother.

The air was now stiff and dry, not happy and hearty like it had been only moments earlier. Grace hated to bump heads with her children, but it was always something with the combative Leah. She wanted Leah to understand that everyone wasn't going to agree with her ideas and that no one could make them. Sometimes it was easier just to let things go than to fight. Grace could sense the tension, and she had to break it.

"Leah, I think it's beautiful. I'm sure it's the best idea. I just don't want them to give you any unnecessary problems during your senior year. They will make something out of nothing in a minute. We all know how this school is, and we know how political they are," Grace said.

Leah did not doubt that Grace meant well, but her mother's meager attitude sometimes angered her. How could a woman who ran such a stern house bend so easily around other people? It was as if she feared being approached or confronted even if she wasn't wrong. In Leah's earlier teen years, it made communication hard for them and kept her grounded for weeks at a time. But as she got older, Leah learned to choose her battles with her mother to keep the peace until she graduated. She had also learned to use her leverage with her dad to get her perspective over. She could tell this wasn't one she was going to win even though she knew Brad agreed with her. "I understand what you mean, Mom. I don't want anything stopping me from getting into

Howard," she replied.

"Howard? Howard University? In Washington, D.C.? I thought we talked about ULM or LSU. We'd even looked at Texas A&M," Grace said with a bit of shock in her voice.

Leah put her napkin on her plate. "All of those schools are great. I'm considering some of them for my graduate studies, but I want to go to an HBCU. It would be such a new experience- one I've *never* had before. When I did my research on Howard, it has so much history! The academics are strong, and the campus is beautiful. I think it is the perfect place to work on my first degree," she said.

"Oh," Grace said curtly. "Well, we never talked about Howard."

"Mom, don't tell me you're one of those who thinks that PWIs are better than HBCUs?" Leah replied.

"What's a PWI?" Blake interrupted as he raked the last of his salad in his mouth.

"Predominantly white institutions and HBCUs are historically black colleges and universities," Brad responded.

Leah's eyes grew big, and she gave a nod of approval in her father's direction. "I see someone is up to speed on their modern terminology," she said.

Brad laughed. "I do review applications, so I have to know terms that matter. Besides, I'm smooth. You know, I'm hip. I can relate to the youngsters when I need to."

"Dad, don't ever again," Leah laughed.

"Like ever," Blake followed up.

Brad looked at his wife. "Let's take her to Howard and see how she likes it. Then, she can decide from there."

"I'm open to that," Grace said, forcing a slight grin on her face. More than anything, she didn't want to ruin the mood completely. It seemed like they were going from one uncomfortable subject to another, so she changed the subject again. "We can talk about all of that later. It's Friday night with both of my children and my husband at home, so I bought ingredients for coke floats. This won't happen again until your Thanksgiving break, and even then, y'all will manage to find a million things to do. I figured I might as well make the best of it," Grace laughed as she dug in the refrigerator. She pulled out the ice cream, root beer, and coke for the floats. She placed everything on the giant island in the center of the kitchen.

Grace let out an internal sigh of relief. She had planned floats just for fun, but they turned out to be the perfect way to smooth out a rocky evening.

"Mom, you don't want me to be great for the Christmas formal. You know coke floats are my favorite," Leah said as she walked over to the counter.

"What are you talking about, Leah? The milk in milkshakes is good for you, and soda is a great energy booster. It's perfectly healthy!" Grace said.

Leah burst out laughing. "I have no idea how you came up with that justification, but let's go with it tonight."

Brad and Blake picked up the empty plates from the table and put them in the trash. Then, they put the dishes in the dishwasher and met Leah and Grace at the island. They had already begun fixing everyone's floats.

"A lot of ice cream and a little root beer," Leah said as she handed Blake his float.

Sipping the floats was like tasting happiness, and the

stiffness slowly left the room as giggling and cheerfulness came back. They talked about the days when Blake and Leah could barely get things off the countertop without help. They sipped and snickered until the room was full of memories, and their cups were empty of ice cream and soda.

"Oh goodness, you two have brought back some memories!" Grace said as she chuckled and wiped tiny tears from the corners of her eyes.

"What can I say? I'm the joy of this family," Blake joked.

"Right, baby, it's all you," Grace said, grabbing the bottom of his face.

"Did I hear Mom and Dad say they will do the dishes?" asked Leah.

"The jokes continue. You know what? Your mom and I will finish loading the dishwasher and put everything away tonight. You guys are free," Brad told Blake and Leah.

The twosome made a beeline for the hall that led to their rooms before Grace could object. "Aw, look how determined they are to help," Grace sarcastically said as she grabbed a pot from the stove and moved it to the sink.

As she turned around to grab the other dishes, Brad grabbed Grace and leaned his forehead against hers. "I just wanted to get you alone. We've done the parent thing; now, it's time for the you and me thing." He kissed her on her neck and whispered in her ear, "Remember that negligee I bought you a few weeks ago."

Grace was blushing as she nodded her head.

"I get hard just imagining you in it." He gave her full-butt cheeks a tight squeeze and then massaged her wide hips and ran his hands up around her waistline.

"But the kids-" she started.

"The *teenagers* are sixteen and almost eighteen now. Let's give them the keys and let them catch a movie in town. Then, let me show you how to make the best of an empty house," Brad whispered as he was kissing her on the neck.

Grace was hesitating, and he could tell.

"Gracie, they aren't kids anymore. We have to let them get out there; we have to trust them. Tonight, I need you to be a little less mom and a little more wife so I can be a little less dad and a lot more Big Freaky." He stroked her cheek, and Grace kissed the palm of his hand.

"I know you are right, Brad. I know it's time to loosen the reins, and I've been thinking about it. I know keeping them sheltered can be worse than letting them out. It just makes me a little nervous," she admitted.

"Relax. Please relax," Brad begged, as he kissed her neck once more, knowing it was her magical spot.

Grace wrapped her arms around his waist and relaxed. Brad continued kissing her neck, moving up to nibble one of her ears, and then back down to her neck again. Chills ran through her body, and Grace could feel her nipples harden.

She took a breath and whispered, "You're already started my engine, so you might as well take me for a ride."

TREKKED.

CHAPTER 3

It was pitch black, and Madyson could not see anything, but she could feel everything. Wetness was all around her, and she was muddy. She could feel sticks and grime and perhaps bugs under her feet and touching her skin. She could hear creaking and night songs being chirped by animals. The night was black; the air was thicker than the mud on her clothes, face, and arms. Her head was pounding, and a sharp pain ran through her left hip. She wasn't sure if she could move or if she was even alive. It seemed like a dream. *Yeah, it has to be a bad dream,* Madyson thought to herself. She laid there a moment longer, believing she would wake up in a minute. She would be in her bedroom, and her parents would be downstairs. Her dad would be getting ready to go to work, and her mother would be logging on to work from home after they had chatted over toast and tea. *Come, Madyson. Wake up,* she told herself. *Wake up!* But it didn't work because it wasn't a nightmare. Madyson and Ben had been chased by the trucks and run off the highway into the woods. This place was not her home. Her parents weren't around.

"Ben," she whispered.

Nothing.

"Ben," she whispered.

Nothing.

Maybe Ben has already gotten up. Maybe he's looking for me, she told herself.

Madyson rolled over and realized her legs were in the deeper part of the muddy water, and her head was near the shallow area. Madyson's legs felt heavy, and she could not lift them. Madyson focused on wiggling her toes and then making movement with her legs. She sighed in relief as she pulled them up and bent her knees. Madyson felt around, still trying to adjust her vision to the dark. The moon shone brightly, and after a few moments, she could see its light reflecting on the metal of the car. Madyson began crawling toward the car, thinking that if she made it to the car, it would be easier for Ben to find her. Madyson continued crawling until she felt the back bumper of the vehicle, which was crushed. She ran her hand down the side of the car and felt the bumps and folded metal on the body. Madyson found the handle of the back door and continued to move her hand down the side of the car until she found the front door. Madyson assumed she would feel a handle, but instead, she felt an opening and then a seat. She climbed into the car and laid her head on the seat. She let out a loud sigh, feeling slight relief to find something familiar. Maybe her phone was near. Madyson reached into the console for her phone; she checked the floor and felt nothing. Perhaps it had fallen on the passenger side of the car. Madyson reached over to the passenger seat and felt warmth and clothes and then skin. She had found Ben.

"Ben!" she cried. "Ben, wake up! We're okay!"

She shook Ben, but he didn't move. She felt his hands; they were warm, but the tips were cold. She didn't know if it was the iciness of the water or death setting in. Panic had made her delirious for a minute, but Madyson knew what to do. She began feeling Ben's pants, then jacket, and finally his neck. Madyson remembered that she could check his pulse by finding the right spot on his neck. Madyson moved her index and middle fingers around; maybe she wasn't feeling the right spot. She had made all A's in her emergency first aid classes. She had done her internship at one of the best hospitals in the state, but today she couldn't even remember how to check a pulse. Madyson took a deep breath to calm herself; then, she moved her fingers around Ben's neck again. Finally, she felt a faint pulse, but she knew Ben was not in good condition. Tears filled her eyes, and her mind began racing. Madyson's heart started pounding as water poured down her face. She let out a wail and then soft whimpers.

Madyson leaned her head on the steering wheel as she tried to figure out how they ended up in the backwoods of Louisiana in the middle of the swamp. Her mind replayed the images of the men at the store, the mad chase down the road, and the moment the car lost control. Madyson was so lost in her thoughts that she didn't hear Ben's low grumble, but she felt something touch her thigh. She let out a fearful yelp before she realized it was Ben's hand. She grabbed his hand quickly, "Ben! Are you okay?"

"No," he whispered, "I'm hurt. My leg…"

Madyson looked over at his leg, but she had a hard time seeing in the dark. The moon shone brightly through the passenger side of the window. She pushed Ben's leg over, trying to adjust it so she could use the moonlight to see. Now, she could see a huge gash that exposed the white flesh inside his thigh.

"It's to the bone. I can feel the air touching it," Ben said as he winced in pain.

"Oh, God," Madyson muttered. "I can't find our phones. Let me look one more time. We have to call the ambulance!"

She felt around in the dark, hoping she had missed the phone the first time.

"Madyson, we don't have time, and our phones don't work anyway," Ben whispered.

She looked in the back seat, still searching for the phones.

"Madyson," Ben repeated. His breathing was slow and deep. "We don't have time. Those weird ass rednecks back there are coming. I don't know what they want, but it ain't good. This wasn't an accident. We don't have time. We have to get out of here right now."

****

"Damn it, Danny! I told you to run them off the road into the bushes. But you had to go overkill like you always do!" Randy angrily sloshed through the woods, kicking up mud and water with each step.

"Well, Randy, if you hate how I do it so much, then you should've just did it. The little bitch could drive better'n I thought. I did what I had to do or we woulda lost 'er," Danny battled back.

"I told ya'll to let me do it," Joe chipped in.

"Oh, shut up!" Danny and Randy yelled back.

"Let's keep going a lil further. They probably already dead, which means all the fun is ruined. If they're dead, I'm leavin' 'em. Just two niggers; let 'em rot in the woods," Joe said. Small tree branches cracked and snapped under their boots. The ground went from grass to soft mud to sinking mud as they went deeper into the woods.

"Watch where ya goin'," Randy barked. "You know this is the swamp. They can't be that deep in here."

Randy stopped and looked around with his flashlight. The car had gone off the road into the woods; the damage to the trees was noticeable, but in the dark, it was still hard to see the direction in which they went.

"Wait. That looks like the door right there. The car can't be far," Randy said as he pointed. The car door was deep into the woods, which meant the car had landed much further than they had expected.

"It's no way they alive out here," Danny said.

"Hell n'all," Randy followed up as he took a cigarette out of his pocket and lit it. "Let's go see the bodies and figure out what to do from there. Might as well get *some* fun out of the night."

We'll be lucky to find the bodies if 'gators don't get 'em first," Danny chimed in.

"Maybe a gator will get you first, and we won't do shit to stop it," Randy responded. He couldn't admit that talking about alligators made him fidgety.

Joe burst out laughing. "That's a good one. Swamp soup they call it."

Boots continued to slosh through the swamp. Joe flashed the light through the woods, looking for the rest of the car. Danny aimed his gun, ready to fire. Randy had his tucked over his shoulder as he puffed on his cigarette. They tried to move slowly and quietly, partly to find the girl and slightly because they were all nervous. Suddenly, there was a loud splash.

"What was that?" Joe blurted.

"Hell, anything," Randy yelled. "We're in the middle of the swamp. Keep ya gun ready in case any of these deer or gators get wild out here."

"Or water moccasins," he said.

"Don't talk like that. You know damned well I'm scared of moccasins." Everybody knew this, so Randy couldn't help but admit it. In high school, they had gone on a fishing trip. Randy thought he was the first to catch a fish. He had his chest puffed out. As he reeled it in, he bragged about how everybody else was an amateur and he was a fishing pro like his daddy. He reeled and pulled, but when the line came up, it was a log with a moccasin wrapped around it. Randy shrieked like a girl, threw the whole fishing pole, and took off running. The snake was gone when the teacher pulled the pole from the water, but Randy refused to fish anymore. He spent the rest of the trip sitting on the bus watching everyone else. Before the end of the day, the word was already around the school. For years, they called him Runnin' Randy; they said he could clear a mile in thirty seconds if you put a water moccasin behind him.

"Can't be too damned scared, Runnin' Randy," Joe slid in.

"Oh, shut the hell up," Danny and Randy said in unison.

****

"I have a jacket in the back seat. Tie it around my leg," Ben whispered. His breathing was getting deeper.

"Where is it?" Madyson asked.

Ben could hear the panic in her voice. She wasn't thinking; she was doing. She was losing focus.

"Madyson, I need you to calm down. A reckless head won't save either one of us, okay. Think about what you have to do, not where we are."

That was hard for Madyson. She was undoubtedly in a scene from a horror movie, and she had no idea how they were going to get out. She took a deep breath and felt around the back seat once more. This time her hand fell directly on the jacket. Something caught her ear, too. In the distance, she could hear noises, like people talking.

One of the voices was a country twang, slightly high-pitched for a man. The other was low grumbling, still country. They weren't close, but they were loud. And there was at least one more, but she couldn't make out the voice. She couldn't understand what they were saying, but she knew they were the voices of the men from the store. Just as Ben had said, they were behind this. The voices were far away, but they were certainly getting closer.

"I just heard somebody talking. They are coming this way. We've got to move." Madyson began wrapping the jacket around Ben's thigh like a tourniquet, securing the knot just above his knee cap. She tried to remember what she had learned in her nursing class. It was much easier when Madyson was practicing on a dummy or a classmate who was not injured. She checked the knot and pressed the area just above the tourniquet. Madyson got out of the car and went around to open his door. She jerked on the handle, and Ben used what little strength he had to push, but the door wouldn't budge. It was dented inward, which meant it was also jammed.

"You're going to have to crawl!" she yelled. She heard the voices getting closer, and she knew their time was limited. She ran back to the driver's side of the car.

"I really can't move," Ben told her.

"Damn it, Ben, you have to! I am pretty sure I just saw the head of a flashlight. We don't have time to waste," Mayson said with more force than she knew she had.

Ben turned to the side and began trying to muster the energy to get out of the car. But he had no energy; he had lost a lot of blood. And even with his leg tied, he was still losing blood quickly. "I can't, Madyson. I just can't," he said.

"Okay. I've got you," she said. Madyson wrapped her arms under his shoulders and slid him out of the passenger's seat to the driver's seat. The voices were getting closer; Madyson couldn't make out what they were saying except the curse words.

She helped Ben ease onto the wet, marshy land where the car was now sinking. Madyson squatted next to him, not wanting to sit in the muddy water, even though she was already soaking wet.

"We have to run," Ben said. "They are looking for us, and they intend to do God knows what to us." He grabbed Madyson's hand. "Let me be straight up with you. I don't know how far I will ma-"

"Ben don't say that," she cut him off.

"-I don't know how far I will make it," he finished. It was no more comfortable for Ben to admit than it was for Madyson to hear it. However, he considered it proper preparation for the inevitable.

"No, no, Ben, don't say that. We are in this together, and we will get out of here together," she said in a trembling voice. "Let's just get you up and get moving. When you start moving, you will be okay." Madyson pulled Ben's arms as he used the car to help him stand up.

They started moving through the woods, going in the opposite direction of the men's voices. They weren't sure where they were headed, but Ben and Madyson knew they had to get away.

****

The three men looked into the car.

"There's no way they're not dead. How the hell did they get out?" Danny said, pulling back his cap and scratching his head. He looked around the swamp, thinking they may have been ejected from the vehicle, but there was no sign of a body.

"Not sure, but it shouldn't be hard to find 'em," Randy said. "Looka there; blood on the seat and a hell of a lot of it. This should be easy." He shined the light in the back seat. "Let's go. We should be able to get these two handled easy tonight. We oughta be home way before sunlight; my boys got a soccer game in the morning."

They headed deeper into the woods. The men's feet seemed to be nearly suctioned by the dense mud as they tried to move through the woods. At times, they struggled to lift each foot and place it in front of the other. Joe fell into Danny and nearly knocked Randy onto the ground.

"Got damnit!" Randy yelled, "I'm gonna smack the shit outta you. Shoulda left you at the house."

"Well, whose truck would you use?" Joe yelled.

"By golly, you're right, Joe. I guess that brand new 4x4 I got ain't shit", Randy said sarcastically, "Just come on and watch where ya going."

They continued trudging through the water; it was getting deeper, and the mud was getting even thicker. Randy was moving more slowly, and they knew his nerves were setting in. The deeper the went into the swamp, the more likely they were to see snakes, alligators, and nutria rats. Louisiana swamps were nobody's friend. Still, Randy would risk almost anything for a good hunt. And intrigue had led him through these waters more than anything else.

"They can't be this far out," Joe whispered.

They were still sloshing when a sudden noise made Randy stop.

Ya'll hear that?" he asked.

"Hear what?" Danny asked.

"That noise," Randy said. "Something moved."

The trio stopped. There was another series of small splashes.

"You heard that?" Randy said as he shined his light back toward the car and then around the swamp.

"I did. I heard it, Randy," Joe said.

"I did, too. That means they ain't far," Randy said.

They heard a rustle in the woods again. This time it seemed a bit closer. They all flashed their lights in the direction of the noise. They saw the flash of yellow in the distance.

"Git 'em!" yelled Joe.

Their feet barely touched the mud and glided over the swamp-like glades on ice as they chased the flash and echo in the dark.

CHAPTER 4

"I still can't believe Mom and Dad let us take Mom's car to the movies on a Friday night," Blake said excitedly. He did a little dance in the passenger seat.

"Calm down; you act like she let us flip the G-ride. I drive this Volvo to school every day. Anyway, trust me- this is all Dad, Blake. All Dad. I don't know what he said, but I'm glad he said it. Mom worries so much, and I'm like 'Mom, your kids are lame and proud!'" Leah laughed.

Blake shoved her shoulder. "Nah, you're lame! Everybody knows Blake is the man on and off the field."

"Yeah, yeah, yeah, big head. Calm down. I still have to remind you to put on deodorant every morning. If half of those girls knew that they'd chill out, onion armpits!" The two burst into laughter. Their chortling was interrupted by the blaring bass coming from the radio; it was shaking the car.

The local station usually played the Club Mania Mix until twelve on Friday nights, and tonight was no different. It was a mix of Louisiana bounce music, hot rap tracks, and a few re-mixed love songs. Leah started shaking her shoulders and chanting every few words of the song.

"I don't know how you listen to that," Blake chimed in. "It is seriously trash music."

"My little pop music, country-lover, you've got to diversify. How are you possibly going to do the shuffle at Mom's family reunion next summer if you don't work on your rhythm now? Dad's got more swag than you!" she laughed.

"The definition of swag is debatable," he argued, a little more curtly than he needed to be.

"That it is not. Even your pop culture committee wants to twerk like Big Freedia!" Leah said as she jiggled her hips in the driver's seat.

Blake shook his head and mumbled, "Just ghetto."

Leah rolled her head back and let out a deep laugh. "Baby Brother, I couldn't be lucky enough to have the hood love me."

Blake rolled his eyes. "Where did Mom go wrong?"

Leah realized he was serious, and this time she wasn't going to let him get away with comments like this. He was a little too arrogant.

She cocked her head to the side and went for the gut. "Mom's kept you locked in the house for too long. You do know that our school is the exception in society, not the norm. Everywhere you go won't be mostly white and run by nearly an all-white staff who only listens to country music and the National Anthem. You've got to learn to be more tolerant of others, or you will have a rude awakening when you leave home."

Blake glared at his sister. He hated it when she acted as if she was so diverse and in touch with society. "I am tolerant and kind to *everyone*. It's so funny how you have become 'woke,' as they say, now that you date Rashawn. You spent one day in the hood, and now you are Angela Rye and shit. I still can't believe Mom dropped you off at that school in the hood that day, and she knows those basketball games can get crazy!" He folded his arms.

Undoubtedly Blake was getting angry, but Leah was laughing so hard she swerved to the left a little as she drove down the road. "You know who Angela Rye is?

I'm guessing you and your little crew can't stand her, right? She's too loud and outspoken, a troublemaker is what they like to call her. She's always on the wrong side of justice, or am I being too nice about the way I'm saying it?" she exclaimed. Blake's face was turning red, but that didn't stop his sister. "How could you be so stereotypical? First off, the school is on the highway; how is that hood? Second, his father is a CPA, and his mother is an assistant principal; he comes from a very solid and hardworking family. I know what you are trying to imply, and it won't work today. And Rashawn and I don't spend all our time talking about race issues but hanging out at his school opened my eyes to a lot. Like it or not, Blake, those are *our* people!"

Blake was seething on the inside, but he didn't have much to say. Leah was a lot more open to hanging around different people and enjoying it. When they went to see their mom's family for holidays and summer trips, Leah tried to line dance and make jokes; it was easy to tell that Leah felt the same comfort she had at home. This was the only time he ever saw Leah dance, and she was pretty good. She would do old school dances with the grown-ups and all the new ticks and rolls with their teen cousins. Though Blake did not think he was better than his mom's family, he did not exactly feel comfortable when she occasionally took them to the family gatherings. He usually sat quietly, watching, and only engaging in small talk with whoever came to talk to him. When his father traveled with them, even Brad would be outside talking about football and barbecuing while drinking a beer. During those times, Blake would follow his dad around, but he was mostly a silent by-stander while Brad went on-and-on about what a great athlete Blake was.

Most of Leah and Blake's time was spent around their schoolmates. They went to a school where most of the students were white, and there was only a small population of black and Hispanic students. It wasn't that Blake didn't recognize he was bi-racial; he just felt he could better relate to his white classmates. They had more things in common. Leah, on the other hand, could relate to anyone. She was nice to everyone, and most people were nice to her, including her teachers. However, some teachers only tolerated her, and it was obvious that they didn't like her. They accused Leah of being combative and too opinionated. If they could exclude from her school activities and class discussions, they would because she wasn't afraid to speak up. Outspoken Leah didn't go where she wasn't welcome, but she didn't let others make her feel uncomfortable about places she had a right to be. Leah said there was a difference between being welcome and having your opinions and beliefs being respected. Many of their classmates respected Leah, but she wasn't welcome into their social circles. That was one of the greatest struggles she faced at their school. Her ability to use her voice was something she took pride in, but her pride sometimes made her brother feel uneasy.

Blake knew his argument about Rashawn was faulty, but it was the perfect comeback when she made him angry. Leah had been passionate about black heritage, and the more she learned about black history, the more she wanted to share it with others. One year, she did a social studies project on great unsung black women heroes of the slavery era. She had researched three women, shared how their roles were significant to American history, and discussed why it is essential to share their stories. To say her presentation was poorly received is a vast understatement. The school threatened to fail her, arguing that some of her sources could not be verified and that she had to re-do the project or fail it. Leah assumed her mother would dispute such claims like a modern-day civil rights activist. Leah was ready for the fury and fire of standing up for history and her right to celebrate the women who were half of her culture and fully part of her history. Grace asked Leah to reconsider the project, arguing that their majority white, conservative school was not ready for such a topic, no matter how profound it was.

"But Mom, how will they be ready if we never challenge their norm?" Leah contested.

Still, Grace urged her to consider complying, saying that the school issue was only a battle and that Leah was really made for war. However, Brad wasn't having it. He knew firsthand the struggles his children would face as they tried to fit their culture into an environment where only black conformity was welcome. Watching his little girl begging for the right to celebrate her history was something Brad refused to do. Unscheduled and unannounced, he marched into the school, demanding to speak with the principal.

The secretary was a short, fat woman with stubby fingers that had been painted pink. Her brown hair hung just below her shoulders. She shuffled nervously through papers as she tried to figure out what to say. "The principal isn't available right now. She will have meetings all day. Maybe you can call and schedule a meeting tomorrow," she told Brad. Brad knew Mitzy, the school secretary, and he knew her trick. They had gone to school together, and nothing about her had changed. That's why Mitzy seemed perfect for her job.

"Mitzy, don't try me. I'm not rescheduling shit, and she's not busy! You know why I'm here. Now, you can go in there and tell Bridget I said I can call the school board and the state of Louisiana Board of Education to file a complaint if she likes. Considering her history, I don't think she wants that," he said feistily.

Mitzy tapped her toe for a minute and then crossed her arms. She finally spun on her heel and wobbled to the principal's office. After a few minutes, Bridget the Principal came out.

"How can I help you Bra-, I mean Mr. Crane," she said curtly. She had graduated a few years behind Brad, and her husband had graduated high school with Brad and Grace.

"Don't try to bullshit me, Bridget. Are ya'll still on this racist shit out here, telling a damned fifth-grader she can't do a history project about black women?" he yelled.

Bridget the Principal, pushed her hair behind her ear, and swallowed hard. "Well, from what I understand, Brad, her sources can't be verified."

Brad's face was red now. Bridget's answer was rehearsed and collaborated. He knew good ole boy bullcrap when he heard it. "Yeah, I heard that was the petty shit ya'll tried." Two students were entering the office; they made an immediate U-turn when they saw Bridget the Principal's face. "So, I'm going to help you out. He reached into his work bag and pulled out four books and a folder. Here are the books she used, and she used one online source from a credible website. Here are the guidelines for the assignment." He slammed it all on the counter. "Now, find another way to bullshit us. Come on. Go for it." He glared at her.

Bridget the Principal reached over and thumbed through the books and pretended to look at the papers. "Looks like the teacher might've made a mistake. I'm going to submit this to her and make sure she corrects herself," she stuttered. "Brad, I had no idea-"

"You tell that bitch I'll have her job if she ever makes my daughter feel like this again," Brad said as he pointed at Bridget. "And if you team up with them to discriminate against either of my kids again, I'll have your job, too. You won't get a damn job in this country when I finish with your ass."

"Brad, there's no need- "she started.

"Bridget don't play with me. If there weren't a need for it, I wouldn't be here. And you feel free to tell that alcoholic ass husband of yours he can try me if he wants to, but I'll have something waiting on him," Brad said. He stormed out of the office.

And he was serious. Although some of the community gave Brad the side-eye for marrying a black woman, he was a smart and well-connected businessman. There were two things he treasured: his wife and his children. Regardless of how people felt about his choice, they knew never to harm his family. That was what made his children feel safe in their community. Their mother often avoided dealing with the challenges of living in a rural southern town; she would either conform to avoid or ignore to soothe. Her son had learned to do the same, but her daughter was a firecracker that could not be put out.

Remembering how Leah had always loved their history made Blake feel a little apologetic for the way he spoke to his sister, but he hated when she insisted that he did not like his black family. He loved his family; he just didn't always feel as if he belonged to them. Blake stuck out and struggled to relate, but he also didn't try. He preferred to stay where he was familiar- his white friends, his majority-white school, his white-ish world. His sister knew it, and he was embarrassed.

They rode in silence with the bippity-bop of the radio rumbling out of the speakers and filling the car. Blake was still thinking about Leah's comments, and Leah wished she would hold back sometimes. Hurtful silence is the worst silence, especially when you are trapped in the car with it.

"It's pitch black already, and it's only seven forty-five. That's how you know fall is here," Leah said to fill the silent space.

"Yeah, and I am glad, too. That means Coach won't try to keep us at the school all night anymore."

"But Mom is going to be even more panicky about me being out late," Leah chimed in. She checked the time; they were right on track to make it to the movies on time. Rashawn was texting her, but she knew he was just checking to see where she was. Leah's eyes were glued to the road; driving at night always made her a little nervous because any animal could run out in front of the car in the country. Early nights also meant a lot of deer and a few wild hogs.

Leah passed the dead end with the broken bridge and noticed that a detour sign had been moved to the side of the road. "Must be finishing some road work this evening. Funny, they must've just started because I just passed through here yesterday, and that sign wasn't moved," Leah said.

"I don't know why they'd do work down there; it's just a dead-end a few miles down. Maybe they just set it there for the night," Blake replied. "I swear they do some pointless stuff out here."

Leah peered down the road. "Must be something going on. I hope nobody is trying to hunt back there. If you go the wrong way, it runs directly into our property, and Dad would have a fit."

"Only one person hunts on that property, and that's me," Blake mimicked. "And I hate hunting, so I guess you know what that means!" He said, waving his finger. The two burst into laughter.

"Dad is the most non-Louisiana Louisiana person I know. 'Hell no, I'm not chasing deer when I can buy a cow at the store!'" Leah chimed in.

"Like father like son," Blake followed up while pointing at his chest.

Leah's cell phone rang. She clicked the button on the steering wheel, and the call blasted through the car speaker.

"Hey, my Queen," the voice said.

"Hi, my King!" Leah said back. "I promise, Rashawn, we are about fifteen minutes away. I mean a real fifteen minutes, not what you call "a woman's fifteen minutes."

"I guess I'll know for sure in about twenty minutes," he joked. "The line isn't too bad, but cars are pulling up. I'm going to get our tickets. You said Blake is with you, right?"

"Yes," Leah said nodding her head.

"Alright, I'll take care of his ticket, too. I'll be at the front waiting on you guys."

"Okay, cool. We will see you in a minute. Bye." Leah pressed the button to release the call. "Well, lucky you, Blake. Rashawn, Mr. Black Power," she said, laughing and holding up her fist in the air," bought your ticket. I will get our food when we get there, even though I am sure he loaded his pockets at the dollar store."

They continued their ride in silence, occasionally talking about people and things from school until they were in the parking lot of the movie theater. It was a Friday night, so their expectations were met with a large crowd. Leah decided against driving the parking lot, hoping they might luck upon a close parking space; they only had a few minutes until the movie would start. Blake and Leah got out of the car and made their way to the front of the movie theater. When she got to the front, there was no Rashawn. She called him.

"Where are you?" she asked.

"I'm on my way from the car."

Leah took a deep sigh. "Here I am rushing, and you aren't even at the front like you said you would be."

"My ma texted me and said not to stand in front of the movie theater; it's not safe for me. She told me to wait in my car. I didn't see you guys pull up, but I'm only a few feet away," he said.

Leah ended the conversation and dropped her aggravation. He was right; a young black boy standing in front of a movie theatre alone was not safe. Sometimes Leah did forget.

******

"So, what's new with the company?" Grace asked.

Brad laughed. "Is this what we've been reduced to, conversations about work? Gosh, either we are getting old or boring."

"No, no, no, I mean, we haven't had the chance to really talk for a while, so I thought we might need to start there," Grace said softly.

"We have candles and wine. You're buck naked, and

we need to talk about the company? Hell, I'm not doing something right then!" Brad shook his head as if he were distraught.

Grace laid back on Brad's bare chest. "No, you do it all right!" she said with a soft chuckle. "I was just trying to keep up with things."

"Let me sum it up for you right quick. The company is doing excellent. Thank you for suggesting that I do a little outreach to some local schools and offer financial support and teacher appreciation. It looked really good when I talked to the owner of my new project. He said his mother was a teacher, and he was so impressed to see me honor them. Of course, I was happy to see him happy; that means he will make me happy, too," Brad spat out. Then he pasted a huge cheesy smile across his face.

"Well, a happy you is a happy me," Grace chimed in.

"You know what would make me happiest?" He looked Grace in the eyes. She waited for him to finish. "I still wish you would consider leaving your job and then just take care of the kids and the house. They will be leaving soon, and they need as much time with you as possible."

"And you like me here at home, too. This is not just about the kids," Grace retorted.

Brad stroked her black, natural hair, which was up in a bun that was now messy and frizzy. "I will not deny that. I love it when my wife is home to take care of me. Your cooking and the energy you have when you get a few days off during the holidays makes me nostalgic every time."

Grace snuggled closely into his arms; she felt his naked skin close to hers even more intimately. When he said words like these, it made her heart quiver and reminded her of why her love for him had never faded. "I've been thinking about it more often. I love working, and you know my career means a lot, but I kind of want to be able to see Leah whenever I want, not when it's a good time for my vacation. Blake's going to be a lot more active on the field next year, and it would be nice to travel with the team and not feel exhausted for the rest of the weekend. The hard part is that I have almost twenty years with the department. I love my job. Not to mention, the money is pretty good, especially since my promotion. What about my retirement?" Grace took a deep breath.

"The money is good, but our money with the company is great. You don't have to work anymore; we are very comfortable, Grace. But I understand you are a strong woman who has worked so hard to get where you are, and I would never discredit that. You are no less of that woman by leaving; as a matter of fact, I've only been able to build our company because of your support. This is not just my success; it is our success." Brad hugged Grace and kissed her neck.

Grace had spent many nights helping complete paperwork, even explaining some of the laws to Brad, who was more of a numbers and logic person. She had filed documents and attended a few meetings as a part of his team until he could afford to hire more people. Even now, she often filled in when the secretary could not come in or if he needed help with a project. Brad did not feel that what Grace did for the company reflected the totality of what Grace had done to support him. She often comforted him when the company was struggling and convinced Brad not to close the business during his first five years. She did all of those things while being a good wife to him and a great mother to their children. Her faith in him paid off for their family, and he wanted her to enjoy what they had.

Grace rolled over onto her stomach, put her hands under her face, and looked up at him. "You drive a hard bargain, fast talker. You are really good, really good. I don't want to lose my retirement, though. What if something happens?"

"Something has happened, and it's magnificent! Our company is successful. Money has been invested. I have IRAs, 401Ks, 403Bs, and E, F, Gs. We have stock and money put away for our kids. Woman, what else do you need? I even have money in a shoebox. We are protected!" He threw his hands in the air and started laughing. "I think your question is, 'what about you having your own?' Let me make this deal with you. How about, I will draw up an official contract- signed and notarized or whatever you want. I will pay for your retirement and put you on an official salary or contract for any work you do for the company. If you don't like that option, why don't you look into some part-time online work, and I will still work out something for your retirement."

Grace smiled. "You really want me to come home."

"Yes, I do," he said earnestly.

Grace thought for a minute. It was a reasonable offer, almost one she couldn't resist; that's why Brad was a successful man. Brad continued, "You don't have to decide today. Think about it, and we will talk again."

Grace didn't tell Brad, but she didn't need to think anymore. She slid down under the sheets and showed him how proud she was of the company.

TREKKED

CHAPTER 5

Madyson was running full speed, barely feeling the tree stumps, sticks, and mushy swamp mud and water underneath her feet. The men had seen them, and they were much closer than she thought. They were coming for blood; she had seen the long shotguns that two of them carried.

She looked behind her; Ben was in the distance, but she had hardly noticed until now. He could barely keep up with her. Madyson stopped and ran back to help him.

"Ben," she said as she looked back and slowed down, "We have to move faster. They are right behind us." Madyson bent over; she was heaving and trying to catch her breath while waiting for him to gain speed.

"Madyson, don't wait for me," Ben said as he struggled to catch up. "I'm coming, but don't wait for me. We have to move as fast as we can." Ben was stumbling and struggling to make it through the mud, but Madyson didn't want to leave him behind.

The men could be heard coming quickly, cursing between their teeth, and yelling and threatening each other.

"You're a dumbass," Madyson heard one tell the other.

"I'm not dumber than your wife," another yelled. Flashes of light could be seen between the trees.

She looked at Ben again. He was leaning against a tree. "Run, now!" Ben whisper yelled. "It's neither of us, one of us, or both of us, Madyson. Please, run. You can get help for me."

Ben knew that if the men caught him, there would be no need for help. These kinds of men wanted blood and death as a trophy. The blacker the blood, the bigger the trophy. Still, he had to say something for Madyson to try to get away; she had a better chance than he did. He couldn't imagine both of them dying because she tried to save him. Someone had to try to survive. Ben stumbled toward Madyson. He looked into her eyes and touched her hand.

He was quiet for a minute. His mind flashed back to all the times Madyson and he had spent together. He remembered how their friendship was always so natural. Their parents bought houses across the street from each other during the same year. They were nearly the same age. They had gone to school together and shared almost every critical moment of life together. Madyson knew Ben better than any girl he had ever dated, sometimes better than he knew himself. Even if Madyson did not always agree with his radical blackness, she didn't try to change him. She took him for who he was and found a way for him not to miss the beauty of the world by being overcome with the pain of man. She had always been perfect for him.

Between gasps of air he said, "I love you, Madyson. I always have, and I always will. You...are the love of my life. I have been too scared to lose you because I knew I wasn't going to ever fit in with your friends and your life." Ben gasped for air. "I don't know what is going to happen, but I have to tell you now, so you know just how much you mean to me." Ben gave Madyson's hand a gentle squeeze.

Her eyes got big; she wanted to cry, but she knew

they both needed strength. "Really, Ben. This is the shit you tell me now! I needed this when I was getting dumped by horrible jerks in college!" She nervously laughed a little. She was scared, and she had to get help. But she wasn't sure how she was going to do it. "I love you, too, always have. I'm sorry for all the times I chose people who didn't give a shit about me over you. You've always been there, and you're always going to be here. So, don't talk like this, okay? Even if you can't come, I'm going to get us help." She kissed him on the lips, and their lips locked for a moment. The fear they'd always had of crossing the line of friendship was no more, and they both felt regret that they had not admitted their feelings sooner. Ben kissed her on the forehead, and Madyson took a deep breath; it was the first time she knew how love felt. Madyson wanted to talk about feelings and look at the stars, but they were trapped in the swamp, and three men were trying to kill them. Madyson could hear their steps getting closer, and Ben knew they were running out of time.

"Run, okay. You have to." He reached into his pocket and put a cold metal object into her hand. Take this with you in case you need it. It's my lucky pocketknife. My dad said a man must always keep a knife because you never know what you need to fix. Use it if you have to."

"Ben, we're-" she started.

"Take it. You are the strongest right now, and you will have to use it if we need it anyway. I may drop it or anything, so you hold it, okay?" He closed the knife in her hands.

 Let's go!" he shouted. Madyson tucked the knife into her bra.

They ran as fast as they could. At first, Madyson felt

Ben's fingers interlocked with hers, but their hands were quickly separated, and Ben was leaning against another tree. Blood had entirely soaked the jacket that was tied around his leg. Madyson looked back and then slowed down. One of the men was coming into view, and his speed picked up when he saw how close he was to Ben. Madyson's eyes grew big with fear, and she knew there was nothing she could do.

"Run!!!" Ben yelled, just before being struck over the head.

Madyson turned around and began running as fast as she could. It was even harder to see without her eyes having time to focus. She was running into trees and stumbling over roots. At some point, she was sure the lump she felt under her foot was a snake or maybe even the tail of an alligator. Eventually, she heard a set of footsteps turn into a troupe of feet hitting the ground. She knew that at least two of the men were behind her.

"Git that bitch!" she heard one of them yell.

She knew they meant it, and if she stopped, they would catch her. Madyson was winded, but she wasn't tired. She was used to running, not quite this fast, but she knew she could probably make it further than they could. Thoughts of Ben were flashing through her head. What would they do to him? Would he be able to fight for himself? Madyson knew that if she wanted to save Ben, she had to save herself. She knew she had to focus less on the journey and more on the destination, which was wherever she could find safety.

Madyson thought about her mother. She had to make it back to her mother. They were so close, and if Madyson didn't make it home, her life would never be the same. Her father loved her dearly, but she was her mother's baby girl. She was probably calling Madyson's older brother and sister, panicking right now. It had been at least two hours since they had last talked.

The footsteps had disappeared. Madyson slowed down but didn't stop just in case she was mistaken. She was right; there were no more footsteps behind her. She could finally stop. Madyson ran behind a tree, bent over, and put her hands on her knees to catch her breath. She had run at least a mile, and she had no idea how to get back to her car. She stood around for a few minutes longer to make sure she was in a safe zone. She didn't even hear the men's voices anymore. She felt around until she found the trunk of a large tree. She put her back against it and slid down to the ground. Madyson put her face in her hands, and tears began pouring downward. She was lost. She was cold. It was dark. Ben was gone. She had no idea where she was or where to go. Her only hope was to get out alive.

Madyson was not equipped to handle this. The most she had done was pump her own gas when her dad didn't have time to fill up her car or when she was away at school. Madyson was a runner, but she only ran around the university lake or on the treadmill in the gym. She was a manicure and mall girl. She wore gloves to load the dishwasher, so her polish didn't chip. The men were gone, but she didn't know how she would make it through the night. She looked up at the moon, remembering her short time as a Girl Scout. They had taught them that the position of the moon determined the time of night. Based on what she remembered, it would be midnight very soon.

******

Grace rolled over and faced the lamp on the

nightstand. Brad was fast asleep, but Grace's mind was racing. The kids had been gone for a few hours. Blake had sent her a text saying they were minutes away from the movies.

Even though she was enjoying the night with her husband, Grace wished she were with her children. It wasn't so much that they were more exciting than a night of wine and sex with her husband. It was just that it was a Friday night, and so many things could happen. She didn't even let Leah go out on weekends unless she was dropping her off and picking her up. Sometimes, she let Rashawn bring Leah home, but Grace frowned upon that because they lived so far out that it was a long drive home for him. Grace hoped Leah was responsible while they were out.

Leah was going to be eighteen in a month, but she didn't always know how to control her emotions. She talked recklessly and didn't consider the consequences. Sometimes even when she considered the consequences, she still didn't care. At home, Grace could ground her. At school, Leah's grades kept her a little more balanced. However, in the world, anything could happen. Grace tried to talk with her, to reason with Leah about how life was. Yet, it seemed the more Grace attempted to teach, the more Leah resisted. They butted heads so often that Grace sometimes tried to hide from her child just to keep the peace. She hated the conflict with her daughter, and there were times when she sat in the bathroom and cried.

These days, Leah was always talking about history. Grace knew history, far more history than Leah did. Grace felt that history had to be what it was- gone. They couldn't live in the past, and if they wanted times to be different, they had to be different. Leah would sometimes puff her chest out when she talked about Big Mama, but she didn't even know enough about Big Mama to be so arrogant. Big Mama had passed away by the time Leah was four.

Grace and Big Mama lived a life that few would talk about in Cradle Creek. That life wasn't easy, and it certainly wasn't kind. Big Mama had to make decisions that Leah would never have to make, so when she picked arguments over things like the colors of the school dance, Grace couldn't see the significance of such a battle. It was unimportant and unnecessary. Big Mama had stood toe-to-toe for bigger battles, so a public debacle over a red or purple backdrop seemed trivial to Grace.

Grace worried that Leah's conflicts could lead to problems for Blake, too. Things were fine now. Coaches liked him; he got along with everyone easily. But if Leah was seen as combative, it could cause others to believe Blake was the same way. Blake had a clear picture of his future and the goals he wanted to achieve. Grace didn't want anything to interfere with that, especially things she felt would not matter to Leah in the future. Why make Blake's future suffer for Leah's ego?

Grace couldn't act like there wasn't some truth to the things Leah said. Cradle Creek was a community that took pride in their hypocritic Americanism. Their "land of the free" was built on the discrimination and isolation of black people in the town. Those black people had to be quiet, work, and go home, and never engage in the community. Ironically, it was built on land that was once the property of an all-black village. That, too, was part of the past that Grace had to accept. The land had been sold and stolen, but there was nothing she could do about that, except appreciate that Big Mama was one of the few blacks who still had land to pass down to her children.

The fact that Brad often encouraged Leah was the one thing that frustrated Grace. The way his eyes lit up when Leah talked about changing things and the problems on the news aggravated Grace. He gladly supported Leah's histrionics several times when Grace felt he should have been calming her down. Having an ally only made Leah more intense and adamant. If Leah would just focus on the path before her instead of the world around her, she could find solace in a great career and personal achievements. That's how Grace had managed to escape the burdens of her blackness in Cradle Creek.

Grace stared into the darkness and focused on a piece of hardwood floor that the moon shone on. No matter how much blackness suffocated the rest of the room, she could still see the boards in the moonlight. The beauty of the brown wood could not be denied, and the tiny imperfections in it- the dents and scratches from high heeled shoes, dragging beds and dressers, and old age- only made it more beautiful.

Grace checked her phone once more to calculate how long the movie would last and how long it should take them to make it home. She felt Brad's hand rub her thigh. Grace rolled over into his arms, which were already awaiting her. Brad kissed her on the forehead, and Grace took a deep breath.

******

Karen Johnson poured another cup of coffee at the bar and stood staring into the living room. She checked the time once more; she had not heard from her daughter. This wasn't like Madyson. She had grown up, and she followed instructions well. Madyson knew her mother would be up worried, and Karen was. She picked up her phone and dialed Madyson's number again. She even entered it digit by digit just in case something was wrong with the contact information. It went straight to voicemail.

Karen laid her phone down and took a sip of coffee. She rubbed her eyes with her fingertips and looked at the clock on her phone. She was just about to pick it up again when she heard the door to the garage open. Karen stood up and watched her husband come up the hall into the kitchen.

"Shift just ending?" she asked as her husband walked through the door.

"I'll be damned if they didn't put most of those new hires on my shift. They say they all passed the certification class, but most of them acted like they didn't know anything. I felt like I had a kindergarten class all day, and then I had to meet this month's goals by the time we clocked out. Hell, I said I would save the paperwork for tomorrow," Johnnie Johnson came over and kissed his wife on the cheek.

Most nights he made it home on time, but the end of the month meant his shift might work late if they didn't meet their goals in time. Johnnie a good supervisor, so most times, they did. However, he hated it when they had new employees because he said it slowed down the team's momentum. They sent the new guys to him because they said Johnnie was patient and a fast teacher. Most guys who got promoted came from under his team.

"Dinner's in the microwave. Nothing fancy tonight-chicken fried steak with gravy and peas," Karen said dryly.

Johnnie licked his lips and pushed the button on the microwave. "It's much better than the tuna sandwich I had for lunch. Went off and left my lunch pail this morning, and the only reasonable thing they had at the café was that." He paused for a minute. "You okay, Karen?" he asked.

"I haven't talked to Madyson," she said. Karen looked down at her cup to keep from crying.

"How long has it been?" he asked as he got a fork from the drawer.

"Almost four hours since I last heard from her," she responded.

Johnnie scooped a mound of potatoes onto his fork. "Oh, honey, you've gotta chill out. Madyson is a grown woman now. It's no telling what she and Ben haven't gotten into. You said they were planning to make a few stops along the way and do some hanging out, right?"

Karen ran her hand through her hair. "Yeah, but every time I try to call her phone, it goes to voicemail. I tried to call Ben, too, and his phone does the same," she said in a shaky voice.

"Look, sometimes we rely on technology too much. Maybe their batteries went down, or they don't have a signal. You and I used to travel all the time before everybody could afford a cell phone. Our parents didn't hear from us unless we made it to a hotel phone, so don't worry yourself. It's no telling where Madyson and Ben didn't end up," he said with a gentle smile on his face.

"Everything you say makes sense, but it's just not like Madyson to not call or text. It's just that the South can be a dangerous place for two young black folks."

"Anywhere can be a dangerous place for black folks," Johnnie interjected. "But that doesn't mean Madyson's in any trouble," he stammered after he saw worry creep over his wife's face. "This ain't forty years ago or even twenty years ago, Karen. What we went throu- "

"-Is no different from what they can go through. Don't you watch the news, Johnnie? It ain't stopped; they will come right through your damned front door. At least that night, they hid behind a hood. Thank God you could drive a truck as fast as you did, or we would've been hanging right over that fire."

Karen took her coffee cup over to the sink and poured the brown liquid down the drain. "I've called twelve times. Madyson would never refuse my calls." She rinsed the mug and put it in the dish rack.

Johnnie sat down at the table in front of the window and looked outside. He jerked his eyes away from the night and shifted them down to his plate. "Did you call Ben's parents?" he asked.

"Yeah, but they are used to not hearing from Ben for days. He's always gone with work." Karen slowly dried her hands on the towel that hung from the sink; she was staring into the white rag's fibers.

Johnnie was almost finished with his dinner. He put his spoon down and looked over at his wife. "Well, there you have it. Karen, you're gonna worry yourself sick behind that girl. You know and I know Madyson has a spirit of her own. If we don't hear from her by late morning, then we will worry. But I have a feeling that phone will be ringing in the middle of the night. I'm going to take a shower, and I want you to take it easy." Johnnie stood up and went to put his plate in the sink. He walked over to his wife and rubbed her shoulders.

"Our daughter is fine," he whispered. Johnny was trying his best to convince both of them.

CHAPTER 6

"That movie was absolutely crazy," Blake said as he walked out of the theatre behind Leah and Rashawn.

"I was lost after the first five minutes," Leah followed up.

Rashawn laughed. "Yeah, because you had your face dug into my shoulder the whole night! The movie wasn't even scary!"

"In my book, scary and bloody are the same thing, but you two were all into it. I was so scared I held my pee until the end of the movie. Next time, I'm picking the movie," Leah whined.

"We'll be watching a chick flick," Blake said.

Leah stuck her tongue out at him playfully. She let go of Rashawn's hand and crossed the hall to go to the restroom.

Rashawn and Blake leaned against the wall, waiting for her to return. They didn't often talk, mostly because Blake felt that Rashawn might judge him. Blake usually didn't know what to say anyway. Rashawn was tall and lean with muscles running through his arms. Blake assumed this was what made him such a good basketball player. He was brown skinned with dreads that stopped just above his shoulders; he had the top of them pulled back by a rubber band. Blake looked down at Rashawn's shoes; they were pretty cool. Blake thought about telling him, but he just looked at his own feet instead.

"How's the season going?" Rashawn asked.

Blake broke his stare and chuckled nervously. "It's

okay. I'm starting varsity now, which is cool. I still have some things to work on if I want a college to pick me up."

Rashawn's ankles were crossed; he switched them around, so his weight shifted. "Yeah, I noticed you were struggling to get down that field a few times. I checked out a couple of your games on the local station. Your goal is to get a solid focus before you throw it. I know it seems that the other team is coming so fast, but don't let that control you. A sloppy throw can make you miss contact every time, but a solid throw can connect you for the touchdown."

Blake was a bit shocked. "How does a basketball guy know so much about football, especially being a quarterback?"

"Most men watch more than one sport, lil bro. But my brother played football and got a scholarship to LSU. I played football in junior high and part of high school. I love basketball, so I stopped playing football to focus on the sport I like the most. I'm just a football fan now," he chuckled.

Blake was learning more about Rashawn in five minutes than he had learned in the seven months he'd been dating Leah.

"You're pretty cool, man," Blake said. "Everything you told me is true. I'm so freaked out about messing up and getting sacked that I try to throw the ball at all costs. I will try to be more focused."

Rashawn chuckled. "I played quarterback for a little while, so I know how it feels when you have that pressure. I date your sister, too, so I know even more about pressure." Both of them leaned over in laughter.

Leah came out of the restroom, and she was surprised to see them so involved. "Well, what do we have here?"

"Nothing, sis, just talking about football. Did you know Rashawn used to play?" Blake asked excitedly.

"Why, of course, I do. I told you," Leah said, twirling her finger, "He's a great guy to get to know."

The trio made their way toward the exit. The crowd was thinning out, and they were part of a small group leaving out of the side door. The temperature had dropped, and it was cold outside.

"Oh my gosh, it's freezing!" Leah said.

Rashawn took his jacket off and wrapped it around her. A police SUV passed just as they were preparing to step off the sidewalk. They paused to let it drive by and then continued across the parking lot. Rashawn had his arm around Leah when the police SUV passed them once again. This time, he hit the brakes and backed up.

"Aw, shit," Rashawn muttered.

The officer rolled down the window and looked at them.

"Good evening, officer!" Blake said with a chipper voice.

"Aren't you friendly," the officer said. He looked all of them over before continuing. "What are you all up to tonight?"

Leah and Rashawn looked at each other. "Nothing," Leah said, "just caught a movie like everyone else coming out of the theater."

"Hum, I noticed this guy right here was circling the building earlier. What's your name?" the officer asked.

"My name is Rashawn Blackston, and I wasn't circling the building. I stood in front of the theater for a minute, and then I went to my car. I was waiting for my girlfriend and her brother," he replied. Rashawn fidgeted around. He was about to put his hands in his pockets, but he reconsidered.

The cool night air made the tips of his fingers cold. There was a slight chill in the wind, and light blue clouds could be seen against the black sky. No matter how cool it was, putting his hands in his pockets was a risky move that he had been reminded to never make in front of a police officer. He shook them a little and pumped his fists, hoping to warm his hands.

"First off, I didn't ask you all that. I asked one question; I saw what the hell you were doing." The officer stepped out of his truck and rested his hand on his duty rig.

Blake butted in. "Officer, my sister and I are in no danger. This is her boyfriend." His voice was light and friendly; he was quite sure it was a simple misunderstanding.

"Oh, I see we have a little ass kisser here. Of course, you weren't in danger, and I wasn't talking to you, boy. I suggest you get quiet," he said to Blake. Then, he turned back to Rashawn. "Give me your I.D."

Blake was stunned and confused. Where he lived, they knew all officers, and they got along pretty well. He nor his sister had ever gotten a ticket, and they usually appreciated his kind nature. This one was different; the officer seemed agitated and aggressive. He acted as if they had done something wrong. Blake felt nervous.

"I'm digging into my pockets to give you my identification," Rashawn said as he reached for his pocket. He thought twice and changed his mind. "You know what; you take it out for me. It is here in my left back pocket."

"Me, take it out? What do I look like digging

in *your* pockets?" the officer retorted.

"No, officer, the question is what will you say it looked like if I dig into my pockets. My hands are up, and I am not moving. If you'd like my license, it is in my pocket- no weapons, no drugs, just some paper from the candy I ate in the movies. My license is in my wallet with a few dollars, my social security card, my debit card, and my school I.D. In my other pocket is my cell phone," Rashawn explained.

Rashawn stood there for a minute, eyes straight forward on the officer- partly watching him, partly praying for this to be over. His phone was repeatedly vibrating; he knew it was his mother. It was always his mother when things were going wrong.

After a few more seconds of staring, Blake was more confused. It made no sense to him that Rashawn would not just give the officer his information. He was only making it worse by refusing to cooperate.

Blake stepped forward. "Look, I will give you his wallet." Blake reached over toward Rashawn to grab his wallet from his pocket; the officer's hand immediately went to his gun holster.

With Rashawn's hands still in the air and Leah's now in the air, they both yelled, "No!"

Blake stopped just short of putting his hand into Rashawn's pocket. The officer was already pulling his gun out.

"Blake, don't ever do that shit, man!" Rashawn yelled before he could catch himself. He took a deep breath. "Put your hands up and be still. Just trust me. Be still," Rashawn said in a tone that was soft and instructional to Blake. Blake turned to face the police and put his hands in the air. This was a news story that Blake had always questioned and whose truth he had always denied. The way these moments went was always based on how the criminal behaved himself. How he spoke. What he said. Whether he was respectful. Tonight, Blake was all of those things, but somehow this situation still left three teens with their hands in the sky, and an officer reaching for his gun.

"I heard ya say something about school I.D.s. What's ya name? Where do ya'll git ya schoolin'?" he asked with his hand still resting on his holster.

"Sir, I go to Bluefield High over there across the river. My name is Rashawn Blackston." His hands were still in the air, and the tips of his fingers were freezing.

There was a sudden twinkle in his eyes. "You the one they say can do the dunking over there at Bluefield, might take that school to a championship? Maybe go to the league."

"Yes, sir. That's me," Rashawn said with his hands no lower.

"Who is the welcoming committee you have with you?" he asked, looking at Leah and Blake.

"As I said earlier, that's my girlfriend and her brother. We just came to catch a movie," Rashawn replied.

"I'm Leah Crane, and this is my brother Blake Crane," Leah said.

"Damn, you gotta be just like this brother of yours. Did I ask you to talk?" He said sounding annoyed.

"Actually, you did ask for all of our names," said Leah. Leah's fly mouth was part of her nature; she struggled to hold back her emotions.

"Crane…Crane…Crane? Of Crane Construction out yonder?" he asked like he was good friends with the owner.

"Yes," Leah said. "That's my father."

"You've got to be kidding me; there's no way in hell you're his kids. Try again," the laughing officer said.

Leah couldn't take it anymore. "As a matter of fact, we are. He's got a dark-skinned, black ass wife, and we are his two half breed kids," she said with an attitude. She had reached into her black woman soul, and her neck was shaking as she laid out her family tree. Her eyes rolled to the sky as she finished the last syllable. Leah was direct, and she hated it when people wasted her time trying to be indirect. "You can call him yourself if you'd like. 318-555-"

He adjusted his holster. "They said it, but I didn't think it was true," he mumbled. Aloud he said, "You've got a helluva attitude, don't cha. No need for all that. I heard he had quite the family, just never seen ya'll in person."

"And why would you? There's no way in hell you'd ever be my dad's friend or my mom's for that matter," Leah snapped back.

The more time the officer wasted, the more reckless Leah was becoming with her words. They had been outside the theatre for 20 minutes now, and the parking lot was nearly empty.

Rashawn knew Leah was aggravated, but this was not the time or place to lose her cool. "Chill, Leah. Everything's okay," he said calmly.

"Fuck him," Leah said, jerking her head to the left. "If you want to shoot us, just shoot us, but don't waste my time. We aren't scared of a bully. And it ain't just my daddy you have to worry about. We'll call every organization across the U.S. if you try us tonight."

"Your paw needs to get a hold of you. I know that mouth you have didn't come from his side," the officer said as he reached into his back pocket.

"Leah, please chill out," Blake mumbled. Leah was ready to read the officer his rights, but her brother's voice- so small, weak, and frightened- stopped her. Rashawn let out a slight sigh of relief.

"Here's what I'm gonna do. I have a lot of respect for your dad, so I'm going to let ya'll go with a warning," the officer said.

"A warning about what!" she yelled, "Walking while black?"

"Loitering," he said, looking over at her.

"But we weren't-" she started.

"Leah, just be quiet," Rashawn said in a pleading voice.

"What'd you say your name was, Rasheem? I'm starting to like you a lot more than I like these two," he said. "I'm going to let you go with a warning, but ya'll get straight home and no hanging out anywhere else."

Leah was seething with anger, and her face was bright-blood red. *The audacity of this dirtbag,* she thought to herself. They waited for the officer to get in his truck before they lowered their hands and then walked to their cars. The walk was quiet, and Leah knew her brother was still confused and probably a little hurt. Rashawn put his hand around Leah's waist, and she put her head on his shoulder. Rashawn looked over at Blake and gave him a small nod; Blake gave a little nod and looked down at the ground.

Just as they made it to Leah's car, a black Mercedes came speeding through the parking lot. It pulled up next to Leah's car, and Rashawn's mother jumped out of the passenger side.

"I've been calling you, and you haven't moved in over thirty minutes. What's the problem?" Mrs. Blackston said.

123

"We got stopped by the cops."

She threw her hands in the air and rolled her eyes toward the sky. "For what?"

Rashawn looked down. "He said loitering, but Mom, we were just walking out of the movies. We were on our way straight to the car; we never stopped. He kept yelling at us, and he told me to give him my license. There was no way I was digging in my pocket because I just knew what he wanted to do. As soon as Blake tried to get my license, he went for his gun."

Rashawn's father was now out of the car, and he was heading toward them. "Where is that son-of-a-bitch?"

"He left," Leah said. "But I got his badge number and his truck number. I'm texting it to Rashawn now." She was already typing on the screen of her phone.

Rashawn's parents had been through this before with his older brother, but his experience had been a lot more violent. The police pulled him over for a missing taillight that led to an arrest. The officer slammed him around and busted his nose, alleging that Rashawn's brother "smarted off" to them. They finally arrested him and locked the seventeen-year-old in a holding cell with prostitutes and two drug dealers on their third strike. The police made him wait for hours to call his parents. The arrest was the lucky move for him. Rashawn, who was ten at the time, was angry that his brother had been mistreated. However, his parents were relieved to bail him out.

When Mr. Blackston arrived at the jail, his son was already sitting in the waiting area. The police chief was apologizing, stating that they had no idea he was his son. "And what does his being my son have to do with being arrested for a taillight? This is bullshit, Chief, and

I suggest you get your men in order before you catch a hell of a lawsuit," he retorted.

"And what is that supposed to mean, Blackson? I'm a black man just like you. I would never want your son hurt!" the chief insisted.

Mr. Blackston stood face-to-face with the chief and looked him directly in the eyes. "Yeah, but we all know you go easy on those white boys with the shit they do in this community. They harass and interrogate black folks unfairly and make some fucked up assumptions about us. I've been pulled over for driving a Mercedes in the wrong part of town at night. I've been asked if I have dope on me, even though they had already run my license plate and gotten all my information before they stopped me. Don't play with me!"

"Blackston, I have a son and daughter. They have to drive around this city, too, so how dare you make such accusations against me. I am only on the side of justice!" the Chief yelled.

"Yeah, yeah, yeah," Mr. Blackston said. "You're full of it, and just because you stopped coming to the NAACP meetings doesn't mean we don't know who you are anymore. You moved to one of the most expensive parts of town to get away from your people, and your children go to one of these white private schools. After spending most of your life at the same church, you left to go to one of these "non-denominational" churches where they lie and say they see no color. Every year you run that television commercial of you and your family during back-to-school and Christmas. And people across the city say you're so nice and a great family guy, but we know the truth. It's your way of saying you aren't like the rest of these- what did you say at breakfast that day? 'Street niggas.' Let me remind you of something; when they get tired of you, they will throw you away like anybody else. A nigga is a nigga regardless." Mr. Blackston stormed out of the office, leaving the chief standing at his desk in a stupor.

Two days later, Rashawn's parents received a phone call from the police department's attorney offering to compensate them for the inconvenience. "I don't want your dirty ass money," Mr. Blackson rattled off. "You tell your boss to hold the motherfuckers accountable for what they did to my son. You know who's doing their job right and who's out there screwing around on the force. Clean it up; that's the only thing that can rectify the wrong. Don't ever try to buy me; I'm not a sellout."

"So often, boys like you don't get to come home," Mr. Blackson told his sons. "This town doesn't like to talk about what happened here, but that's why it's so important that you always remember what I taught you. Don't think about whether you are right or wrong; think about what you need to do to get home. I will handle the legal stuff. If doing right still gets you killed, at least you died with dignity. I promise I won't let this city rest until the whole goddamn world knows your name."

Their father was an accountant with a large local company, but he was well-connected in the community. Mr. Blackson also did independent contract work to help some of the city's largest firms and organizations. He even provided a lot of financial backing for community activities in low-income neighborhoods through his fraternity. Though Mr. Blackston wasn't very public, he was well-respected for his work, and that carried social weight for him;

therefore, when he had any problems, he always had a list of people he could call, both black and white.

And here they were again, seven years later, facing the same kinds of problems, in a town just over the bridge.

"I'm sick of this," Rashawn's mother said. "He can't even go to the movies without being harassed. I hate to call in favors, but we will take care of this Monday morning, and I am posting it online. Everyone else may be afraid to speak up, but I'm not."

"Let me just take care of it," Rashawn's dad said to his wife.

"Oh, I know you will take care of it, and I will, too. I just can't sit back this time, Black. I've had enough." She put her hands on her face, rubbed her temples, and took a deep breath. "Leah, are you okay? I know you guys aren't used to this type of stuff."

"Yes, ma'am, I'm okay. I was just so angry," Leah replied through her gritted teeth.

Rashawn started laughing. "Yeah, for a minute I thought she was about to give the officer the business. She was turning red and everything. I was like 'If she hits this man, we are all going to jail tonight, or somebody's going to die.'"

His parents and Leah chuckled. "Now, he knows I am never foolish enough to hit an officer. I just don't like this kind of stuff," Leah said.

Blake had gotten quiet and was standing slightly behind his sister. The experience was unnerving for him. He was having trouble processing why the officer was so ready to shoot. Even more so, why was Rashawn's family so familiar with this kind of stuff?

"When I kept calling that phone and my baby boy didn't answer, I told his daddy 'Let's go'!" Mrs.

Blackston said.

Rashawn came over and laid his head on his mother's shoulder. "My mama always knows."

"It was my womb! My womb felt him calling for help!" She burst out laughing.

Rashawn's dad was shaking his head. "She swears her womb quivers when something is wrong with these boys. I'll give it to her tonight; she was right."

"And I'm always right. Last year, we were running late for Rashawn's second playoff game, and I told his dad to floor it to the school because something was wrong. By the time we made it, my baby boy was on his way to the hospital for a hairline fracture," she grabbed her chest and shook her head.

"Maybe she is on to something," Mr. Blackston said.

Blake was still quiet, still shaking on the inside and still struggling. Rashawn's mother saw it. "Come here; little Blake, is it?"

"Yes, ma'am." He said as he walked over to her open arms.

She brought him into her chest, laying her chin on the top of his head. "It's okay. The best news is you walked away." She pulled him back. "This world won't always be as kind as you, as honorable as you, as pure as you. You just keep pouring into this world, and don't let this world pour into you." She put her hand under his chin. "It's okay."

Rashawn's dad turned to his wife. "What are we going to do to get everyone home? How do we want to carpool so we can get Leah and Blake home?"

"Oh, no, sir! That's not necessary," Leah said.

"You can't possibly drive home alone tonight!" Mrs. Blackston exclaimed.

"Oh, we'll be fine," Leah replied. "As a matter of

fact, when we get to the parish line, my uncle is one of the supervising sheriffs out there. Everyone knows our family; we will be okay. I'll call my mom, too." Her uncle wasn't good for much, but Leah could trust that the officers wouldn't give them any problems.

Rashawn's mother was nodding her head in approval, but she disapproved. "So, we will at least follow you to the parish line. Then, we will head back home as long as you promise to call me or Rashawn when you make it. What am I talking about? I know you two will be on the phone before either of us can pull up to the house. So, Black, what do we want to do?"

"I'm going to ride back with Rashawn, and we will follow you while you follow Leah and Blake."

"Sounds good," she replied. Even though Leah was sure they wouldn't have any more problems, she didn't argue. They got into their cars. Leah turned on the engine and then reached into her pocket for her phone. Her mom had texted her several times.

Hey Mom. We are on the way. Sorry, we are a little late. Leah clicked send. Leah waited a few minutes, and eventually, her mother replied.

I will see you when you get home. Grace texted back.

Leah knew the tone of that message, and she wasn't sure if her mother would be willing to listen when they got back. She probably would never let Leah and Blake go out at night again. She would be dropping the high school senior off as if she were in junior high and sitting outside waiting on her until Leah went off to college.

Blake had his face down staring at the palms of his hands.

"You okay, Blakester?" Leah asked.

"I'm okay," he replied with his head still down.

"Nah, you're not. I know tonight was very scary for you; it had me pretty freaked out, too. I honestly didn't know what that officer was going to do to us," Leah admitted.

Blake still said nothing.

Leah took a deep breath. "Look, Blake, don't let this change who you are. Just let it make you more alert about the ways of the world. You have good folks in this world, and you have jerks, like that cop."

Blake was still quiet for a minute. He finally said, "I would always blame them for stuff like this. They said something. They did something. They should listen; they should act differently or talk differently. You know."

Leah looked at the highway, searching for a way to respond. She looked into the black night like the answer would line the sky. All she saw was beauty in blackness, but all the world saw was darkness in blackness.

"The first time I experienced the pain in my blackness was when my teacher said she didn't think I could play Little Jenny in the Christmas play because my hair wasn't straight enough. It wasn't just what she said; it was how she said it. I was in second grade, and I knew something was wrong. I never told Dad; I never told Mom. I just took the role of an elf." Leah's voice dried up a little. Thinking about that experience still made her feel uncomfortable. Thinking about many encounters she had growing up in their community was hard. The way she was treated didn't get better for a long time; she just got better about how she handled it. She hung out with people who liked her and stayed away from those whose parents gave her the side-eye at school events or always had an excuse about why they couldn't come over to Leah's house.

The air was silent and thick when Blake suddenly cut through it like a knife in a pound cake. "I was four the first time I noticed something different. Dad and I were at a restaurant with an indoor play area. I went in to play in the ball bin, and a woman ran in and got her son out. She claimed it was time to go, but I saw it in her eyes. She looked at me with an iciness that said she saw something different. When I was six, my teacher told a parent who was her friend that she was so over the mixed-breed she had to teach because 'Brad couldn't keep his Johnson out of colored girls.' Like, who says 'colored girls?' And what are we, dogs? When I play on sports teams, there is an automatic assumption that I am supposed to be so athletic and save every team. And that may seem like something small to complain about, but the pressure is crazy. Some of my teammates didn't like me because I actually was good; they would say stuff like 'Of course he's good; we know that's all they're good at.' Even now, they go out to eat after games and, depending on whose idea it is, I may not even be invited. That's why I tell you to come pick me up." His voice trailed off. Leah heard a small sniffle. "I've felt like an animal for years. I once heard my friend's dad tell another dad that I looked like a monkey. I was in freaking seventh grade, seventh grade! That's when I thought that if I just change something about myself- you know, walk different, talk different, change what I watch and only hang with certain people, that would make things better. It was weird because my friends are allowed to love everything black- rap music, swag, fashion, even slang- but they look at me differently when I use any of this stuff. Why am I expected to be a stranger to my own culture? I started to hate half of myself because I thought my black side was ugly and useless. Some days I felt like a prisoner in my own body. Sometimes," he paused, "I even hated that mom was black, and I blamed her for making us half black. Like, who does that shit? Man, who turns on their Mom, who is loving and kind and the most perfect woman ever, just because some redneck pricks can't see past her skin?"

Blake was on a roll, and Leah had never heard him talk about the problems he faced. Even when she brought them up at dinner, Blake usually sat quietly or even asked to be excused. Leah knew he had to get it out. She kept driving slowly and listening quietly.

"Tonight, I realized that there is no excuse for the way people are treated just because of the color of their skin, and I shouldn't have to change who I am just to make somebody like me. Not ANYbody! This year, we had to go to the schools to talk to the little kids. When the other black players and I walked in, all the black kids got excited because there aren't that many of us. And you know what I did, Leah? I talked to them, but not like talked to them TALKED to them. I treated them like their blackness might rub off on me, the same way that the lady acted when she grabbed her son out of the ball bin with me when I was four." Now Blake was definitely crying. "I am so ashamed, but I am also so confused."

She looked over at her brother. He looked different- like a little boy—one who was lost and cold and scared. The tears on his face had made him age backward for a moment. Much of what Blake said stunned her entirely, but she didn't want to act too shocked for fear that he would close up again. Leah chose her words softly, calmly, and earnestly.

"Blake, being black or even half-black, is a gift we can never repay. Our ancestors shared a journey to and in this country that is unmatched. I understand the confusion you felt; when I first realized people saw my skin before they saw me, I tried to figure out how I could make them love my skin. You should've seen me in the bathroom about to fry my hair every day trying to straighten it so white girls wouldn't keep asking me to touch it. Maybe I could be smarter or quieter or even whiter, but that didn't work, and I wasn't happy having to wear a mask every day. I didn't want to hide anymore and have to play fake for people to pretend as if they liked me. Blake, you are perfect in every way. Your skin makes you no less, and their skin makes them no more. Sometimes people assume that having Bradley Crane as your dad makes life easier, but sometimes even money can't fix your problems. I know you think I am in way too deep with this culture stuff, but there is so much we don't know. Slavery and inventors, movements and so much more than you can imagine. I know people are always saying, 'Oh, let's move past slavery and the Civil Rights Era.' But the problem is all of the mindsets, traditions, oppression, and brutality that were connected to that era still exist and pervade our society. *Per-vade.* I've been waiting to use that word ever since I learned it a few weeks ago." She laughed softly to herself. "Anyway, we can't change what people want to be, but we can be the new generation of young folks who don't play that shit. Like, we're gonna hug and sing kumbaya and celebrate each other's heritage, fight against injustice together, and speak up. And, no, everybody won't be on board, but what do Mom and Dad always say?" She paused for a minute.

"Blake! What do they always say?" she asked again.

He scratched his head. "Do you want to be grounded for eternity?"

They both doubled over in laughter. "Okay; what else do they say? Have *you* done *your* part? Because that's all we can control."

They were near the city limit line, and Leah could see Rashawn's parents still behind her. She pulled over and rolled down the window. Rashawn's mother pulled up next to her.

"I called your parents to let them know why you are late. They are waiting for you. Please let us know when you make it home, okay, baby?" she said.

Leah would rather battle some type of lie than have to discuss this with her mother. "Yes, ma'am!" she replied to Mrs. Blackson.

Leah pulled off toward home, and Rashawn's family headed back toward town. "Mom's never going to let us out again." Leah looked over at Blake; the red in his eyes was now a slight pink.

"Never. We had fun, but we might as well treasure it until you graduate." They both chuckled.

******

Randy stomped his feet in the mud. "The damned flashlight would go out right now! We could've had her little ass," he proclaimed.

Danny butted in, "Well, not really. I mean, she must've been a track star or something because she was so far ahead of us; I was ready to give up a long time ago. I mean, hell, we caught one." He looked back at Ben, who now had a rope around his waist as Joe dragged him. His head was slumped over, and there was a gash on his forehead that drained blood down his face.

"I'll tell you what, for a cripple, this'un damned sure gave us a fight. Whew, he was one of the most bullheaded ones we done had," Joe said as he wiped his head.

"That good cluck put a stop to him. Glad I had my hammer to slow him down." Danny made a swinging motion.

"That ain't what I want, though," Randy said with a lost stare in his eyes. "That'un that believes she done got away. That's what I want." He reached in his pocket, fumbling around for his lighter and his cigarettes. Just as he pulled the lighter out of his pocket, it slipped from his fingers and fell on the ground.

"I'll be damned!" he yelled. "That there's my good lighter. See if you can find it."

Danny pulled out his cell phone and used the screen to shine the light on the ground. "What color is it?"

"My black one that my daddy gave me," Randy responded.

Danny looked around a little longer, searching behind Randy's shoes and in front of them. "I hate to tell you this, but we ain't gonna find that lighter in this thick mud."

"It couldna fell that far. It's got to be down there. Keep looking," Randy barked.

Danny and Randy searched for a few more minutes, digging the toe of their boots into the mud. They pressed their heel in, dragging it back to see if they could feel it. Danny finally called it quits.

"My phone is on twelve percent, and yours don't work in the woods. You know Joe's phone is off. We can't get stuck out here in the dark with no phone. I can't find it," Danny said.

Randy kicked the mud. "Damn it!" he yelled. "I need a smoke. Let me borrow yours."

Danny reached in his pocket and handed his lighter to Randy, who lit his cigarette immediately.

He ingested the smoke and nicotine and then stood for a minute, observing the darkness as if he were expecting to see Madyson in the black night. "Yeah, that's the one I want."

"Well, what you wanna do?" asked Joe.

"That's why I'm trying to figure out," he replied.

Randy started walking forward, sloshing his boots through the mixture of water and thick swamp mud. As he slammed his foot down, mud and water splashed up, hitting Joe and Danny.

"Ain't no damned way you can see a nigger in the black night like this," Danny barked.

"But shit, we can all smell nigger meat burning! It's a different kind of stink…like, like a skunk mixed with rotten deer meat," Randy barked

Danny walked closer to Randy. "Yeah, yeah, like the dumpster when the trashman forgot to come by."

Joe kept the jokes going. "Kinda like that brother of y' urn smells?"

Randy's head snapped to the side. "Hey! Hey! Damnit, don't ever bring my brother into this. I don't like to think about how he pissed on the family's name with that no-good nigger he's got."

"Well, you started it; now you wanna cry about your brother. You ought to be used to it by now; they've been together forever," Joe countered.

Randy stopped in his tracks, "One more word out of you, and we'll be dragging you like that coon behind ya. I'm trying to right his wrongs by taking care of business, and here you wanna lull on 'bout shit can't neither one of us control."

Randy started sloshing again. They were quiet for a minute. Joe was shining a smaller flashlight he had found in his pocket while dragging Ben's body behind him. His steps were getting further and further away from Danny and Randy. His arms were growing heavy, and Ben's limp body kept getting stuck in tree roots and mud. He finally stopped.

"What are we doing with this body anyway?" he asked irritably.

Randy swung his head around but didn't stop walking. "What do you mean?"

"What I said, 'what are we doing with him?' I mean, what's the point of me dragging him if he's already dead?" Joe was annoyed even though he was used to this type of treatment.

"I don't know what we'll do with him. Might take him to my shed until I can figure something out." Randy said without looking back.

"And how the hell do you plan to do that with your wife always at home?" Joe asked.

Randy stopped and turned to face Joe. "See, that's the problem. My wife knows her place; that sow of yours needs to learn hers. You ain't got no balls; that's why you're hen-pecked."

Joe's eyes got big, and Danny and Randy could see the whites even in the pitch-dark night. "Funny how you can whine about that half-breeding brother of yours, but you think it's okay to make jokes about my wife's health!"

Danny, who had been quiet, chimed in. "Well, she is a big gal, Joe."

"She just had the baby!"

"That baby is almost a year old!" Randy blurted out.

Joe dropped the legs of Ben's corpse. "That's it! I've had it. Find her your damn self. I'm headed home to my wife; she appreciates me a hell of a lot more than you rednecks!"

Randy and Danny burst out laughing. "Wait!" Danny cried.

"I'm sorry," Randy apologized sarcastically. "It was just a joke."

But it wasn't a joke. Randy and Danny had petite wives. Even though Danny's wife had a couple of rotten teeth, nothing was worse than a fat wife in their eyes. It made Joe's wife the constant butt of jokes, even though his wife wasn't exactly fat; she was just fat for a white woman. It wasn't just the wife jokes that made Danny, Randy, and Joe clash; Joe was the water boy of the team. He always had the physical work, and they always got to make the decisions. Joe hung out with them because they had always saved him from the bullies who made fun of his dirty and worn-out clothes in high school. When he met Randy and Danny, his white tennis shoes were filled with brown stains, and the big toe of the left shoe had a hole in it. Randy bought him new shoes, and slowly he went from being their friend to becoming their friendly punching bag-always the butt of jokes, always the working man, always the last one to know everything. He often grew frustrated with them, but besides his dirt-poor family who always needed something, he didn't have anyone else.

Danny wasn't much different from Joe, but everyone in their community respected Danny because of his grandfather, who was the only sheriff in the area for many years. His family didn't uphold the dignity of his grandfather, though; his mama, Jennie, dropped out of high school and married a man who couldn't keep a job. That man was Danny's father, and he usually beat Danny's mama black and blue. Everyone in the community knew about it. Jennie had once shown up to the school to check Danny out. She had scratches going up and down her arm and a dark black ring around her eye; she was shaking as she signed him out of school.

"Jennie," the school secretary said, "Do you want us to call the police? I can even call your daddy directly. You don't have to go back. He can't come on school property. We'll be sure of that."

Jennie never looked up. She yelled, "Just gimme my damned son, okay!"

The secretary called Danny to the office. He was so embarrassed by his mama's appearance that he stuck his head in the door and told his mama he was on his way to the car. He knew not to complain or ask for help because his daddy wasn't afraid to give Danny the same ring around his eye that he gave his mama. So, he just held his head down and walked out of the school.

During Danny's senior year of high school, his daddy was found with a gunshot wound to his temple. Danny's mama said she found him in the car shed like that after she heard the gun go off. But there were rope marks around his wrist and marks that coincided with gagging on the side of his mouth. Nobody asked questions, though. They buried his daddy and cashed in the $25,000 insurance policy to pay off the trailer.

Danny had started hanging out at Randy's house as much as he could because it was how he ran from his dad. His father didn't dare come out there causing a ruckus because Randy's dad was well known in their community, and he wasn't slow to pull a gun on anyone who caused problems on his property. Randy's family was considered one of the better families in their community; they had a small business hauling logs. They made enough money for Randy and his two brothers to have nice trucks in high school. There was one problem that held their entire family back; they were racist. It was not a secret that most people in their community were, but people in the community tried to reserve their racism for sideways looks, isolated living, and private talks. Randy's family was known to refuse to hire black drivers; they had been sued a time or two for turning them around when they came to pick-up logs for their company. It was rumored that Randy's father was a part of the Klan, but he swore the Klan was beneath him. It was always hard to tell if Randy's mother was genuinely racist or if she just followed along with her husband. She didn't say much, but she honored whatever his father ordered, never objecting to his behavior. Randy was a kid after his daddy's heart. At the heart of his father was hate for blacks, Latinos, Asians- anybody that wasn't white. Randy decided he had to be just like his dad in order to have his heart. It worked; they threw around racist banter like a tennis ball on an indoor court. It was the language of affection between the two, and Randy knew he could always ease his father's anger by reminding him that of all his sons, he was the one who understood him. Therefore, he excused Randy's problematic behaviors.

Randy hated how hard it was to find people to do exactly what he wanted. Though their country town wasn't the most progressive, most people didn't openly admit they had prejudiced or racist ways. They reinforced their beliefs through their lifestyle and relationships. They used terms like "the good old days," "when I was growing up," "when we had morals," and "before things changed." Most of them didn't preach white power directly as much as they cultivated a climate of whiteness where it was understood. That didn't fit Randy. He was open and loud with his hate, and he didn't know when and where to turn it off. It wasn't that he didn't know; he didn't care. Then, Randy found Joe and Danny- two men who had so many other problems that they had to find a reason to hate someone other than those who disappointed them most.

Danny had tried to fill his grandfather's position as the head sheriff in their area; he took the test five times before he passed it. Some people swore the sheriff's department finally helped him get on the force because they knew his grandfather and Danny wanted it so badly. By the time he passed, there was no position open in his area, so he worked the jails instead. A job finally opened out in Cradle Creek, but it was given to a black officer with more experience. Danny finally left the force. Danny said that niggers had taken the good jobs that belonged to whites, and his grandfather was rolling over in his grave. He wanted to redeem his grandfather's honor by making every black person feel the way he felt when he was denied the job once held by his grandfather.

"It just ain't right," he said one night after his sixth shot of whiskey. "That job belonged to me and my son and my son's son. My granddaddy worked his blood, sweat, and tears for Cradle Creek; he's the only reason they have so many sheriffs out here now. These blacks keep going everywhere they ain't got no business. Because of affirmative action and shit you gotta give it to 'em. They don't have to earn nothing; we just give America away! Not me; I'm not doing it. They're gonna pay. They're gonna pay!" He tossed back another shot.

And Joe was just a follower. It was a horrible reason to be a racist, but Danny and Randy were his only friends. Joe worked alongside blacks at the paper mill every day, but at night and on his off days, he spent most of his free time making all the wrongs of society right with Danny and Randy. He had allowed them to convince him that if there weren't so many entitled blacks on his job, he would already be promoted. He gave little consideration to his constant tardiness and the fact that he quit school his twelfth-grade year.

"My family's company is completely full. Matter of fact, we might have to lay some folks off soon," Randy lied. He just didn't want to see Joe every day because Randy was sure he'd get sick of him, then he wouldn't have anybody to use anymore. "I woulda gotten you a job with my brother, but he says you got to have a high school diploma. You don't want to work there anyway; he just fills his company with blacks and Mexicans. He's always promoting them and everything; I hear about it all the time. Hell, I don't know how he makes money," Randy griped when Joe quit his job at the mill the first time. The real reason Randy couldn't get Joe a job with his brother was because they didn't talk.

But tonight, Joe wasn't following along anymore. He was done with feeling like the scapegoat of the group. He dropped Ben's body, turned around, and started heading in the direction from which he came.

Randy turned around, too. "Are you serious, Joe? Of all the times you wanna grow some balls, you wait until tonight?"

Joe kept walking.

Randy took his ball cap off and scratched his head. "I guess we might as well hold off until tomorrow. Hell, we can't see a thing anyway. I'm not giving up, though."

Danny chimed in. "Do you think there's any way she's alive out here?"

"I don't know, but I won't be satisfied until we drag that corpse of hers out of here. All the damage that gal did to my truck, I gotta get a little satisfaction out of this," Randy replied.

They sloshed back to the car in silence, with Joe in front of them. He was using the GPS on his phone to get back to the highway. Randy knew Joe was furious, but he couldn't understand why he was angry now after all these years. They had always made jokes about their wives, well, mostly his wife. Joe usually laughed it off. Randy had to think of a way to fix it or finding the girl would be nearly impossible. When they made it to the highway, Joe got into his truck and drove off in silence, leaving Danny and Randy to ride home together. Danny tossed Ben's body into the bed of the truck and got in the front with Randy.

Randy lit another cigarette and let smoke float up to the top of the truck. "He's pretty pissed, huh?"

"Definitely."

Randy flicked ashes out of the window and turned on the left signal. "Let's let him sleep on it."

******

Madyson leaned around the tree, afraid that the men might see her shadow. They were inches from her, and she was scared to breathe too loudly. She could feel sticks under her feet, and she was careful not to shift any weight because the slightest move could alert the wolf pack. She could hear them cursing, and the blonde one with the longest beard had a cigarette hanging from his lips.

She saw the trace of their figures in the partial light cast by the moon; she could still remember their scary faces from the gas station. She saw one of them dragging Ben's dead body. Madyson knew something was strange about them, but she never imagined being hunted in the woods. She leaned her head forward to put it against the wooden trunk of the tree, and then she winced in pain, nearly yelling aloud. There was a knot on her forehead. A large one that protruded and now was throbbing with pain. She was sure it was a concussion. *I don't know if this can get any worse,* she told herself.

Her moment of self-loathing was interrupted when she heard the men yelling. The fat one was angry; he dropped Ben's legs and started walking away. It wasn't long before the other two started following him; the one with the brown hair grabbed Ben's legs and dragged him with them. Madyson let out a sigh of relief. She felt stuck in the woods regardless, but at least she no longer had to run. Maybe she could finally start trying to find her way out. First, she needed to rest. She was tired. Her feet were heavy. Her head was pounding, and her eyes felt as if sandbags were pressing them downward. Madyson turned around, so her back was against the tree. "Just ten minutes of rest," she said in a low mumble.

******

It was almost two in the morning, and Leah and

Blake had made it home about an hour earlier. Brad closed the bedroom door behind Grace and him. They were finally getting over the shock of Mrs. Blackston's phone call and were trying to figure out how to handle the situation. As much as Brad didn't want to have the conversation, he knew there was no way they could pretend that their children wouldn't face some tough problems because of their race. They had minimized the discussion with the kids, trading questions for hugs. Instead of asking what happened, they focused on telling the kids how magnificent they were; it was a nearly perfect way to avoid being asked uncomfortable questions or listening to frightening details about what had happened.

"The answer is *not* telling them they can't go out alone anymore, Grace," an agitated Brad said.

"Well, you tell me what the answer is then. At least, if one of us is there, we can handle it," she retorted. She grabbed disinfectant spray from the cabinet below the bathroom sink and began spraying down the counter. Mrs. Blackston's phone call had interrupted their night of romance. Both parents were now fully dressed. They had waited anxiously on the front porch for their children to arrive. Grace had grabbed a basket of laundry and begun folding it to help calm her after the emotional encounter with her children

"We can't handle everything for them. I think Leah did a great job tonight," Brad said.

Grace's head popped up, and she paused. "Blake was obviously distraught. I could see that he had been crying. Our children were terrified. Terrified! I can't carry on as if nothing happened. That's insensitive of you!" she yelled in a low voice.

Brad looked up from the dresser, where he was

placing some of the folded clothes in drawers. "No, Grace, *you* were terrified. When the phone rang, you went to pieces, even though Mrs. Blackston told you they were okay. I had to beg you not to call and make them nervous." He grabbed more clothes from the top of the dresser and began placing them in drawers. "And maybe Blake needed to be terrified. If he doesn't see the way of the world now, he will have a rude awakening when he goes off to college."

Grace stopped folding clothes and sat on the bed.

"Everyone isn't like that-" she started.

"-but a lot of people are," he picked up. "And ignoring reality isn't going to make life any easier for our children, Grace. When people look at them, they are black. Not the Crane kids. Not honor students. Not even *half* black- black. And we live in a part of the South that claims to be the Bible Belt, but these people are full of more hate than love. Jumping joyfully on Sunday and loaded with hell on Saturday night. Calling their sick conversations bar talk and table talk, and on Sunday, they completely disregard what's going on in the news and social media—talking about how they just look on the inside. Can't be true, Grace. How can they look inside others when they know they are filled with nothing but pure hate? It's no way in hell they can be looking on the inside." Grace knew Brad's rant had been brewing for a while, and what he said wasn't just about what happened tonight. It was about what he saw in their everyday life. The things they had both tried to ignore.

"Leah said that the cop reached for his gun before Rashawn could explain to Blake why he shouldn't do that. Blake *has* to learn what is okay for him to do and what is not okay when a police officer stops him. I'm not telling you this because you don't know. You do know. You live it; I'm sharing this with you because it's the epiphany I had tonight." Brad looked down at the dresser in a blank stare for a minute.

He left the dresser and walked over to his wife. "Honey, we have to do better. We can't keep them locked up, trying to hide them from the world. Blake wants to go to a Division 1 school, and Leah is already applying to colleges. This is reality. If we don't have the right conversations with them, it can cost them their lives. If we don't teach them how the world can be, they will not know how to fight the battles they will have to face."

A tear rolled down Grace's face. "I just wanted life to be different for them because it was so hard for me. Living out here, being bullied because of my color is a pain I've struggled to get over. Working a job where I wasn't promoted first because knowing the profession wasn't good enough; I wasn't the right color, either—being hated by your family because of my color. I didn't want our children ever to think their color made them different or bad. I wanted them to know kindness and love for everyone."

Brad wiped her cheek. "You don't think our children know love and kindness? Look how Leah took care of her brother and how angry she was about what happened with Rashawn. She wasn't even thinking about herself. Did you hear our son tell us tonight that he has to do something about what goes on? You've done a fantastic job. We have taught them who we expect them to be, but now we have to teach them about the world, or it will suck them up. It's not easy for me either. I am a white father of two black children, and, at first, it was really hard for me to relate to some of the things they go through. But as they were growing up, I saw it. They weren't invited to friends' houses that I had known forever. They were *mistaken* for kids from the special church program when we would go to the mall. It's hard when your children get treated differently right before your eyes...but that's why I want to do everything I can to protect my family. That includes preparing them for the world outside of Cradle Creek.

Grace leaned her head into Brad's chest. "If my Big Mama were here, she would've taught them everything she taught me."

"Your Big Mama is here, and she is right in there," he said as he touched her heart. "I completely believe Leah is like your Big Mama reincarnated. She is a fighter, and she isn't scared. You worry about Blake; I am worried about her. She has no understanding of injustice, and she has no tolerance for mistreatment. That's exactly what makes her so dear to my heart."

Grace looked up at Brad. "I worry about her so much, too. I tried to calm her spirit, but she thinks I just want to change her."

"Why? Why try to calm her spirit if that's who she is? There is nothing wrong with our children; there is something wrong with this world. We both should be doing more to teach them, not just you. When we got married, I thought I knew and understood a lot of the difficulties we'd face. I greatly underestimated that. I don't ever want you to think you have to teach them about their challenges or their culture by yourself. As their father and your husband, it's my responsibility, too. We just can't keep pretending like the world doesn't exist."

Grace stood back up and began placing the rest of

the folded clothes into the basket. "I know we can't, but as a black mother, you always hope you can change the world before they go out into it."

He took the basket from Grace and placed it on the floor. Then he put his arms around her waist. "What do you think you do every day when you clock into that office and then come home to work with two of the most awesome kids ever created? The world is a big place, but you are certainly doing your part."

"You surely know how to lay it on a girl real heavy," Grace said with a smile. Brad leaned down, kissed her on her forehead, and then moved his lips to her nose, and then her lips. He kissed her with a passion Grace had not felt since their wedding night. His hands moved down her waist, then to the top of her butt, then below her butt, where Brad massaged two handfuls. His lips moved from her lips to her neck before he lifted her and pulled her legs around his hips and laid her on the bed. Brad kissed from her navel down to the top of her pants. He slid her pajama shorts off. That night he helped her forget the worries of the world all over again.

CHAPTER 7

Madyson's eyes peered open, and she squinted as she tried to see into the still, dark morning. She pinched her eyes shut once more and then opened them again.

"Madyson," a voice said.

There was something in front of her. Somebody. There in the swamp, where she thought she'd never be found.

"Madyson," the voice said again. Then, several voices joined in telling her to wake up. They sounded like chimes blowing in the soft spring sun and cubes of ice clinking against a glass of her mama's homemade lemonade.

Madyson looked straight ahead and then to the right and left in the other voices' directions. Standing before her were five women: each looked similar, yet different. One woman was dressed in an old brown dress that looked like a potato sack with a string around the waist. She had a long scar that stretched from her forehead diagonally across her nose and through her lip. The woman next to her, who looked a little more polished, wore a long full dress that scraped the ground. It was apparent that a petticoat was underneath it. Her hair was pulled back, and her dress was not new, but it was beautiful with its dingy white color and blue trim. There was another who had on a mid-calf length dress. It was draped with beads, and she had layers of pearls on her neck. She wore thick stockings and a low heel; she had a tiny shimmery hat on her head. She laughed sheepishly and leaned into another woman who had on large clear-rimmed glasses with two-toned lenses. Her hair was in a Jeri curl, and she had on a shiny polyester dress with a high neckline and a tightly pleated skirt that stopped at her ankles. Around her mid-section was a skinny black belt. The last woman had on a Christmas sweater that danced with sparkly mistletoe and dark blue jeans. Her hair was rolled tightly, and her eyes shone brightly.

To that one, Madyson said, "Momo, what are you doing here?"

"What do you mean, what am I doing here? I told you I'd never leave you!" she said in her usual chipper tone.

"Yeah, Momo, but here in these woods. Who are these women with you? How did ya'll get here?" she questioned. "Did my mama send you?"

The woman next to her grandmother looked familiar, and Madyson realized it was her great grandmother. She was still confused because her grandmother had been gone for at least five years, and she had not seen her great grandmother since she was a young girl. Though Madyson felt relief at the sight of their faces, she struggled to understand where she was and why they were there.

Momo let out the soft chuckle that Madyson loved so much. It sounded like cotton candy coming out of a plastic bag- sweetness being freed. "These," she said as she pointed at the women, "are your grandmothers. My mother, grandmother, great grandmother, and great-great-grandmother. Five generations of Williams women who have come here to see you!" Williams was the maiden name of Madyson's mother.

"To see me? Why? Oh, this is too weird," Madyson

said as she pounded the sides of her head with the palms of her hands.

"Calm yourself, my child. It's not as weird as you think. We are with you more often than you know. We heard you were in some trouble-" her grandmother began. The women nodded their heads.

"Am I ever, Momo! This was supposed to be a fun road trip to celebrate entering my last year of nursing school and Ben's launch of his business, but I stopped to use the restroom. Then, these crazy men were following us and chased us. We had a wreck in this swamp, and I lost my phone. And Ben. Ben, the men got Ben," she stammered. "The men got Ben, and he's gone. This wasn't how this was supposed to go." Madyson said. She started crying and placed her head down between her knees as she used to do when she was a little girl.

She looked up at her grandmother. "Grandmother, they killed my best friend. Ben is gone, and I feel so lost." She began sobbing more heavily.

"Madyson, Madyson, calm yourself, my sweet child. Yes, Ben has gone to eternity, but it is not that time for you." She felt her grandmother touch her head. She looked up.

"You are the seventh generation of Williams women, which means you are so special to us. There is a mission for you to defy the odds and do great things for this family. This journey will not be easy, but you can make it. Everything you need to survive this journey is within; stop fearing man. Look within; you have what it takes to survive. It is within, and we are with you."

"Yes, we are. We certainly are. You can do this, Madyson," the women mumbled.

"But I don't know if I'm strong enough, Momo," she cried.

"Madyson," said the lady who was dressed in the burlap potato sack and had a scar on her face. "I am your great, great, great, great grandmother. You see what happened tuh my face, dear chile? My massas wife grew angry wit' me 'cause he was so fond of me. She 'cused me of sleepin' wit' him. And what was I tuh do? Makin' him angry could mean my life. I was a slave, considered only property, and I had tuh do what he told me tuh do. Trus me, it was nevuh 'cause I wanted tuh. 'Magine having a man who admires you for nothin' more than the way you work a washboard and fulfillin' some strange likin' that most white slavers had. He beat me with the same hand he used tuh make me lay wit' him. And he raped me long 'fore I started to submit tuh him like I was 'posed tuh. My mistress hated me eithuh way. She slashed my face wit' a razor 'cause she said I thought too much of muhself. Her words was, 'You ain't nothin' but a ugly nigger bitch now.'"

Madyson's mouth dropped in horror.

"Don't let that startle you, dear girl. What she did tuh me made me run fuh my freedom like nevuh before. I had heard the stories of ole Moses 'scaping up North, and, though I was scared, I knew if she could run back an' forth I could run, too. When I got up North, I didn't nevuh look back. You may be scared jus' like I was, but don't let that stop you," the old woman waved her finger as she was talking. Madyson knew this woman had to be Grandma Mae, the escaped slave her family still bragged about generations later.

The grandmother in the petticoat leaned forward. "Oh no, chile, we Williams women don't let anything stop us. You are so strong and smart. We've been watching over you for a long time, and you are special. Now, that mother of yours could've done a little more, but-"

"Yes, she could've, but that isn't what we are here to talk about," her grandmother interrupted, and the other women nodded.

The grandmother in the petticoat continued. "I opened up one of the few black-owned hotels up North. Black politicians and well-noted blacks and whites stayed at my hotel. All the abolitionists knew about Lila Williams' hotel. I prided myself in my place and nice accommodations that were often better than the white hotels. When the white folks burned my first hotel to the ground, well me and my husband worked our fingers to the bone and hired some men to help us build another from the ground up. Don't let these white boys scare you, Madyson! Don't worry about them and what they *might* do; think about you and what you *can* do!" she said with fiery energy and a glimmer in her eyes. Madyson had heard about Grandmother Lila and how strong and fearless she was. To see her up close lit a tiny fire in Madyson's chest.

Madyson's grandmother saw the light in her eyes, and she began smiling, too. "I told you she was a great woman, and that's why we are here today. You came from great women who escaped slavery, integrated schools and communities, got an education, and had great children! It's in your DNA, Madyson. You are a fighter!"

As excited as they made her feel, Madyson's reality made her question her grandmother. "But I am alone and lost in the swamp," Madyson said in a low voice.

"You are surrounded by love, and you have everything you need. You are not a little girl anymore;

you are a young woman. Do not be afraid of where you are; the earth is your friend. We are with you, and you have everything you need to survive," she said.

Then Grandma Mae looked her in the eyes and said, "Madyson, the real fight, the thing you *must* survive is the war in here." She pointed at her head.

The women turned and began walking away, deeper into the swamp, disappearing behind the trees. Madyson wanted to call them, but she knew they were leaving and there was nothing she could do. As they faded into the distance, sleep overcame Madyson again, but this time she felt peaceful, even in the dark swampy woods.

*****

Randy pulled up to the old gas station, slammed his truck in park, and got out.

"What's the deal with ya'll, man?" he yelled.

Danny scratched his head. "Man, my wife is hot as a radiator with no coolant. She was sitting up waiting on me when I came in this morning. Said she's had enough of me disappearing all night one weekend a month."

Joe was still sitting in his truck. He had calmed down, but he was still a little salty. "Mine, too," he said. "She had all my shit on the lawn last night, talking 'bout she knew I was with some waitress from the bar. I had to sleep on the couch and everything. Say what you want, but this shit ain't worth it. You may think my wife's a fat ass, but she's still my wife, and I love her."

Randy rolled his eyes at Joe's jab. "So, you guys gonna be some cowards or what tonight? Hell, we shoulda been back out there by now. She might be gone by the time ya'll get your shit together."

The cashier, Danny's mother, Jennie, came outside. "Whatever kind of bull corn ya'll have going, I don't want no parts. Danny, you and your friends been hanging around here for two days. Go on about your business!"

Danny turned his head sharply and looked at his mother, who was standing in the store door. "Really, Ma?"

"Yeah, really," she retorted. "Anytime you get with Randy, it's some bull. And don't you look at me like that, Randy. You know I don't fancy you too much." She didn't, and Randy knew it.

"Now, Miss Jennie, why you wanna treat me like that?" Randy said with a smirk on his face.

"I reckon you think this is a joke, but I'm not playing with your ass. I may not be too fond of the blacks, but I ain't joining no Klan or starting my own shit. I got enough problems trying to keep myself and these two grands I'm raising fed." Danny's mom stuffed a rag into her back pocket and put one of her hands on her hip.

Danny butted in, "Aw, now, Ma, chill out."

Randy put his hand up and interrupted. "Naw, let your ma carry on. I like that feistiness in Ms. Jennie. Besides, I'll stop her when she's lying."

Jennie had allowed her son to be friends with Randy because his family was well-known. His brothers were pretty decent boys, but she knew something was strange about Randy. Despite how noble his parents pretended to be, he didn't even have public decency. He was defiant and crass. He married a girl, and they had two kids, but she was rarely seen or heard. It was said that he beat her mercilessly, and Danny's mother believed it. Randy may not have hit his wife all the time, but he used his iron fist when he was sick of her or himself. Danny's mother could see the signs in any woman. That was one reason she had grown less tolerant of him over the years. With the way Danny loathed her ex-husband for beating her, she couldn't understand why he would be friends with Randy.

"I already said what I gotta say. No hanging around this gas station, you hear. Go on about your business," she repeated. She turned and went back inside the store.

Randy gritted his teeth. It took everything within not to read Danny's mama for the white trash filth he felt she was. She wasn't worth it. He had other things to do.

"Give us just a second, Ms. Jennie. I promise I will get out your hair," he said instead. Then, he turned back to Danny and Joe. "Well, look, how about ya'll meet me in an hour. You stay as long as you can since you're some wussies. I don't think it will take long to get this one if she ain't made it out yet. I would've been out here sooner, but I had to get my wife in order about her whining. I guess that ain't something ya'll know how to do. I'll be damned if a woman ever tells me how to walk and when to talk in my own damned house. And my daddy said the same went for my ma, too." He looked toward the door of the store; Ms. Jennie was gone inside.

Danny didn't take kindly to Randy's comments, but he owed him too much money to fight with him. Instead, Joe butted in. "Yeah, Randy, we know you won't hesitate to show your wife who' boss, but you forget mine's got a frying pan and a mean left hook. She also has two brothers. She ain't afraid to use neither of them," he said.

But Randy didn't care for the joke or anything else Joe said after that comment about *his* wife. He glared at him and said through his teeth, "You don't know shit about my wife but what you think you heard. You keep smartin' off, and I will give you the ass-whipping you think she gets."

Joe had a quick flashback to the past twenty years of friendship with Danny and Randy. Randy's comment was Joe's reminder that he would never be seen as a friend in the eyes of Danny and Randy. Learning to think fast and speak up would never help him and letting them use him had never changed how they treated him either. Even when they got caught trespassing on a black guy's land, Joe was the one who went to jail. Randy took two days to get him out, claiming that he had to wait for his trust fund to clear so he could have the money. Randy had money, and they all knew it; he certainly had no problem coming up with $250 for bail.

"You know, last night, my wife asked me why I'm friends with you. She told me I was stupid because you just want to use me up. Then she said she wasn't coming to get me out of jail for whatever mess you get me into. I would just sit there like the last time, and she'll be gone when I get home. When we went to get the doctor that you said killed your paw, I said okay even though we all knew he had a bad heart and ate like shit."

"You son-of-a-bitch!" Randy pulled back his fist, but Danny grabbed his arm before he could bring it forward to strike Danny while he was sitting in his truck. Danny didn't flinch.

He continued," When you told me we should kill that guy's dogs and do a number at his house because he made them dogs eat your cows on purpose even though they came on his land, I understood. We found out he didn't know anything about what happened, and I still went with you to do the job. When one of them cut us off at the red light out here, even I was pissed about that. Had it not been for your brother pulling him over, we woulda did what he deserved. But chasing down this girl is just enough for me. I seen her face flash in the dark last night, and she's scared shitless. I tried to act like I didn't until I seen her face again in my dream this morning; woke up in a cold sweat and my heart was pounding. She ain't much older'n my oldest girl. Then you wanna gripe and moan the whole time. When I came home, I was cold, wet, and tired. My wife is making chili tonight, and the game is about to come on. I'm out of this, and I won't be back." Joe started the engine of his truck.

Randy was furious, and they could see it. "I guess since the little nigger at the job gave you a fifty-cent promotion, now you love 'em."

"It's three dollars an hour! That three dollars has helped me out of a lot of shit that listening to you got me into," Joe said, waving his big sausage-like pointer finger. "Say what you want, Randy. I ain't doing it no more."

Joe put his truck in reverse and gunned the engine as he backed out. Dust and rocks flew up in the parking lot as he swerved onto the road and took off down the highway.

"Shit!" Randy reacted. He took a deep breath and sighed as he watched Joe speed off down the highway. He felt around in his pocket and grabbed a cigarette and Danny's lighter that he had borrowed the night before. "Joe's pretty pissed. He might be serious this time. Well, see you in an hour?"

Danny definitely wanted to back out now, but he owed Randy money. And Randy was his only friend. "I can't stay out all night, Randy," he said.

"We don't need all night. I will take care of this one quick. This little bitch has caused more problems than she's worth," he said. Randy walked to his truck and got in. "I will meet you at my house, and then we will ride in my truck. I know where we need to start, too."

"Okay. See you then," Danny replied. Randy backed out of the parking lot and sped off down the road.

Danny stood there looking for a minute. Then, he turned and looked at his mother, who was straightening shelves in the convenience store. He walked in to speak to her before he left.

"Hey, Ma. I was just letting ya know I'm leaving," he said.

Jennie was putting a can of peas on the shelf; she turned around and looked at him. She began putting cans of peas on the shelf again. "When I, err, loss your daddy," she said, slightly stumbling over the words between *when* and *daddy*. "I thought it was the best thing for my family and me. I didn't want him to kill me and certainly not in front of my two kids, so losing him seemed like the best thing that could happen to me. I was hopin' they'd never turn out like him or that ugly version of me. Now, you ain't no wife-beater, and you done pretty good about providing for your family, but you know, and I know you doing some things that just ain't right by God."

She paused for a minute and looked at him. Danny dropped his head.

"You ain't got to like nobody; hell, I prefer that some folks stay out of my way and sight myself. But letting your hate for some folks rule your life will only ruin your life. I can tell you that firsthand. I never told ya'll this, but that sister-in-law of Randy's ain't half bad. When she was a girl, her grandma lived down the road from us. Course her house was nicer, and she owned a lot of land from what I'm told. I don't know how she got all that, but somehow, she did. Anyway, every month they would come down to our house and bring food from their garden- greens, tomatoes, peas, corn, all kinds of stuff. I never asked for it, and at first, I was downright ugly when they brought it. Your daddy was gone, and so was your pawpaw, so I needed all the help I could get. I had been on such a rampage when your daddy was alive that most of the people around here didn't want to mess with me. I thought I was too high and mighty to go to the food stamp office. I had already used the money from the insurance, and times were tough."

"I remember that, but I thought the church gave us that food," Danny interrupted.

"Son, not one church around these parts would even talk to me after what I was accused of in this community. Randy's family brought us a basket from their church once, but that was the only church and the only time. That lady brought me food for three months before I could even look her in the face and say thank you. When the holidays came around, she did a little more. She bought rice and ham and turkey so you kids could have a good meal. She never asked for anything in return, and even though ya'll went to school together, that girl never said anything other than hello when she saw me at the school or a game or something. I knew what your granddaddy believed, but everybody ain't the same. Sometimes people ain't what you been told they is. And when you learn that you feel outright ashamed because it's so hard to get them thoughts you been taught out of your head. Sometimes strangers treat you better than the people you know; sometimes, the people you hate are the ones to teach you about love. Hell, your grandpa cut me off when I got married and pregnant at seventeen, not exactly one of his gleaming moments. The point is, remember that everything you do has a consequence. You might pay the price, or your children might pay the price, but the price will be paid." She walked toward the front of the store, and Danny followed her. He had questions, but he had no rebuttal for what she said because he knew she was right. His family had faced hard times over the past few years. Even when he got a bonus from working in the lumber yard, something always came up. If the car wasn't broken, something in the house was. When they finally got one child out of daycare and into school, his wife was pregnant again. Five kids took a lot of money from his wallet. He took in a deep sigh and let out a big breath.

"Mama let me ask you a question," Danny said. He looked down at his boot and then up at his mother. Age had not been kind to her. Her face was covered in wrinkles; her hair was almost entirely gray. Even though she was tiny in stature, her skin sagged, making her eyes look sad even when she was smiling. Danny felt sorry for her; she never remarried, and just when he thought she could live a little, his sister was taken in for smoking and making meth. The kids had to go with family or end up in foster care. Naturally, she took them and tried to be thankful that she got her grandchildren before the system did. But she was tired and old, and it was easy to tell taking care of a six and eight-year-old was wearing her down. "Did you kill daddy?" Danny finally asked her.

She stared at cans of carrots that she was holding in her hands. For a minute, Danny thought she might cry, but she pursed her lips and answered. "I didn't kill your daddy. Your daddy was kind, handsome, and sweet. He talked to me like poetry and loved me like chocolate candy. That man who used to beat me black and blue, threatened me, and locked me in the bathroom when ya'll went to school wasn't your daddy. I killed the devil, or the devil would've killed me.

******

"We'll do your mom's truck first, then my truck, and you guys' car last," Brad said as he and his son picked up two water buckets off the garage shelf. He handed one to Blake and sat one on the ground. He grabbed the soap and two pieces of old sheets that had been ripped up.

"You have to be the cheapest man with money. You won't even get our cars detailed professionally," Blake laughed.

"That's where you are mistaken; I get each car detailed once a year- carpets shampooed and everything. I even get the little special air fresheners," he laughed.

I know you mean it," Blake said as he grabbed his bucket off the ground. "I've never seen a man with so much money be so coin conscious," he laughed.

"I'm frugal about certain things, son. I don't believe in paying for things that I can do myself. We pay a water bill each month. Why on God's green earth would I buy more water just to wash the cars? That's just crazy to me. I can make time to save money," Brad said to him as they walked out to the cars, which had been moved from the garage and parked outside Brad's work shed.

"Okay, I can understand that, but what about the time you wanted us to grow our vegetables and fruit? Honestly, Dad, you knew that would be a fail," Blake said, slinging the first soapy sponge across the hood of his mother's car.

Brad couldn't resist laughing as he thought about how they spent two days planting the small garden and making big plans, and then they never even watered it again. "You might be right about that one. It wasn't about saving money, though. I thought we'd be healthier, and we'd be spending time together. I didn't know if we were going vegan or vegetarian, but your mom is quite the gardener. You know she and Big Mama used to grow a huge garden when she was growing up." He sprayed water on the two cars they were washing. Grace's SUV was now full of soapy foam.

Blake paused, holding his sponge over a spot on the window for a moment. "Dad, we eat far more racks of ribs and chicken wings than normal, so I think the correct term for us is *meatatarian*." They both started laughing. "Seriously, does my mom know how to grow a garden? She used to get on the ground and pull up weeds? She can't stand for a speck of dirt to be on my clothes," he said.

"Your mom is prim and pretty, but she is also a country girl who can survive off the land any day. When I first met her, I thought she was the best, always answering all the questions in class and coming to school smelling good. Then, when she finally gave me a chance to hang out with her, she could talk about anything. Aw, man! I was in love!" Brad had a huge smile on his face as he reflected on their days in high school. He imagined Grace sitting in the desk that was in front and to the left of him. Her hair was in small single braids, and she always smelled like soft flowers. Even if she had already answered one or two questions, Grace always had her hand up in class. "Gosh, she stole my heart," Brad said. He had a smile on his face, and he was staring into space as if he could see their childhood days clearly.

"Thanks, Dad, but nobody asked for the weird stuff," Blake scrunched his nose, so his father sprayed the water hose at him.

"One day, you will know the feeling," he replied. "What about you? Girls?"

"There are a lot of hot girls at my school, but honestly, I struggle so much with feeling comfortable about who to date. If I date a white girl, will her family accept me? Will someone say something that I don't know how to respond to? If I date a black chick, what if I'm not 'black enough' for her? What if my friends out here don't want to talk to me anymore because of it? I'm embarrassed to even say the last part, but it's true. I used to like this girl named Mindy Stevens-"

"Yeah, the little cheerleader. I know her family," Brad interrupted.

"Right. And they know ours, which was the reason they didn't want us to see each other. We were talking and texting for a while. We even video chatted a few times, but when I asked her on a date, her dad was not having it. He told her he wouldn't buy her a car for her birthday and everything. It really hurt her. She finally broke down and told me that they got into an argument about it. Her dad told her he didn't care who we were or what kind of money we had; he didn't believe in races mixing," Blake said. Brad could hear the hurt in his voice.

"Sometimes, I regret not moving away from here. The South can be a hard place for anybody who's not white. Progress has been slow; people haven't changed. It's even more frustrating to know I've had coffee to talk business with some of these guys, yet I know how they feel about my family," Brad took a deep breath.

Blake was drying the vehicle, but he paused for a moment. "What would moving change, Dad? We've traveled a lot of places; the scenario may change, but the hearts of so many people do not. I remember when we went to New York, and we saw people protesting the Stop and Frisk Law on the court steps. It's obvious that this law was targeting minorities, but they didn't want to change it. I was really young, but I clearly remember seeing those crowds of people and how angry they were. The whole time we were in New York, I thought it couldn't happen to me, but now I know it could. They could've frisked me with you standing right there, and there was nothing we could do about it. There was the time we went to Puerto Rico, and that waiter at that fancy restaurant referred to us as 'la familia con la negra mujer' when they were bringing our drinks out. He could've said table twenty-six because we had a big card on the table. But that's not what he saw; he saw a dark-skinned black woman with a white man in a fancy place that was majority white people. So many times, we've been traveling, and people act a little shaken when they figure out we are your family. Honestly, it was always easier when I was little because I felt protected by you. I could act like things didn't bother me because of how much people respected you. But I'm not a little boy anymore, and the world doesn't treat me like one either."

Brad finished drying off his truck and leaned against it while Blake finished the last part of drying off his mom's car. "Blake, I know things are changing for you, and you are seeing things in a different way, a more real way. I don't want your self-confidence to be rooted in being accepted by others, not even a woman. You don't have to act like other people to be accepted out here. Hell, most of these people didn't like me before I started dating your mother, and they damned sure don't like me now. They didn't stop anything for me, and I don't want them to stop anything for you. There are more good people than rotten ones in this world, and when you are doing the right thing and being true to yourself, you will meet them. Those are the game-changers. Those are the world changers, and they come from different races, from different countries, with different beliefs and looks."

Blake was now standing across from his dad. His father's words made him feel good, and there was a warmth just below his heart. Still, some things lingered in his mind. "Dad, all of those things are easy for you to say because last night never happened to you. We go places, and people judge the rest of our family and never judge you."

Blake's words were strong, but they were true. and Grace agreed that they had to be more open and truthful in their conversations with their children, but it happened faster than he expected. The burn of the conversation was stronger than he thought it might be. Brad would rather take a straight shot of cheap vodka than face his son's truth about race and his own white privilege. He swallowed it though and then chased it with words he'd never been able to admit before. "My greatest challenge has been that I cannot relate to what you are going through. I know what happens, and I am angered by it, but I cannot personally say what it feels like to be a black person. Sometimes, I feel it is the greatest intimate connection that I may never be able to have. But I am still your father, and your pain hurts me, too. Your struggles keep me awake at night, too. I love you so much, and the way the world treats you angers me." His voice quivered, but Brad wasn't a man to cry. "Come on. Let's clean up your mom's truck together, and then we'll grab some pizza, the universal food of love."

******

The air in the car was so stiff and thick that a hacksaw probably couldn't cut it. Grace had jazz music playing so low that it could barely be heard, and Leah was intently staring out of the window as if the shrubbery on the side of the road was uniquely interesting. They had been to town to order the rental pieces for the school dance and to check out dress options for Leah. It had been fun, but the teen and her mother were avoiding the discussion of what happened the night before. Leah's parents had handled last night's incident better than she anticipated, but she knew something was brewing inside her mother.

"I think it is so cool that you were able to convince your club sponsor to change the colors of the winter formal," Grace finally said.

"Yeah, it worked out. Unfortunately, I had to do quite a bit to convince the sponsor, but I got it done,"

Leah replied. "However, having all of the work turned over to me is her sweetest revenge. I'm glad you could come with me to order the rental pieces."

"Well, sometimes we have to pay the price to get what we want," Grace said.

Leah gave her mother the side-eye. "It's not about getting what we want; it's about getting what we deserve. There's a difference between paying the price and being punished."

The car in front of them had been driving slowly for the past several minutes. Grace turned on her signal, got into the left lane, and passed the small car. She continued, "Well, there was always the option to leave it as it was."

"You're just not going to let it die, are you? You have to win the argument or prove you are right, don't you, Mom?" Leah said in a frustrated voice.

"Leah, your tone is-"Grace started.

"My tone is aggravated!" Leah yelled. "What is it with us? Why is it that everything I say or believe or do is a problem for you?

Grace looked at Leah with shock. "Leah, that's not true. I'm just trying to get you to understand that you don't always have to go against the grain," she said.

"And I'm trying to get you to understand that you don't always have to go with it. It amazes me that you are always telling Blake and me to be leaders, but when I try to lead it's not right unless it's what you want me to do or how you want me to lead."

Grace looked at her daughter quickly. Leah had struck a nerve. Leadership was one of her most frequent arguments for making the right decision; it was nearly impossible for her to argue with that point. A part of Grace wanted to use her parental authority to silence Leah, but she knew she was supposed to be doing more listening than objecting today. So far, Grace was already failing. "Leah, I want you to lead, but why does your leadership always have to be so conflictual?" Grace asked matter-of-factly.

"Conflictual? Talking about Big Mama, the woman who raised you, is a conflict? We raise thousands of dollars hosting a school formal each year, and asking for some new decorations makes me problematic?" Leah was yelling, and her face was red. She could feel her tear ducts swelling. *Damn it,* she told herself, *get it together. You are not a cry baby.* Leah was never the type to cry but knowing that her mother could never seem happy with her had turned her frustration to pain. "The part you dislike about me is the part that used to be so much of you. Over the years, I have watched you fade into the background, and I just don't get it."

"Leah, I'm just saying that sometimes life is easier if you don't make a big deal out of everything. Let some stuff go," Grace said.

"By birth, I'm biracial. Half black and half white. But in America I'm black, Mama. Because of that, people treat me differently, and you know it. The lives of people who look like us aren't easy. Turning a blind eye to everything won't make it go away," Leah replied.

"If you keep making everything about race, you will never see that life can be beautiful. You will always see a problem," Grace raised her voice.

Leah cocked her head to the side. "Whoever said I didn't think life is beautiful. Can't I be conscious of the problems and happy to be alive at the same time? How can you be so one-dimensional? I know you can't believe what you are saying. There's no possible way you can think we should ignore color, and the problem will disappear. Or maybe you want Blake and me to live in that kind of world. That's total cow crap, and you know it," she said. Leah wanted to say *bullshit*, but she knew the chances of being slapped to graduation were highly possible.

"You just don't get it, Leah."

Leah looked at her hands and said in a low voice, "Yes, I do. You were raised by a strong and fearless woman; I hear you were once fearless, too. What changed you? Education? Money? The loss of Big Mama? Having children? Or marrying a white man?"

Grace shot her a look that seemed like anger, but it was rooted in hurt. What upset Grace so much was that Leah believed she was smart and had the world figured out. Grace pulled the car over to the side of the road, a few feet from the "Closed Road" sign that had been moved. "Let me tell you something, Leah Crane; your father and I have worked our fingers to the bone for you. We have done our best to give you all the things we never had; we support you in everything you do. I don't give a damn how much of a strong black woman you *think* you are because you read a few books and watched a few movies, you will never disrespect me. One day, you will see that having a big mouth isn't all it's cracked up to be. You'd better learn to humble yourself now, or you'll pay a gruesome price down the road." Grace put the car in drive and took off.

Leah sat quietly for a moment. She stared out of the window; then, in a low voice she said, "I've been reading and learning so much about how my people struggled at the hands of others all over the world; the greatest burden is when your own mother is your oppressor." Leah never turned away from the window. Grace knew the conversation was over, and Leah was done.

The rest of the ride home was silent. Leah's words struck her, but the tone of Leah's voice struck Grace even more. Her daughter was trying to breathe, and Grace was suffocating her. She was a forest fire in a barrel, begging for the chance to set something ablaze. She wanted to burn down the old, dry, useless forest and make room for the re-birth of beauty and purity in the world around her. Grace had been extinguishing the fire every time Leah started to burn. The worst part was that she had no idea how to tell Leah she was sorry.

******

Madyson felt the light before she saw it. She opened her eyes, squinting them to block the sun. She winced; her head was pounding, and she could feel the pain more intensely directly in the center where the knot was. She used the tips of her fingers to press down on her forehead, and she felt the lump still there. It had gone down just a little. Madyson tried to open her eyes again, but the sun was still shining directly into them. She put her hand up like a visor and slowly pushed her lids open. She remembered where she was and how she got here. It took her a minute to get the feeling in her arms and then her legs, and she was sure she had a concussion that had left her unconscious for a while. She sat up and looked around the woods, trying to remember the direction from which she had come. She was having a hard time judging the path she should begin walking to find her way back to the highway. Madyson thought back to the dream she'd had; it still seemed so real. She remembered the words of her grandmothers, and a half-smile briefly crept upon her face. She felt comforted, as if she weren't in the swamp alone.

Madyson stood up and lifted her head back to the sky. The swift move made the sky and trees above her spin. After a few moments of dizziness, she gained her balance. "Grandma, I know you and my ancestors are with me. Guide me! Dear God, protect me!" she said. It had been a long time since Madyson had talked to God. She hadn't even gone to church since she was away at college. Her parents attended church faithfully on Sundays. Her mother urged Madyson to come with her when she was home to visit, but Madyson was either tired or needed to go back to campus early. She usually didn't have time for a morning prayer, but today she was pleading for help. She felt a little guilty. However, Madyson was sure that God had sent her grandmothers to her, and she knew she needed Him to help her if she was going to get home.

Madyson brought her head forward and looked into the woods. Madyson knew she was facing the direction from which she had come because there were broken plants and a slightly visible line in the mud where they had been dragging Ben's body. The only problem was that the mud became water with deeper mud underneath it, making it hard to follow the tracks. She would follow it as long as she could; she hoped to make it to the car. That would mean she just had to continue walking forward to get out of the swamp.

Madyson had a subconscious worry- when were the men coming back? They were looking for her, and they wanted to kill her. Madyson surveyed the woods around her once more. There were tall trees- oaks and cypress- dripping with moss as they waved above her head, and cypress knees were jutting up out of the swampy water. Madyson was ready to find her way out of the swamp. Just as she lifted her foot, she saw a flash of metal. The flash was dull and quick; she almost missed it. To her left, near the base of a dwarf palmetto, was a cigarette lighter. It was the one she had seen the men looking for when they were chasing her. She reached down and picked it up. Madyson pressed the starter, and it flicked a small flash of fire. She pressed the starter again, and this time a flame popped out. Her eyes lit up as brightly as the flame when she considered how handy the lighter might be. She thought about putting it into the pocket of her shorts, but the pockets were damp, and she was afraid the lighter wouldn't work when she needed it. Her shirt had started to dry, and it had crisp patches where dirt had dried on her shirt. Madyson slid the lighter into her bra next to Ben's knife and started her trek.

Madyson could hear mosquitoes; even more so, she could feel them pricking her skin. She was itching and had welts on her arms. She recalled her Girl Troop days. They had been told that mud was a great way to ward off mosquitoes. Madyson didn't know if it was more dangerous to dig her hands into muddy swamp water or to let the bugs continue to bite. They were big, so big that when she smashed one on her arm, she heard a loud crunch. *The key,* she told herself, *is to not focus on the mosquitoes.* Then there were the slithering sounds and the pops and flops that she knew belonged to snakes, alligators, nutria rats, and all kinds of swamp monsters. She was sure that several of the bubbles she saw in the water were sets of alligator eyes, and she had seen one when she was running from the men. *Focus on the destination, not the journey,* she told herself. This place was enough to drive anyone crazy, but the thought of home and her family kept her sane. Madyson was sure her mother was looking for her now. She was so far in the woods that even if she could use her cell phone, she knew they couldn't locate her.

The sun was going down. Madyson had been walking for about thirty minutes, which meant she was unconscious much longer than she thought. She had to find her car within the next forty-five minutes. She stopped and leaned against a tree to rest for a minute. She was tired, and now her body was also screaming with hunger. Madyson could taste her mama's buttermilk pancakes and strawberries with whipped cream. The breakfast sausage and sunny side up eggs would be perfect right now. Her mama would have coffee, and she would have grapefruit juice while talking about all the latest "wives of whatever reality show" drama. Her older sister would be tuning in on the phone, chipping in snarky comments now and then while she fixed bowls of cereal for her boys and oatmeal with tea for herself. Her mama's smile was so clear and stretched from one ear to the other, creating rosy apples in her cheeks. Only Madyson, Karen's baby girl, made her smile like that. Madyson knew she had to see that smile in person again. Her daddy, if he were off work, would say that they sounded like cackling hens, and he was glad that they found those shows to be entertainment and not real life, to which her mother would say, "What do you mean? I do spend everyday shopping, planning parties, and talking about the latest petty gossip." Madyson, her sister, and her mother would barrel over in laughter as her father left the room, shaking his head and laughing with a cup of coffee in his hand. The conversation was always spontaneous, but the Saturday breakfast was a regular when Madyson was home.

She stepped away from the tree and bent over to stretch her back before starting her journey again. Madyson had lost a few more minutes of light, but the break was worth it. Just as she prepared to trudge forward, she heard the sound of splashing and moving. Then she heard the sound of voices; they were in the distance, and she could not make out what they were saying. But she knew at least one of the voices was from the men. They were back.

******

"I told you to meet me in one hour, man," Randy griped. "Now, it's getting dark, and she might be gone by now."

"You could've always come alone. And if she was found, we'd know by now. My wife's friend told her the sheriff's department got a call about a missing girl in the area. They told them they hadn't had no emergency calls, and they wasn't going looking for no trouble. They put an alert out on her car, but the last known hit was twenty miles out. You know only one phone company gets service in this area and there ain't no service in these woods, so I think we are good on that. Whatever you wanna do, do it tonight before it gets late," Danny said.

"So, what are you, gotdamn Detective Tibbs? You heard what everybody else done heard. We have time, but we need to make it happen fast," Randy rebutted as they pushed through the woods and muddy swampland.

Danny's conversation with his mother played in his mind. The hunt was becoming more than he expected and certainly more than he wanted. He realized he could lose everything. Danny questioned how he had gotten so far in with a man who was so dark and dangerous. Randy's own family didn't deal with him much, and once his father died, they dealt with him even less. His younger brother steered clear of him and tried his best never to know what he had going on. They talked, but it was usually an empty conversation with the same topics over and over. How was the family? Did he go hunting lately? Was he ready for the summer, winter, fall, or spring?

Randy's older brother didn't talk to him at all, and Randy preferred it that way. Randy considered him to be a betrayer of the family's name and culture. Randy once said that if his brother needed a kidney and he was the only one who had it, he'd sell it on the internet before he'd give it to his coon-loving brother who was contaminating their bloodline. Danny thought that was mighty cruel, but he didn't dare defend Randy's brother. Since Danny's grandfather was a known member of the Klan, he knew it just meant Randy was true to his beliefs and passion for the white race.

The whites needed somebody who cared about them. Danny believed everything his ancestors had worked for and built in this country was going to waste by the Blacks and Mexicans. They were moving into the good neighborhoods and using affirmative action to get jobs they didn't deserve. He hadn't worked with many blacks since he left the Sheriff's Department, but he thought about how hard it was for Joe to get promoted on his job. Once, Joe had to retake a class on diversity because he failed the test on his job. *How can a job try to make someone like blacks, Japs, border crossers, and everything else that had no natural right to be in the United*

States anyway? he had said to himself. It was the very reason his wife had to quit her job and go home with the kids. For years, the daycare by their house was owned by a good white family; everybody in the community respected them. After thirty years, Mrs. Lisa decided to sell the daycare and retire. With all the nice white girls who worked there, the one black girl decided to buy it, and it was said that Mrs. Lisa sold it for little of nothing. It was no way he was letting his kids stay there; he didn't trust her kind even if she did say she would honor the lower price Mrs. Lisa let him pay. His wife made some decent money keeping books at the parts yard, but her anxiety ran high every time she thought about leaving their two little ones over there. They couldn't afford the other daycare, so the only option was to quit her job and bring them home. Since then, Danny's family had been struggling financially, but their integrity reminded them that they did the right thing.

And there was his mother today talking as if she didn't understand all of this. Of all people alive, she should know. She was a hardworking white woman who couldn't even qualify for food stamps because they were all sucked up by welfare folks who didn't want to work but wanted to eat steak and shrimp all day on the taxpayers' dollars. There she was bragging all high and mighty about some black woman giving her greens and tomatoes out of her garden when Danny was sure that same woman was collecting food stamps and every other government hand out possible. He had no proof, but he knew how those folks were. Danny and his wife had been getting food stamps for a little over a year now, but they were different. He was a working man, and his wife was taking care of the children so they could be safe. They only had steak every now and then because his gout flared up, and he was allergic to shellfish.

The more Danny thought about how he got here, the more he realized Randy was right. They had to make a point, but it had to be made in two hours or his wife was going to lock him out.

"Quit dragging your feet, Danny!" Randy barked. "And be careful; I just saw a moccasin out here."

Just then, Randy heard a splash. "Did you hear that?"

"Yeah, I did. Turn on the flashlight; it's too dark to see," Danny said.

Randy turned on his light, and Danny did the same. This time they were prepared. They flashed the light around the swamp, running the stream of light up trees. He flashed it between trees, hoping to see at least a shadow.

"I know the bitch is here," Randy muttered.

Suddenly there was a series of splashes and the sounds of tree limbs moving. Randy and Danny flashed their lights in the direction of the sound. They saw something run across the stream of light, and they knew it was her. They took off running, trying to shine their lights in the direction of the sound. It was hard to push their feet through the thick mud and water while flashing the lights and running. Randy was cursing, and Danny was yelling as they used all their might and speed to catch Madyson.

Randy wasn't going to stop chasing Madyson, but he realized they were running deeper into the swamp, which could take them to more dangerous waters if they went the wrong way. There was no way he wasn't leaving with his prized buck. He and Danny ran until they realized they didn't hear any more steps. It was dead silent.

"I'll be damned. I know we didn't lose her again!" Randy said as he kicked up mud and water.

Danny ran his hands through his wet hair and leaned down to put his hands on his knees. He was out of breath. "She's fast as hell; I'll tell you that!"

"Oh, shut up! All of 'em can run and catch and throw." Randy spat the words through his teeth. Both men were heaving and breathing deeply, trying to catch their breath.

Randy stood up and began using his light to scan the trees. "I don't know how she managed to get away. She's got to be somewhere close." He grabbed his shotgun and began shooting up into the trees.

Danny followed suit with his light and shotgun, firing three shots into the trees. "What are you doing except waking up gators and water moccasins. There's no way she could be in the trees, man. You're just going crazy now."

"I guess not; I was hoping we'd be lucky enough to see a swamp monkey fall. Damn!" he yelled. They both started laughing.

******

Madyson was holding her breath and exhaling in short, tiny breaths. Just below her, the two white men were trying to figure out where she was. They had been shining lights and cursing, confused about how she got away and where she was.

As she ran, she realized that her only option to escape was hiding somewhere she would be hard to find. There weren't many options as she got deeper into the swamp, and the water got higher. Madyson reached for a tree and felt the body of the bald cypress. It was full of splinters, and she knew crawling it might scratch her legs, but her gymnast background meant she knew how to use her legs. She had to move and move fast, though. If the men caught her as she went up the tree, there was nothing she could do. The man, whom she now knew as Randy, was talking too much; he was griping and throwing demands, as always.

Madyson could hear his disgust with her in the tone of his voice. She moved quickly up the tree and grabbed one limb and then another. She was standing between two limbs and realized she needed to climb as high as possible so that she could blend in. Her black shorts and green top were the perfect summer fashion faux pas that would help her brown skin blend in. Madyson laid down on a branch; it was a thick one that she knew could hold her. She wrapped her legs around the base of it and rested the soles of her feet on the trunk of the tree. The men were just below her, shining their lights as Randy was cursing and trying to figure out where she was. Suddenly, both men started firing bullets upward into the trees.

Madyson's heart was racing, and her first thought was to start screaming, but she could not. Madyson began breathing in deeply and letting out slow short breaths to help her remain calm while bullets were flying inches away from her. She remembered the words of Grandma Mae, *Madyson, the real fight, the thing you must survive to live is the war in here.* She watched the guys with a slight smirk on her face; their desperation was almost comical. One minute they were arguing, the next minute they were stumbling through the swamp or shooting or cursing. Suddenly, both of the men started shooting upward again. This time the bullets and the men were even closer to her.

Madyson closed her eyes again and focused on breathing. After a few shots, they stopped. She rested for a few minutes, using the time to relax and remind herself that she had to be the woman her ancestors expected her to be -strong, bold, and unafraid. However, when she felt something touch her arm and then slide down toward her fingertips, fear ran through her body like mercury in a thermometer. She knew the snake was black because even in the moonlight, she could not see any color, only a shadow of what she felt. It was a water moccasin and a massive one, at least the size of Madyson's wrist. She knew the snake could feel her warmth, which was why she couldn't move. If the moccasin's bite didn't kill her, Randy and Danny certainly would. Science class had taught her that this was one of the most poisonous snakes, and without anti-venom a victim could die in minutes. Madyson closed her eyes and focused on being safe rather than scared. She knew that if she could just hold on, all of her fears would pass.

******

Randy and Danny had been searching the trees for what seemed like forever. Neither was sure how she managed to get away, and they thought she would've been easier to find. Danny wanted to call it a loss- let the girl try to find her way out or let alligators and snakes kill her, but the longer Randy had to search, the more he didn't want to give up. It was hard to admit that they had let a hunt getaway.

"I reckon it ain't nothing we'll see tonight," Danny said. Danny thought that if he called it quits, he could get home to his wife without a lot of lip from Randy.

"Yeah, yeah. You're already past your two-hour curfew. I will go beg your wife to let you in. Damn! Ya'll have no balls. I mean, who's the man of the house?" He said cockily.

"According to my wife-you," Danny responded. He thought back to their argument the previous night, and how his wife had told him that since keeping Randy mattered more than her, she'd make sure he didn't have to worry about a sixth child. That night she slept in a pair of tights and a long sleep shirt. Danny got the point.

"Aw shit, lemme get you back home before you pull a Joe on me. You can't afford to sleep on the porch with five kids, and she can't afford to stay mad," Randy said. They turned and started back toward the car.

"I didn't think we'd leave without her tonight; figured we'd throw her over the same bridge we threw him," Danny said.

"Ain't no way in hell we'd let her have that luxury," Randy said, imagining all the things he'd do to Madyson. "I'd like to tie her up in my shed for at least four or five days, make it slow and painful, but a whole lot of fun. I might try some stuff with this one that I ain't never tried before. With all the stuff in my shed, I'd make her pay for every hour we spent looking for her."

There was a sinister look in his eyes. He was sincere in his desires and serious about his plan. It was no longer about fulfilling his plan to torture and humiliate her; Randy wanted to avenge his honor for the tortured and harassed blacks who had gotten away. The most challenging hunt usually brought the greatest pride-whether it was deer, wild pigs, or a scared nigger. A grin eased across Randy's face as he thought of the joy he'd feel when he finally got his prey.

The twosome headed back to Danny's truck, which was parked on the side of the road. Danny hoped they wouldn't come back a third time for the same girl; they could move on to the next one. It made no sense to keep looking for her night after night in the swamp only to be evaded. Two days wasted, his wife was aggravated, and he still didn't get what they wanted. *Damn, blackies are always messing something up,* he thought to himself. He had chosen to disregard his mother's words, accusing her instead of getting soft because of old age. His mother had never outright said she didn't like blacks, but some things you just know are the family way. If his grandfather knew she was accepting food from "culuds," as he would say, he'd be rolling over in his grave. Danny could remember when he was a little boy, and the mayor of their town was having coffee with his grandfather.

The mayor said the town and city down the highway wanted to meet to discuss some of the problems they were having in the communities. His grandfather laughed and slapped his knee. "When he told them 'I'd eat gumbo from my damn dog's bowl before I sit at the table to eat and laugh with some jiggerboos,' I just about cracked my side!" he laughed with tears in the corners of his eyes. Both men leaned over in laughter. Danny knew that what he was doing would make his grandfather a hell of a lot happier than that hippie "We are One" Martin Luther King bull his mother was talking about. He was beginning to understand why his grandfather disowned his mother. He saw it in her, and when she admitted that she killed Danny's dad, Danny knew his grandfather saw that in her, too. She'd betray her own race one day. Kill her white brother and defend the coloreds.

Still, he knew tonight would be his last night in the woods with Randy for this run. He would have to catch him on the one next month if his wife weren't raising too much hell. He climbed into the passenger side of the truck and slammed the door of the old Chevy. It was the one Randy used for runs like this. He said it was easier to clean out and even reupholster if they needed to.

"You know why I really like my truck?" Randy asked.

Danny shook his head no.

"It makes me feel close to my dad," he said. "I know everybody thinks I'm just this jerk with money from my family and not a care in the world, but my daddy was the only man who understood me; you know- what I valued and respected. How much I love my family, and I love America. The way my family was nothing and my daddy opened his business when he was twenty because he wanted his piece of the American dream. That's why I have to preserve that; I have to honor him." He was smiling, which was rare.

Randy reached into his pocket and grabbed Danny's lighter to light his cigarette.

"I still can't believe I lost my daddy's lighter. That's one more reason I can't let her ass get away." Randy lit his cigarette. "It seems like I'm the only one who has any honor for my daddy these days because my ma has lost her mind. She's getting old, and she ain't doing good...not doing good at all. Anyway, she tells me that my daddy gave her the power to do what she wants with the business and our land and stuff. And you know what she tells me: that she don't trust me to be smart enough with the family business. After Brad tainted the family bloodline and my younger brother ain't worth a shit, I'm the only one that's stayed true to our family values," he said while jabbing the dashboard with his pointer finger on one hand while keeping the other hand on the steering wheel. "I guess they think Brad is the special one because he got his degrees and all, but he's a nigger lover. That shows you how stupid he is right there. That cancels out anything else. If you can't trust him with the woman he chooses, you damned sure can't trust him with the family business. He'd have niggers running the whole company in less than six months, and that's not why my daddy built it. He said once they brought Jim Crow to an end, everything went to the shits. My daddy built that company to preserve the white man and preserve the white family. What does his son do? Bring a damned nigger right through the front door and expect us to act like it's okay. Almost killed my daddy and sure hurt my mama. All the good white girls out here and all those pretty gals at the uppity college he went to, and he falls for one of the only nappy-headed pickaninnies in school. Shoulda seen how they were begging him to give that blonde hair, blue-eyed white girl another chance. And who wouldn't? She was all-American, pure white, and had a set of legs that ran straight up to her cunt. Her family had money, and they liked him. It was like he was hooked on that blackie or something. To this day, I still believe she put the voodoo on him.

You know they all do that kind of witchcraft and sorcery shit. As mad as I was at him, I feel bad for him 'cause I know she put something on him. I know she did, and he ain't been able to shake it." It was obvious that this had been brewing in Randy for a while. He was slinging his hands wildly; cigarette ashes were falling over the truck, and his eyes were beadier. Danny listened quietly, only nodding his head and saying "Yeah" or "Damned right" occasionally.

"I want white families to work without worrying about whether somebody will come to take the job just because they finally want to get off their sorry black asses or because they made it across the border after they committed all kinds of crimes in their own country. Affirmative action. I got some affirmative action, affirming my power as a natural-born American with the right to run this country the way we see fit. After all we did for this country, how dare they take bread from our mouth to give it to those no-good ass moon crickets. I see my ma every week, just like I promised daddy I would, and what kind of thanks do I get? A few more dollars in another trust fund and a couple acres of land. Where is the *honor* in that? She was always weak behind Brad, though. I remember when he married that gal; Daddy didn't even want to talk to him. She tells him, 'Well, at the end of the day, he got a right to choose who he wants. Your family didn't take too kindly to you marrying me 'cause I was dirt poor, but you did.' That was the first and only time I think my daddy thought about putting a smacking on my mama. He didn't talk to her for two or three days after that. I don't blame him one bit. What type of shit is that? I said she must've put the damned spell on my mama, too. Thank God mama was able to break that fix and understand that we needed her most."

Danny just listened. Randy's brother Brad had always been different. He wouldn't hang out with them. He and his father never saw eye to eye even before Brad started dating Grace and certainly not afterward. He sneaked around with her all through high school and stopped coming home when they got back together in college. Danny didn't think anything was right about the situation, and he could understand why they didn't like it or him, but Randy playing the "good son" card wasn't true either. He had caused his parents some trouble over the years, and while he didn't date outside the race, he brought home some wild ones until he found his wife. Even then, Randy's father told him he had to calm down because too many people heard about how he ran his house, and it wasn't good. One thing was true, though- Randy and his father had created a bond because they shared a common belief in loving and protecting their community and people. Danny always respected and admired that. Randy pulled up to Danny's house and put the truck in park.

Danny looked over at his friend, and he could see that this shook Randy. "Honoring your dad is up to the person who values him, and obviously, that's you. If you can't honor him one way, you do it another. Preserving us the way you is and looking out for us out here is the sign of a true friend. You do what's right in your heart, and your family is gonna regret selling you out," Danny told him.

"Danny, you are the friend who sticks closer than a brother. Tonight, I'm doing this for you, me, my daddy, and your granddaddy. I will see you tomorrow with good news!" They saluted each other. Danny walked up the porch to his front door where his wife was waiting with her arms crossed.

"Forgive me, Ashley; I had him running a little late. He gave me hell getting him back on time!" Randy yelled out of the driver's door. Her only reply was a clear and direct middle finger.

Randy giggled as he backed out of the driveway. He turned on his radio and sped down the road. One of his favorite country tunes was blasting lyrics about freedom, America, and the right to bear arms when his phone rang. He didn't want to miss his song on the radio, but when his phone rang a second time, he answered the call, and it blasted through the cell phone speaker.

"Hey, my number one brother," he shouted jovially into the phone.

"Hell, technically I'm your only brother," the voice on the other end said.

"You're damned right about that," Randy replied, laughing.

"Looka here, I didn't know if you heard, but they're circulating a message about some gal and her boyfriend gone missing. You heard anything about that?" he asked.

Randy knew that if his brother was calling, the police were starting to dig. "No, Billy. Why the hell would I know anything about some nappy head girl gone missing?

"Exactly!" his brother replied. "Damned Chief Deputy came all the way out here asking me if I'd heard from my brother. I told him 'Now what the hell does my brother have to do with this shit?'" Randy was quite sure Billy didn't have the guts to say it that way.

Even though the community knew of Randy's

beliefs and dealings, they never actually charged or convicted him for hate crimes. However, they also did not fully know the extent of Randy's hate crimes. They chunked it up to harassment, burning a few crosses, and using a little inappropriate language.

"You tell your chief to call me directly if he's got any concerns regarding Randy Crane. I will set that shit straight for him. That's the damned problem now; they're so quick to run and report lies as soon as one of the blacks comes crying. What has this country come to?" Randy complained.

"It wasn't so much him as it was the one they hired on the force- supposed to be the supervisor out here. Hell, he came in there with papers talking about the last cell signal was a few miles from our area, and they couldn't pick up a clear signal nowhere else, just creating lies and making a mess of things. I told the chief that's the problem with them bringing one of them out here; they don't know their place," Billy complained. Randy was quite sure Billy didn't say it like that either.

"Somebody needs to fix him. I've been tired of seeing him riding around here with his chest out like he's something special. You can't give a nigger shit without him becoming too uppity and thinking he can do what he wants," Randy barked.

"Well, I just wanted to check with you to see if you'd heard anything. If you do, let us know so I can put ole chief at ease. He said our people have always been good and upright, and he was all in a tizzy when that boy came to the office raising sand."

Randy reached in his pocket for a cigarette and Danny's lighter as he drove down the highway. "I sure will. And if I see that black boy, I will let him know personally that it would be in his best interest to mind his business," he barked.

He disconnected the call and turned the radio back up. It was another country tune to remind him that he was a free American with a passionate love for shotguns.

CHAPTER 8

"I see you made good use of the car wash today," Grace said as she walked across the room to hand Brad a glass of whiskey. She sat across from him with her wine. She closed the blinds to the window next to them in the den of the bedroom. "Lights dim," she said. The room started to go dark; then, she reached over and turned on the lamp. Brad had offered to make their home fully technology proficient, but Grace said she didn't trust that. She only wanted enough technology to make things safer and a little easier without making everyone lazy.

Brad looked up from the newspaper, smiled, and said, "I guess you took a listen today."

"No. I just watched from the window. How is he doing?" she asked.

Brad sipped from his glass and ran his fingers through his hair. "Of course, he's still in this space of figuring out and accepting things, but he is doing better than I thought he would. I think that's what bothers me."

"What?" Grace said as she stood up and began taking off the shirt and pants she had worn that day.

"He has had all of these feelings I didn't know about and all of these things he experienced. All this time I thought we were protecting them from this stuff, but they noticed. They saw. They were bothered, even if they didn't tell us. This world is shit," he said before swallowing the rest of his drink.

Grace couldn't help but chuckle a little as she tied her silk robe and walked over to sit across from her husband again. "I think it's the whiskey. Maybe I should've put the coke in there anyway. I forgot how you get when you hit the cup with no mixer. We always knew the world wasn't too nice; we just tried to create our own. Our little outing started well and ended as a disaster. Leah said I was unrealistic if I thought I could raise children who 'didn't see color.' She told me I was her oppressor." Grace said. She brought her feet up on the love seat, and Brad reached down to grab her left foot. He began rolling his thumb on the bottom of her sole and massaging her toes with his fingers.

"My baby girl," he said. "She can certainly bring the dramatics out."

"Some of what she says is right, Brad," Grace said. "No, I wasn't mean or ruling with an iron fist, but when she wanted to talk about black stories on the news or articles from social media, I immediately shut her down and called it negativity. She needed to talk, and in this house I was the only one she could relate to. I was too busy not wanting to relive my nightmares in this community, so I tried to pretend that times have changed."

"Well, they have," Brad said.

"Oh, yeah, certainly. These aren't the kids we went to school with; it's their children. Sure, they've changed a whole lot," Grace replied sarcastically.

Brad shook his head, "Well, you are certainly right there."

Grace continued. "Some of them are completely different, but many of these kids have parents who are determined to hold on to the 'good ole days' as long as they can. They don't believe in interracial marriages, playing with black children, or being too progressive. People tolerate us because of the power and money we have; they don't like us, and you know it. Your business is recognized across the South; you've been on state boards, you're in a lot of social circles, and people want to be known for knowing you. But no matter how successful we are, there are maybe three white girls whose families would approve of them dating Blake; meanwhile, the black girls just want him to give them a shot because they think he is hot- like his daddy," she added with a giggle. "But he doesn't even feel comfortable around black folks, which is largely my fault. At school, they assume he doesn't like black people and that he thinks he's better than everybody. That's like cursing the black community, and we do *not* take that lightly." Grace had to admit that even she didn't like the idea of black people who didn't like being around other black people.

"Sometimes it's strange to think about how people who have so much in common can have so much animosity toward each other- in all communities. It's not just about race, it's about money, too," Brad shook his head.

"And that Leah. She said some words that hurt my feelings today, but I took them with a grain of salt." Grace looked at Brad. "She is just like my grandmother, and it's so…so weird and scary. I was looking at her, and she even has my grandmother's eyes. We were going at it back and forth, and she wouldn't back down. It's like she's even more adamant because of what happened Friday night. It reminded me of how they tried to force my grandmother to sell our land out here because all the whites were running from the city. They wanted to take our fifty acres and make a subdivision, and she told them there was no dollar value for the land her people struggled to buy generations ago. They increased the money, asked for forty of the fifty acres, and then started making threats. They even burned a cross in our front yard, and my grandmother didn't sleep at all that night. She sat right in the front room until the next morning. I remember her calling into work and telling her boss she needed to handle some business. Her voice was rough and dry. She didn't talk to me much that morning, and she shoved me into my clothes more than she put them on me. My breakfast was a little colder than normal, and after she dropped me off at the elementary school, she sped out of the parking lot so quickly that her tires burned rubber. I later found out that my grandma's boss heard what had happened, and he was waiting for her when she got to the city hall. They say he begged her to calm down and let him handle it. Of course, you know my grandma wouldn't be hushed. They went in together, and she came out with apologies and requests for a handshake from the same people who tried to bully her. To this day, I don't know what was said, but we never had a problem again. Still, it bothers me that we were treated that way when Big Mama was such a good person and so kind to everybody she crossed. She went to church every Sunday, paid her bills on time, and minded her business. Big Mama is the same grandmother that fed her poor white neighbors and taught me the true meaning of Dr. King's words and to be upright. Most importantly, she gave love and affection to a grandchild who lost her mother and needed some guidance along the way. And I see her in Leah- strong and firm but committed to what's right. Leah isn't scared, and sometimes that's scary to me."

Brad stopped rubbing her feet for a minute and said, "Grace, what is a leader if she isn't fearless?"

"Useless," she said immediately.

"Exactly. Don't be afraid for Leah. Be afraid for this world. She's going to challenge justice and uprightness whether she is a teacher, a business owner, a store cashier, or running my company."

Grace smiled. "You had to throw that in there."

"Of course, I did. Just in case she wants to because I know she'd do a hell of a job," he said with a smile.

Grace reached down and grabbed Brad's left foot to return the same favor he'd granted her. "I can't deny it, Leah's a tough cookie. I've got to be more understanding of Leah and accept her as she is. You would think that of all the lessons my profession has taught me, the greatest one would be respecting people for who they are. She is a great leader, and she is full of passion. I have to accept who she is or risk losing my daughter, especially when she goes off to college."

Brad and Grace sat in silence for a few moments. They had been forced to realize they could not dictate who they wanted their kids to be. They had to make room for their children to show them who they were and how they applied the lessons Brad and Grace had taught them.

Grace finally broke the silence. "We talked about Blake and Leah. We even talked about Big Mama; let's talk about you."

"Hey, my kids are great, and my wife is happy. My life is good," he said, stretching his arms and then interlocking them behind his head.

"No, no, mister. That's not what I'm talking about. Have you, um, talked with your mother?" Grace's voice softened a bit, and she shifted her focus to Brad's feet.

The question was unexpected and made Brad swallow uncomfortably. "What makes you ask that?

196

You know my family doesn't have much to do with me, and Ma doesn't do much other than her dry ass Christmas card."

"Brad, I told you she's been trying to reach you."

Brad pulled his leg back and sat up. "And I don't want to talk to her. I mean, what could she want now, after all this time?"

Grace looked up at him. "She's been in a nursing home for a while now. I think you know what could be coming. You just don't know how to deal with it, and I get that."

"With what, Grace? She'll be stone-hearted like my daddy was until she dies. What sense does it make for me to call or go by, or do you think I am supposed to be the 'good son' and do what's socially right? Well, I followed my heart and did what I know is right," he said with a slight agitation in his voice. He didn't understand how Grace could try to convince him to see a woman who disowned him because he married her.

"I know you would like for me to think with my scorned wife's heart, and at first I did. But I know I was raised better than that, so I had to think with my social worker head. I also tried to think with my family head. Brad, I don't think going to see her is for you; I think it is for her." Grace slowly reached for Brad's right foot, coercing him to lean back on the love seat and allow her to rub his feet again. Grace remembered that there were pressure points in the feet, and she thought that hitting a few might ease some of the tension Brad felt.

"When they disowned me, I cut them out of my life, too. What's the need to go back just because she's in the nursing home. Nothing has changed, Grace. Why go back to that place?" He leaned his head back and rubbed his temples.

She rubbed his lower calf muscle on the back of his leg. "You've changed, and that's a big reason to go see her. You're more tolerant and patient; you're a different kind of man now. That tolerance you have and the way you negotiate with everyone should be extended to your mother this time. Besides, I went to see her," she said without looking at him.

Brad jerked his head up and looked at her in a bit of bewilderment. "You what? When? And how did that go?" She had not mentioned it even though she did suggest calling his mother when they got a letter in Brad's name. Brad had disregarded it since the letter from the nursing home said his contact was requested and needed, but not urgent.

"Well, she was surprised. She asked me what I was doing there. I told her we kept getting mail from her, and since it wasn't in my name, I didn't open it, but I was concerned. Then she talked to me, not in a friendly way, not with hugs or a reunion celebration or anything. Hell, she wouldn't even look at me very much, but she asked about the kids. How old they were. How they were doing in school- stuff like that."

"Why would she ever give a damn about our kids?" he said through tight teeth.

"Brad, her blood runs through them, too. I find it hard to believe that in all these years, she has never wondered about them. Now, I am not saying you have to go up there with flowers and hugs and kisses, but she asked about you, too. Said that she had read a few things about you in the paper and that you looked like you were doing well without their help."

"And I am. So why do I need to go see her now?"

Brad responded.

Grace paused the massage, and the softness of a loving and caring wife became stern, almost forceful with her reply. "We said we were facing our demons, but I guess our demons are only about the blackness of our children and not about the racism of your family."

"That's not fair, Grace," he countered.

Grace's eyes became enormous, and her voice grew deeper. "Not fair? Our children stood at gunpoint last night because a prick officer didn't see them as Brad Crane's kids; he saw thugs or whatever modern racist term they use. And here you are having a pissy moment when your mother is dying in the nursing home. She's a racist. We know it. She betrayed you. We know it. But Brad, you're not the only one who knows betrayal. Our children know betrayal. I know betrayal. And we still get out there and live and be decent to people who have been shitty to us." Grace pushed his foot down and stood up. "I understand your family hurt you, Brad. I know it's been painful all of these years, but how can you move past that pain if you won't even face it when it's trying to face you? Your mother wants to see you, and I just want you to reconsider."

Grace headed to the bathroom to take a shower.

******

Madyson searched for a spot dry enough for the sticks and Spanish moss she had pulled from the top of the tree. It was especially hard to find a dry patch while using only the moon for light. She used the toe of her soaked shoes to find a spot that seemed a little hard. Finally, the full moon shone on a perfect piece of solid ground and grass. She had found it just as her frustration started to grow. Not far from the spot was a tree with low limbs and a log that was partially in water and partly on land. Madyson hung her dinner on one of the low tree limbs and arranged her sticks in a pile to start a fire. She walked over to the log and pulled it further out of the water so that it was closer to her collection of sticks. She sat on the log and rested for a minute. Then, she reached into her bra for the cigarette lighter that Randy had dropped. It was a lifesaver in the swamp tonight. The sticks were slightly damp, but Madyson hoped they were dry enough to start the fire. She struck the lighter, and a small flame lit. She bent over to light the sticks, and the flame went out. She hit it again, but the twigs would not ignite. She tried again, and a small flame started and then went out.

"Damn," she muttered to herself. Madyson looked around, straining her eyes in the dark, looking for possible dry sticks. She considered getting some of the higher limbs off a tree, but she was too tired to climb again. She needed more light to see. Madyson thought for a minute. Her clothes were too wet to use. She needed something flammable. Madyson reached up and touched her head. Her hair, which was still in a bun, was starch dry. The one thing she had not gotten wet was her hair, and it was flammable. Whether it was braids or a sew-in, striking a match to a hair weave could start a brush fire. Madyson dug in her pocket for Ben's knife and grabbed a chunk of her braids. She took a minute to decide how she wanted to cut the hair for best use. She wasn't sure whether to cut near the scalp or the ends of the braids. She figured the scalp might be a little damp from sweat, so she cut halfway down the braids. The feeling of the half-cut braids touching her ears felt unnatural, so she reached up and cut each braid directly above the scalp, leaving her with a mini afro.

Madyson had shunned natural hair for years, opting for sew-in hair weaves most of the year and braids during the summer and on vacations. She faithfully relaxed her hair between styles. In conversations with other black girls, they pretended that braids and weaves were their favorite choice to make. But inside, Madyson didn't want the same stares and pleads to touch her hair that she heard her sister bicker about constantly. Besides, she felt prettier when her edges were as slick as possible, and her braids were fresh like Bo Derrick's. But tonight, she felt free and more beautiful than ever. Her scalp felt the coolness of the night, and she smiled as she ran her hand over her head. She felt connected with the moon and as if the wind were feeding her soul. Her chest felt open, and even her lips felt as if the fresh, minty air was touching them.

Madyson piled the pieces of dry braid hair on top of the sticks and struck the lighter once more. The hair instantly caught on fire, and flames engulfed the sticks. After a few minutes, the blazed calmed, and a low steady flame flickered. Madyson's eyes lit up with excitement. She had never been able to imagine herself surviving without her cell phone and certainly not in the swamp. The snake that so frightened her only a short time ago was now her dinner, and as hungry as she was, she couldn't wait to tear into it. The moccasin was big and meaty. Madyson had not seen many snakes up close other than at the zoo; even when the Girls Troop took hiking trips, she never actually saw any snakes. But tonight, she knew that if she did not kill the snake, it would probably kill her. So that's what Madyson did. When she figured out where the head was, she grabbed it quickly and began stabbing it viciously. She didn't stop until she ran out of energy; by then, she had killed it. The snake was dead, and she was hungry. Madyson had not eaten for nearly two days, but tonight she planned to feast. She pulled the skin off the snake, trying to remember what she once saw on a television show, what she had learned in nursing trauma class, and her common sense. Madyson grabbed her knife and went over to the swamp stream to rinse it off. She grabbed the snake from the tree and started prepping it by cutting its head off. She knew the venom was near the head, so she cut about two inches below it. After she had removed all the skin, she checked it once more to see if anything looked like a poisonous vein. Then she hung it over the fire and prayed a long and precise prayer that the snake would be edible and that she had gotten all of the venom out. She turned the snake a few times to make sure it was cooking evenly. When it had a crisp-cooked skin on it, she took it off the fire and broke a piece off in the thickest area to see if it was cooked inside. It was. Madyson nibbled on the piece she had broken off. It tasted like chicken with no seasoning.

"Could use some seasoning," she laughed to herself, even though she hardly knew how to cook. Truthfully, Madyson didn't care whether the snake was seasoned or not; she was hungry, and her body was depleted of energy. Madyson thought about Ben; she missed him. Ben would never believe she was in the swamp eating a snake she had killed with her own hands.

The more she nibbled on the moccasin, the more aggressively she tore into it. The more she ate, the more delicious it became. Eventually, Madyson had to catch herself because she was halfway through the five-foot snake. She allowed her body a few minutes to process the food; Madyson was sure she was fuller than she was acting, and she was right. Her tummy was sticking out and moving was a little awkward. She looked at the rest of the cooked snake, and she regretted having to throw it away, but she was already afraid of alligators and other wild animals being attracted to the smell. She slung the rest of the snake into the swamp, as far away as possible. Madyson dipped her hands in the water to rinse them off. She returned to her spot in front of the fire and sat watching the flame.

Madyson thought about her high school and college friends, and how they spent most of their time worrying about their hair and nails and doing just enough to pass classes. Their biggest worry was finishing each semester with a 3.0 even if they partied every weekend. Madyson tried to fathom how she could ever explain this experience to them. They were still caught up in the world of superficiality, where the biggest struggle was to survive three weeks without a nail refill. Their worries now seemed so vain and selfish. Being lost in the swamp and fighting for survival made Madyson reconsider how much she valued her life and the time she had with her family. She seldom thought about how easy and comfortable her life was, often behaving as if her family's comfort was the norm for everyone and a personal right—being alive when Ben had died made her shudder with guilt. Ben had understood life and valued it while she often wasted it away. There, in the swamp with nothing but hope that she could see her family again, Madyson realized that she had lived all wrong.

She sat back and leaned against a tree. The road trip with Ben had changed so quickly. They were supposed to be bragging about a jazz club in Jackson right now. Instead, she had no idea what the men had done with Ben's body, and she was trying to stay awake until daybreak so she could find her way out of the swamp. Madyson was tired. Running in the woods, killing a snake, and trying to survive were taking a toll on her. She wondered where her mother was. She knew they were looking for her. Madyson wanted to make sure she was able to be found alive. Somebody had to be able to tell what they went through. She let her mind drift back to her happy childhood days and how good life was when it was easy. A smile stretched across her face, and moments later, she fell asleep.

******

Brad rolled over and checked the time. It was almost 3 a.m. He hadn't been able to sleep well since his conversation with Grace. Despite the way his family had treated him and Grace, he knew he should see his mother, but a part of him had gained peace after so many years without them. Brad thought about the time when he saw his father at one of the annual expos. Old man Crane was laughing and drinking beer with some of the other small company owners. Brad could never forget how he felt when their eyes locked from across the building, and instead of coming to speak to his son, Old Man Crane shifted his eyes back to his backwoods business associates like he never saw Brad. That was the day when he knew he could not continue to hope his father would change. They weren't father and son anymore. They were just two men doing business their way for their reasons.

A small voice asked Brad why he thought his mother should leave his father when he wasn't willing to leave Grace? He assumed the right side of justice, fairness, and love should've been enough. But they had been raised to believe that loyalty to their own motives came before any of those things. Brad had chosen to be different, and that decision cost him some things, including the people who gave him life. Brad had no regrets in his choices, which was why his feelings about seeing his mother were so complex.

Brad sat up on the side of the bed. His racing thoughts had made him thirsty. He looked back at Grace; she was sleeping peacefully. *Probably dreaming about how many cases she closed this week,* he thought as he chuckled to himself. He went over to the tiny fridge they kept in the sitting area of their room. He opened it to check for bottles of water. It was nearly empty except for a bottle of whipped cream and a bottle of chocolate. Brad debated whether he wanted to go downstairs, but he knew he wouldn't sleep well without some water. Now that he was up, it would be a while before he dozed off again anyway. He made his way downstairs to the kitchen using the stairway that led from their bedroom to the hall. Brad was about to reach for the refrigerator handle when he saw the flash of a tablet screen. Leah was sitting at the table.

"I guess this is why I was so thirsty," he said.

Leah looked up at her father. "Hey, Dad," she said. "What are you doing up?"

"I reckon the same thing as you," he replied. "I couldn't sleep, so I came to get some water since we were out upstairs."

"So basically, you woke up and had nothing else to

do, so you came up with something to do. My dad," she laughed as she clicked the tablet screen off.

Brad turned on the light switch and walked over to sit with Leah. "And what's keeping you up?" he asked.

"Well, I was talking to Rashawn after the game, and I was just about to go to sleep when my phone and tablet got an alert. A twenty-two-year-old girl and her friend are missing. It didn't say a lot- just that they hadn't been heard from in over twenty-four hours, but it struck me," she said.

"This isn't just about two missing people you don't know. I feel like there's something more to this. What's up?" her dad asked.

Leah started tracing patterns on the table. "Dad, I am in my senior year of high school, and Mom and I still cannot see eye-to-eye on most things. Earlier today, we were supposed to be talking about that jerk cop from last night. I couldn't even get Mom to admit how jacked up this community is. I mean, she has a solution to everything, even if the solution is not realistic. There is nothing we could've done make that cop stop being who he is every day, but she doesn't want to talk about that."

"Talking about all of this isn't easy for either one of us, but it's even harder for your mom," Brad said.

"I know, Dad, and that's why I want Mom to be real with me. I'm about to be a black woman without her to run to every day, and I know the world can be a million times worse than Cradle Creek. I know this world is hard as hell for a black woman because I've had to live in it my whole life. I'm too aggressive, too outspoken, and too loud, even if I am the quietest person in the room. I'm not qualified enough even if I have the highest degree in the room. I don't know how to relate even if I've raised the children of everyone else in the room. I'm not connected enough even if I am the plug in the room. No matter how nice I am to everyone, I am the outcast."

Brad took a deep breath and ran his fingers through his hair. "I can't pretend to understand everything you go through, but your Mom is trying. We are both trying to work through the things that we have brushed under the carpet for years. Your mom is always on the side of doing what's right, even when it means ignoring herself or her feelings. She puts herself last every time for everybody. Her job. Us. Hell, she's making me go see my mom tomorrow, and my mother was an absolute monster to Grace." They both laughed.

Leah looked at her dad. "I think she's right about that, though. You have to go see your mother no matter what has happened."

"I know you are right. I just-"

"-hurt? Dad, it's okay. You have feelings, too." She touched her dad's hand. "We've been a family trying to do right by society for so long that we neglect the feelings and emotions in our own house. I know everybody thinks I am Leah the Loudmouth in this family, but I say what's inside me because I know we have feelings."

******

Leaving the woods had taken a lot of time, but Randy came back determined to catch the girl by himself. For two hours, he had been driving from one side of the wooded area to the other. There was a highway stretch that curved around to a road that connected to the swamp and a piece of open land. He had paid more attention to where they came out of the woods this time. He had no idea exactly where she was in the woods, but Randy knew she was still somewhere hiding.

He stopped and got cigarettes and a case of beer to keep him company. He leaned his head back and thought about Joe. He had not heard from him since the argument that day. He knew Joe was gone, and their friendship was, too. It wasn't just because of the wife jokes and being out late; Joe wasn't the same anymore.

"He's a damn traitor," Randy muttered to himself as he sipped his beer. "I'll be damned if Daddy didn't tell me to watch out for his type. They'll be one way when ya together and another way when they get around the blacks." Randy slammed his hand on the steering wheel.

He was still thinking about the disagreement with Joe when something on the radio caught his ear. He turned it up. "...once again, the woman missing is twenty-two-year-old Madyson Johnson of Dallas, Texas. She has brown skin and long black braided hair. She is 5' 3" and approximately 135 pounds. She was last seen driving a small red car with her friend Benjamin Spivey..." The announcer went on to describe him and a number to call if they were seen.

Randy knew he had to find her tonight. It was only a matter of time before their town was flocked with people looking for the missing pair. He changed the radio station to another that was blasting one of his favorite songs about red, white, and blue, and pride. He hoped the music would tune out the racing in his mind, but he couldn't settle down. He had to find Madyson.

TREKKED

CHAPTER 9

Randy jerked his head up and then opened his eyes. He nearly dropped his half-full beer bottle after dozing off. It had been at least two hours; he checked his watch. It was almost six in the morning, and the sun would be coming up soon. He had pulled up close to the woods to watch for a few minutes, but the few minutes watching the woods turned into the woods watching him sleep.

"Shit," he muttered. "Ain't nothing happened yet." Randy took his hat off and scratched his head, then rubbed his beard. He checked his cell phone—no messages or calls from anyone, not even his wife.

"She knows better," he said to himself. It wasn't so much that she knew better as it was that she didn't care. Less Randy at home meant less drama in the house.

Randy started his truck; he was about to put it in reverse when he smelled the faint odor of smoke. It wasn't close, but it was a lingering odor like something was burning or had just been put out. As far out as he was on the property, there was no reason for something to be burning unless it was the one family who lived on the property at the other end of the woods. He doubted it was them burning anything in the thicket behind their house. Randy knew where the smoke was coming from and that it would lead him straight to Madyson.

"When being a smart motherfucker makes you dumb," he chuckled. He put the truck in park and turned it off. He grabbed his shotgun from the seat and slid out of the truck. He reached into the pocket of his jacket for a cigarette and placed it between his dry and slightly cracked his lips. He felt around in his pocket for Danny's lighter and then struck it to light his cigarette. He took in a deep breath, partly to inhale the nicotine and partly to smell the burning woods over the glowing cigarette. She was near. He was going to get her. He rubbed on his sandy beard again and then ran his hand across his eyes. Randy pulled down on his hat, flicked the cigarette on the ground, and crushed it with the toe of his boots. He began walking toward the woods, slightly swinging his elbow as the shotgun leaned over his shoulder.

******

When Brad woke up, the conversations with his wife and daughter were still on his mind. As he stood in the bathroom brushing his teeth, he looked at himself in the mirror. With short brown curly hair, Brad was the child who looked most like his mother. His square jaw and deep green eyes made him look even more like her. As he turned on the shower, he thought about his mother's greatest flaw: not standing up to his dad. Even when she knew he was wrong and she didn't agree, she wouldn't stand up. Her words were, "We're a family, and your daddy makes a family's decision, so we all stand with him."

When Brad was a little boy, he was his daddy's most loyal cheerleader. Watching the way his daddy worked hard for them and made enough money to keep them living well made Brad want be just like him. His daddy's perspective changed when he started hearing rumors that his father didn't believe in hiring black employees for their company. Brad had never specifically heard Old Man Crane talk about race; he always talked about loving the Lord and being neighborly to each other. He bragged about being a good American and a Southern man. Brad knew the rumors were true the day he saw Old Man Crane meet with the chief of the sheriff's department. One morning, young Brad and his dad went to a meeting at a place called "The Breakfast House." It was a tiny one-room restaurant in Cradle Creek. It was wooden and so old that the front porch leaned, but it was often packed with people from the community. It was a special meeting place for the few business owners of Cradle Creek. Brad was only thirteen at the time, so he wasn't particularly interested in their conversation. However, he caught one part merely by accident, which changed the way he looked at his father.

"Well, Sheriff, they can apply as much they want to, but I ain't hiring 'em. I told you when I opened my doors ten years ago, I'm preserving and that's what I meant. Sue all they want," Old Man Crane said. He sipped his coffee.

The Sheriff leaned back and rubbed his big belly. "That's comforting to know, Crane. I will be sure and tell the boys they don't need to worry. I'll tell you they was in an upheaval, scared you might be forced to bend, but I told them 'I know Crane, and Crane is a pure-bred man. He ain't having it.'"

Old Man Crane scooped grits into his mouth. "You can bet your last damn dollar I'm not," he said.

It looked like Brad was focusing on his ham and biscuit breakfast, but he heard every word. It would be a while before he dared to ask his dad outright if he was part of the Klan. But when he did, his father's response was, "Son, I'd never be trash enough to be a part of an organization that terrorizes people; but I understand how they feel. I handle my concerns for my community in a different way." Brad could no longer doubt it. His father was a racist.

And since his father was a racist that meant his mother was supposed to be a racist, too. And their children were to carry the torch of white fear veiled by white power claims. That is what would ultimately ruin the relationship between Brad, his father, his mother, and his two brothers. He expected them to be disappointed, but he never expected his mother to be so stone hearted toward him. She cut off communication with Brad and sided with his father in not allowing him to have any part of the family business. "Whether you can improve the business or not, your practices and our beliefs don't mix. We can't help that you are family, but we can't uphold everything you do," she told him. They talked about his relationship with Grace as if it was filth and the ultimate sin. Brad was the prodigal son, and his mother declared that she prayed he would find his way back home. When he announced his plans to marry Grace, his mother spat her last words to him as if it left a bad taste in her mouth. "I never thought my son would betray our God and our bloodline."

Amidst the ugliness Barbara Crane showed to Grace, she now expected Brad to visit his mother. He wasn't going because he wanted to or because he cared how his mother felt; Brad went because he knew what Grace understood too well. Brad would have no real peace with himself if his mother died, and he didn't see her face one last time. He pulled his gray polo shirt over his head and then slid on a pair of jeans. He slid his feet into his loafers and headed downstairs.

When he got downstairs, his children were already sitting down for their Sunday breakfast. Grace had scrambled eggs, cooked little round sausages, and baked biscuits. Cinnamon rolls were in the oven.

"I guess no one could sleep much. No church today, but still up early," Brad said. He looked over and winked at Leah, who looked sleepy.

"With all the free time we had this weekend, I slept so much I was up before the sun this morning. I had to figure out something to do," Grace said.

"Mom came into our rooms claiming she was putting our clothes away, but she was so loud," Blake laughed. "And of course, all Leah needed to smell was food for her to get up."

"At least we know," Leah said with her mouth full of sausage. Her hair was tousled on top of her head in a bun.

Grace was loading the dishwasher with pots and pans when Brad sat down and began fixing his plate. "You couldn't resist going to that police department and giving them a piece of your mind, could you? I guess that was why you had to run to the office yesterday morning," she said with a smirk on her face.

Brad looked at his two children. Grace continued, "Don't worry; they already know. A few of the officers got word to folks out here, and their kids sent out a group message that made it to Blake and Leah quickly. Not too much trash talk with two hundred kids in one message, you know what I mean. Not to mention, my coworker texted me text early this morning saying her husband had just gotten off, and he was pumped about the way you handed the police chief's ass to him."

Brad responded, "Well, I wouldn't say all of that."

Grace picked up her cell phone and began scrolling

through the texts. "Said you came in like a raging white man, told them those were Brad Crane's kids, and you weren't putting up with their racist shit. The officer was in the office, and you called him all kinds of pricks and sons-of-bitches and threatened to sue. All I could do was shake my head," she laughed. "And you told the officer that if he pointed another gun at your son, you'd blow his damn balls off."

Leah bucked her eyes at Blake and they both started laughing. Even Grace couldn't stop laughing.

Brad, who was eating, put his fork down. "The more I thought about how scared all of the kids were, the angrier I got. And the fact that Rashawn's mom knew something was wrong means this is all too common, Grace. I won't have it around my kids or my kids' friends. The chief called me into the office giving me hell at first, saying he'd arrest me if I ever came into his office acting like that again. I was honestly ready for him to take me in. Then, he asked my name and said I looked familiar. When I told him my name, he apologized, claiming they didn't know they were my kids. I went from being a disgrace to the community to being Mr. Crane. I told him I didn't give a damn whose kids they were, what happened wasn't right. Rashawn's parents filed a complaint with the city, and I'm filing one, too. His dad and I are having breakfast tomorrow to talk about what we can do next. If the department doesn't address it, I'm going to the news, hell, all of the news stations."

"Well, my co-worker's husband was glad you came in this morning. Your complaint wasn't the first one they'd had about some things going on, but the complaints didn't matter because of who they are. It's shameful to think that specific people's complaints arc the only thing that matters when it comes to justice. He said the black officers deal with all kinds of stuff, but yesterday changed the tone of the office for at least a little while. Since there are only three black officers on the whole force, they are sure the new mood won't last long," Grace said.

It was quiet for a minute as the family partook in Sunday breakfast, the usual routine before church. They had decided to take a break from service to spend time together. Brad finally broke the silence. "Besides hitting the pit this afternoon, what do you guys have up for today?"

Grace went to the refrigerator for orange juice to refill her and Brad's glass. "Well, I will be finishing some notes for work and the last of the never-ending laundry for this week. The kids are going to run to the store. We need some groceries, and Leah has to get some things for a school project."

"Yeah," Leah chimed in. "We were asked to do a project on little known history. We have to make boards and have some type of artifact, even if it's a recreation. This teacher does not like technology; as a matter of fact, he still uses PowerPoint. I mean, really?"

"I like PowerPoint," Brad chimed in.

"Our point exactly," Blake shot back. Both teens started laughing.

"Yeah, yeah, yeah. Old jokes. So, what are you presenting about?"

"Big Mama's run-in with the KKK or townspeople or whatever you want to call them," Leah replied.

"Now, Leah, there's no reason to be a fire starter," Grace said as she put Brad's glass on the table.

Leah immediately looked at her dad, recalling their conversation from the night before. He locked in on her for a minute.

"Mom, how am I a fire starter?" She asked. "It's a history lesson of our choice."

"How do you know about Big Mama's run-in with the Klan?" She asked.

"It's not because my mom told me," she retorted.

Grace shot her a sharp right eye, and Leah knew she had gone a bit too far. Her eyes shifted down to her plate.

"Last year, we were setting up for the fall festival, and Sandy Billows and I disagreed about the best way to set up the ticket and food booth. Her grandma was supposed to be there to help, but she really wanted to help Sandy boss people around. When Sandy and I didn't agree, she muttered under her breath, 'She's problematic just like her grandmammy.' I knew you and Dad would have my butt if I were disrespectful, but you know I wanted to give her a piece of my mind. Instead, I just worked on something else and stayed away from them. I couldn't stop wondering what she meant by saying my 'grandmammy' was problematic, so I asked Tasha's grandma that night."

"Where was I?" Grace asked.

"Gone to the football field with Blake, and Dad was on his way behind you. I was so glad because I had been trying to get to her by myself all night. Anyway, she told me about how they wanted our land. Let me clarify that this was in the freaking 80's okay, not like 1943 or something. They had already made a full blueprint for the fifty acres and had put out the word that they would soon be accepting bids for lots on Grandma's land. The trick was they put one price for lots in the paper, and they gave people another price when they met with them in person so they could try to keep blacks out. Meanwhile, they hadn't even approached Big Mama about the land. They thought once they offered the money, she'd be sure to take it. An older woman raising her little granddaughter- she'd sure take the money. When Big Mama said no, all hell broke loose. And the white people were in an upheaval; how dare this black woman tell them no. Sandy's grandmother was one of the families who was buying a lot. But none of them could scare *my* Big Mama," she said with a big grin on her face.

"Interestingly enough, that's pretty much right. So, you want to do this project out of spite?" Grace questioned.

Leah looked at her mother in the eyes and responded, "No, I want to do this project out of pride; it's important to tell this story. This area is mostly white now, but it used to be owned by black folks. Most of them were threatened into selling their land or sold it at a cheap price, so it would be easier for them to get industrial jobs in the city since they couldn't get loans to farm. That's when white people, like my grandfather Crane, started buying land out here to run away from the city, talking about preserving the white family and moving them away from the black men who would rape their women, girls, and the black women who would lure their boys. It's just like now- the black kids at Cradle Creek High fade into the background because they feel they have no voice in this school. Many of their parents and grandparents are still scared of what people around here might do if they speak up. And look at the news- they make false claims that all black people are thugs and criminals because they really don't want to be around us. They don't fear us as criminals; they fear equality because they genuinely believe their skin makes them better than us. Nothing has changed. We always think Jim Crow was about white people wanting to be separate, but "Americans" also found it hard to watch the power gap between blacks and whites get smaller and smaller. Black folks were getting half the pay, being charged higher prices for land and houses, and getting sent to back doors, but they were still making it work. And here was Big Mama refusing to give up her property because she knew what it meant for her people. She knew what it meant for her children and grandchildren. If we can talk about anything that relates to history, I'd rather it be about something that means a lot to me." Leah gulped down the rest of her orange juice.

"Well, I think it's a great idea," Brad said as he reached across the table for the plate of eggs and sausage. There was a smile running from east to west on his face. He loved the fire in his daughter.

Grace folded her arms and looked at her husband. "And for what, Brad? So, it can cause a ruckus, and you'll run up there raising hell again? Yeah, that always works."

The kids knew by the tone in Grace's voice that the conversation was about to get heavy. They picked up their plates, put them in the trash, and headed to their rooms. Their parents rarely disagreed, especially in front of them, but they were smart enough to know that if the conversation didn't leave the room, they needed to.

"No, Grace," he said looking at her. "Because it's what she wants to do. Leah's happy, and her face lights up when she talks about Big Mama."

"Just because her face lights up, that isn't a reason to cause chaos at that school," Grace replied.

"If telling the history of this community causes chaos, then maybe they need it. What happened to Big Mama was wrong. What you saw as a little girl and how teachers and students at school treated you was wrong, and you have to stop running from it. Last night you said I had to face my problems, so it's your turn to face yours." Brad stood up to put his plate away.

"I just don't want my children to go through what I went through. When Big Mama didn't sell the land, I was bullied for the rest of the school year. Teachers tried to fail me; Big Mama had to argue about my grades all the time. They came up with fake reasons why I couldn't even try out for cheerleading, and they even tried to change my transcript when I graduated high school- years after Big Mama wouldn't sell the land. No, they didn't ask Big Mama to sell again or burn another flag, but they still let us know they were angry about it." Grace was crying, and Brad felt guilty, but she needed to get it out. "One day, some girls cornered me in the bathroom, and they tried to beat me up. They said my Big Mama and I were coons who didn't know their place. The only thing that stopped them was my English teacher, Mr. Briggs. He saw them come in the restroom behind me, and he came to the door and called them out. He told them that if he caught them harassing me again, he'd personally call the police. Mr. Briggs was gone at the end of the year. When you and I started dating," Grace looked upward and wrapped her arms around herself, "It was no better. I was an 'uppity nigger' and all kinds of stuff under people's breath. My two black friends and I had to be home before dark; that's why you always had to come to visit me. That didn't matter anyway because your parents would've never let me set foot in their house. Big

Mama trusted me; hell, she trusted you; she just didn't trust the community. You don't know what it's like because as much as you love me and us and you are trying to embrace all that comes with our family, you are still a white man, and life is different." Brad leaned over and wrapped his arms around his wife. Her back went up and down, and her tears soaked his shirt. Grace had never unloaded the burden of being black in their community; she had decided to hide in a quiet life. It was safe for her, but it had been a burden for her until now.

"Oh, Grace, I'm so sorry," he mumbled with his face in her hair. He rubbed her back and held her.

She looked up at him with her eyes still muddled with tears. "But it's true- you can't hide from your family anymore, and I can't hide from mine. I have to respect what Leah wants to do because she is becoming a woman, too. Big Mama's story is special to her, and I never want to hide that from our children. Even more so, I don't want Leah to resent me and think I am ashamed of us. I was only trying to protect my children."

As Grace sobbed, she realized the heaviness she'd been carrying for years was finally gone; crying made her feel so much lighter. She had accepted the pain of her Cradle Creek chronicles as an integrated part of being a black woman. The very thing she often told her clients to avoid was nestled into her life like uncomfortable comfort- complacency had become her norm. The pain of Cradle Creek haunted her, but she accepted it as part of her life while trying to avoid making it part of her. That had not worked; the amalgamation had caused Grace to live in private emotional pain that pretended to be caution and concern but was projected as resentfulness. When hate ran deep as it did in Cradle Creek, one could not simply smother it with love. Hatred had to be called out and dismantled instead of being covered like a pot that would boil over when it was too much to be contained.

Grace finally lifted her head and wiped her cheek. "Who knew how much Friday night would change our family?"

"I think something had to change us," Brad replied. "Thank you for not backing down on me. I'm going to see my mom. You are right; I have to face my challenges, too."

Grace didn't say anything; she just smiled. She seemed calm, and the pink in her eyes was fading back to white. Brad knew she was okay.

"You'll be glad to know I'm heading to the nursing home. I won't be gone very long, but I am going to talk with my mother," Brad said as he stood up. "How about you relax for a change? The kids and I will handle everything when we get back."

"I think I can handle that," Grace replied.

Brad leaned down to kiss his wife on the forehead before grabbing his jacket and heading to the front door.

******

Madyson felt a nudge in her stomach. She opened her eyes and in the center of her stomach was the barrel of a shotgun. At the other end of it was a man with brownish-blonde hair hanging scraggly from underneath his ball cap. Madyson knew who he was, and he knew who she was. He shoved the gun into her stomach.

"I guess the bitch finally ran out of luck!" he said. "Get up. Get up!"

Madyson was frozen for a minute. She had not meant to fall asleep, but she was so tired that she had dozed off. Pain was surging through her head again and shooting directly to the knot on her forehead. Madyson squinted her eyes and looked up; she was face-to-face with her hunter. Madyson slid back against the tree, trying to get away from the gun, but Randy shoved into her stomach again, making her wince in pain.

"What do you want from me?" Madyson asked with her voice quivering.

"Shut up!" He said, "I will do all the damned talking. The last thing I need to hear is your voice whining and begging for a chance to live. Been sitting out here all night looking for you; I almost gave up and quit like the two flunkies I had with me. Just as I was about to leave, luck led me right to you. Your best option is to do exactly what I say, and that will make this quick for you."

Madyson knew "this" meant death, but she was determined to fight until her last breath. Looking into Randy's wicked eyes only made her want to fight harder. It was like staring at the devil; his pupils were black, and the whites of his eyes were red. He was so confident that he had finally won. Randy didn't believe Madyson had a chance to survive, and she knew it. They were staring eye to eye when a loud splash scared Randy. For a second, his focus was broken as he turned to see what the noise was; Madyson jerked from under the barrel of the gun and turned to run, hoping to climb up the small hill behind her. Randy grabbed her leg and began pulling; Madyson kicked, hoping to land a foot to his face. But before she could, he pulled her down and got on top of her. His face was only centimeters from hers. His breath was stale. He smelled like a combination of fish and old sweat. He made Madyson's stomach turn; she wanted to vomit, but she held back. Randy rubbed his hand between her legs and began massaging her crouch. He started pulling her shorts down, getting them just below her hips.

"There's one thing I forgot to tell you; a fighter turns me on, makes me rock hard. I ain't never had me a piece of a nigger girl anyway." He was tugging at his pants' button. "I'll finally get to find out what my brother likes about ya'll so much."

"Please, no!" she begged him.

"Don't waste your breath, gal. Ain't a damned thing you can say that's gonna make this easy for you," he said back.

Madyson had to think fast. Her first thought was to fight him, but she decided that fighting might not be her best option. She looked around and saw a large stick. It was about as thick as her wrist, and it was within arm's reach. Madyson looked down at Randy, who was still working his pants down. When he had them just below his waist, Madyson grabbed the stick and swung it to his head, striking him on his temple. Randy fell to the side, and Madyson rolled over on her stomach as quickly as she could. She got up, pulled her shorts up, and began running as fast as she could. She could hear Randy getting up.

"I'm going to get your black ass," he yelled. He fired one shot. Then he fired another. Both missed her.

Madyson heard Randy's footsteps gaining, but she didn't look back. She was running more slowly than usual; she knew she was tired. She took a deep breath, determined to run faster, but as she exhaled, Madyson felt a blow to her head. Suddenly, everything was black.

******

Leah and Blake pulled into the store parking lot.

"The real blessing of missing church this morning is not having to be in the store on a Sunday evening. Look at this parking lot; it's as empty as the club next to a Baptist church," Blake blurted.

"Remember that time we saw a church and a club in the same shopping center? It's like listening to Lecrae on Sunday after turning up to some old school Juvenile on a Saturday," Leah laughed.

Blake shook his head, "What a contradiction."

"Sometimes a little contradiction is how you get some balance," Leah followed up.

Leah parked the car near the front of Super Mart and got out. She and Blake found a shopping cart in the parking lot, and Leah pushed it into the store. Rashawn had gotten out of his car and was running to meet them; he took the cart from Leah's hand. They began walking the aisles together.

Blake was sure he was a bit more excited to see Rashawn than Leah was. He had not spoken with or seen him since the night at the movies, but Rashawn had asked Leah how Blake was doing. Blake had thought about Rashawn and wanted to call him, but he wasn't sure how to start the conversation.

"Hey, Rashawn!" Blake said excitedly. "Has everything been cool with you?"

Rashawn knew what he meant. "Oh, yeah, man; it's been all good. I was a little shook up that night, but the next day I was fine. What about you?"

"I've been okay," Blake said. Rashawn saw him look

at the ground when he said it.

"You get used to it," he told Blake. "Not okay with it but used to it. Before we leave this store, somebody will think we are stealing. Even if they have no reason to, they will assume we are. They are going to follow us a couple of aisles, maybe even go out of their way to act like we need help. I have learned to focus less on what they do and more on how I respond. I used to get all upset and angry about it, but then I was the only one feeling that way. They go on and do it to the next customer, and they don't feel bad," Rashawn explained. They turned the cart down another aisle.

There they saw a white employee pushing a cart filled with boxes and cans. They had just seen him on the previous aisle. He looked up and flashed a smile. Instead of putting anything on the shelf, he kept shuffling through the same boxes in his shopping cart.

"I mean, what the hell can we steal on the vegetable aisle?" Rashawn said with a slight chuckle.

"Do you ever report people like that?" Blake asked.

Rashawn reached for a can of green beans and began tossing it in the air and catching it. "For what? Most times, the managers are the ones who tell them to do it. The fact that we don't do this stuff proves enough, and don't say that too loudly," he said, pointing at Leah.

"I already heard," Leah chimed in. She had been pretending to look up coupons on her phone while listening to the entire conversation.

"She *will* call the manager and corporate or go to the store's social media page and leave a horrible rating and message. I had to beg her to stop doing that stuff. One time I went to school and one of my teammates said, 'Man, your girl went in on that department store!' I was so embarrassed." He put the can back on the shelf. He looked at the man who had moved down the aisle closer to them, "Then, they miss the people who don't look like me and are stealing jewelry, TVs, and all kinds of stuff right under their nose. When I see it, I don't say anything!" He laughed again.

The employee finally turned around and took a brief look in their basket. "Do you guys need help with anything?"

"Nope!" Leah said sharply.

"If you need anything, just come get me. I am right here." He stepped a little closer and glanced in the buggy again. "In the future, you can order your products online, and we will have them ready for you at the door."

Leah's head jerked around sharply, and she struggled to hold her words back. Rashawn rubbed her back and continued to laugh. "It's just a way of life, and honestly, a look and a rotten attitude aren't even that crucial."

The employee followed them a little longer until they crossed the aisle and went toward the school supply section of the store. Blake looked back at him one more time. Rashawn remembered that look from the movies.

"My mom and dad are also in the NAACP, so that makes a difference, too. They have local trainings and conferences for people my age, so we know how to handle problems like this. They teach us laws, our rights, and stuff like that. It's always free, and you get the best lunch ever. You should come to one; your sister's been," he said with a grin on his face.

She put her finger up to her lip. "Shhhh. Mom still doesn't know; I had her drop me off at the arcade that day. It was pretty cool, too. I learned a lot, so I'm going to the next one. One of the session leaders nicknamed me 'Young Harriet,'" she laughed and polished her nails on her shirt then blew on them. "Now, enough of this male bonding. I still have half a list of things to get, and you have practice for the big game tomorrow," Leah said to Rashawn.

"I am still not happy; I don't care if it is for the playoffs. I prayed for us at early morning service; that should've been enough," he said as he shot an imaginary ball.

They continued to get items on the list. Blake and Rashawn spent the rest of the time talking sports and arguing about the best players.

"I'll admit, you've got a pretty mean arm, lil bro. I showed my brother some of your videos, and he wants to meet you," Rashawn said.

Blake smiled. He felt connected, and it wasn't by trauma or blackness. It was love and brotherhood. He'd never known that feeling from someone who wasn't his dad.

******

Brad walked down the hall and stopped at room 218. The name Barbara Crane was on a tiny white rectangle that had been slid into the sign slot on the door. There was a wreath on the door and a tag hanging from it. Brad knew it wasn't likely that his brothers sent it, so he checked the label. *You are loved, Grace, Brad, & the kids*, it read. He expected nothing different. So much of Grace was just like her grandmother. Brad pushed the door open, and he could see the back of his mother's head. Her hair was in its usually short style and tapered at the neck. Her once solid brown hair was now all gray. She, wearing a soft pink robe with yellow and light blue flowers on it, was sitting in her wheelchair by the window.

"Mom," Brad said as he entered the room. "It's me-"

"Brad," she finished. She turned her head to the right slightly, and then her chair followed. She surveyed him, starting at the top of his head and going down to his feet. "It's been so long since I've seen you," she said softly.

"Yes, it has been," he said, standing face to face with her. He sat in a chair against the wall. "How are you?"

"I suppose I'm as good as I can be for a dying woman," she said.

Brad wasn't sure what to say, so he said, "I'm sorry to hear that, Mom."

"Don't feel sorry for me. Don't ever feel sorry for me. I've had a decent life, even after your daddy died ten years ago. There were some things I missed, but quite often that was my choice, no matter how foolish the choice may have been," she looked down at her dress. "How's life for you? Don't talk to me like a stranger; just talk to me."

Brad didn't know how to not talk to her as though she weren't a stranger. After nearly twenty years of not talking with her, she had become a stranger. However, he concluded that this moment wasn't about him; it was for his mother. It was she who needed this meeting, so he put his anger and hurt aside to make what might be their only visit a pleasant one. Brad reached back to his memories of his time with her as a little boy. He was her heart, and she doted over him. Barbara took pride in everything she did for Brad-whether she was fixing his school lunches, ironing every wrinkle out of his clothes, or brushing his hair. From that place of childhood love and happiness, he talked to her.

"Business has been great over the past few years. We went from local supply contracts to state and now the entire Southern region. I've been able to add a few new people to the team and even add on to the current building. God has blessed us," Brad said with a smile on his face.

"Yes, I heard about your article in the Southern Construction Digest. You've done so well, Brad. And the children, how are they?" she said, looking out of the window.

Brad knew she had already asked Grace these questions; maybe she just wanted to hear his answers. "They are amazing kids, Mom. Leah is an honor student and is involved in all kinds of activities at school. Blake plays ball, and scouts are talking about him already. You know we stay on him about those grades, and he maintains."

"Good parents do good things for their kids, so I know you are doing just that. The last time I saw them," she said, looking down at her hand, "you were in the grocery store. I was in the fruit section, and you were checking out. That little girl had long curly hair. That boy was chunky and giggling up a storm, reminded me of your father. I reckon they look a lot different now."

Brad took out his phone and began showing her a few pictures of the children. She stared long and hard at a picture of Brad with each child on his side. Suddenly, teardrops hit the phone screen. She tried to wipe her eyes, but the tears continued to fall.

Brad stood up and walked toward the window. He couldn't understand why she had the right to cry. His parents had disowned him by choice. They told him he wasn't welcome. Barbara didn't even call or try to sneak to see them. Here, in her room, she even admitted that she had seen him and the kids in public and didn't even speak.

"Don't mind my tears," she said. "Sometimes, you look back and realize some things weren't worth it. After your dad died, pride was the only thing that kept me from reaching out to you. I didn't know how to tell you that I was wrong and that I wanted to see my grandbabies."

"Humph," Brad said. He was at a loss for words. Her grandbabies. She didn't even deserve the pride of using such words to refer to his children.

"Can I show you something?" she asked.

Brad looked back at her. "Sure."

"Gimme that box over there," she said, pointing to a box under a coffee table by her bed.

Brad bent down and picked up the box. He handed it to his mother, who took the top off. Inside was a stack of newspapers. She took the first one out, unfolded it, and handed it to Brad. She took another one out, unfolded it, and gave it to Brad. She took out a stack of carefully cut articles and handed them to Brad. He thumbed through them, scanning the titles and pages. They were articles about him- his company's new location, the company's expansion, the company's big contract, the company's holiday give-a-way, and other stories about his company. Then, there was an article that made him stop. It was an article about Blake being recognized for varsity accomplishments during his freshman year of high school. *Her blood runs through their veins, too,* Grace's voice played over in his head. Brad's mother handed him one more piece of paper. It was a newspaper photo of Leah being honored for all A's during the school year.

"My decision may not have been the best, but I thought about ya'll all the time," she said. "You were my firstborn, the one who made me a mother and the sweetest baby out of all my sons. No matter what happens, a mama can never forget that." She looked over at Brad, who was still staring down at the articles.

He looked up at her. "Mama, why now? All these years you went without talking to us. Never called or asked to come by, and you knew where we were, so why now?" he begged.

"I've wanted to call you since the day your father died, but pride and guilt wouldn't let me do it. I even picked up the phone a few times, but I put it back down. I just didn't know what to say...or how to say it...or if you wanted to hear it. I know your wife told you to come 'cause she came to see me first. She showed up on a day when I didn't care if I was coming or going in the next five minutes. I knew you were coming when she said she would talk to you; I just didn't know when. I didn't know how to tell her thank you; kinda hard to look somebody in the eye that you treated so badly. I just sat here patiently waiting each day, but I had no doubt that Grace would get you here."

Brad couldn't believe she said Grace's name. She had called Grace many things, but none of them was her name. Most of them were not pleasant. He didn't know if life had changed her or if Grace's kindness had moved her.

"They say I have four months, Brad," she

continued. "And I know it ain't no lie; I can feel it. I didn't want to leave this earth and never have seen your face again." She looked down at her hands. Brad sat down in the chair again.

Barbara took a deep breath. "There's some business I have to handle regarding the family, and I want to talk to you about it if you don't mind." Brad nodded for her to go on. "When your daddy died, he left everything to me- the business, the land, the house, and the money, of course. He told me I was free to do whatever I wanted when he was gone; he just wanted me to be happy. I don't want the family business to go down. It meant so much to this family and this community. Truth is, my other two boys ain't equipped to handle it. Randy would have all kinds of scheming and plotting going on, and Billy would run it into the ground before the first year is up. I want somebody who knows what they are doing and will keep the business for maybe another few years. Would be nice to keep our name on it. So, I wanted to talk to you about it."

Brad was shocked. His mother was making an offer that had been his childhood dream. And often, he had still considered what he could have achieved if he could have merged his father's logging business with his architect and construction company.

"What do I owe for something like this?" Brad questioned, figuring the price would not be so much financial as emotional. Who would he have to leave? What stipulations would there be?

"Nothing at all. I figure I already charged a hefty enough price you didn't deserve to pay. Regarding the land, I left each of your brothers some twenty acres, and I left you sixty. To balance it out, I gave them a little more money, though I know money is the last thing that matters to you. That's what the letter was about. I know you didn't want to read mail from me after all these years, but I thought that would be the easiest way to get it to you," she said.

Brad had a hodgepodge of emotions running through his veins and head and heart. He was angry that his mother thought this was supposed to fix all the years he was without her. He was a bit sad that she didn't have long to be with him. Brad couldn't deny his happiness in knowing his dream would come true. Yet, he felt so much confusion about how all of this came about so quickly.

"Brad," Barbara said softly, "please forgive me."

A tear slid down Brad's face. He got on his knees to put his arms around his mother. She kissed the top of his head and allowed the warmth of their hearts to swallow the moment.

******

Five women stood before Madyson again. *Maybe they are here to get me this time,* she thought. They were still so beautiful and so peaceful as they came toward her. The swamp was no longer scary, dark, and wet. She could see light streaming between the tall trees, and the beauty of the women manifested beauty all around. "Grandmother," Madyson said. "Grandmothers," she corrected herself. "You can take me with you. I am okay. I am at peace."

"You are almost home, dear child. Do not give up," her grandmother whispered. "We are carrying you. You can do this. Reach in, Madyson. Push out. You are almost there." Then, as quickly as they came, they were gone.

A splash of water woke Madyson; she leaned her head back and gasped for air. For a moment, she was bewildered and had forgotten what happened. When she saw Randy in dirty jeans that were wet below the knees and a confederate shirt with holes in it, she remembered everything- the swamp, the woods, and this man.

Randy let out a sinister laugh. "You thought you could outsmart me, you little black bitch," he said.

Madyson tried to lunge at Randy, but her arms were bound behind her back. She looked down, and her feet had been bound. "I underestimated you. I did, Madyson. When I saw you, I thought you were a little rich whore who wouldn't last a minute out here. I thought you'd be an easy catch and a fun prey, but you have proven me wrong. I guess all of ya'll have a little gorilla in you. Uppity nigger or poor ghetto nigger, you're all the same," he said, circling around her.

Randy leaned close to her face, breathing his hot breath directly into her nose. "I'll never let you win." He grabbed Madyson by the throat and began choking her. "This is going to be long, and it will not be fun. I'm going to fuck you in every way possible."

Madyson could hear the filth in his voice. He meant every word of it, and she knew he did. She could see it in his eyes- hate, anger, and death. He wasn't looking at Madyson; he was looking through her, at something deeper. It was what fueled his rage and what he felt justified his torture. Madyson knew she wasn't his first victim. He had done this before, and with each chase, he felt energy and thrill. Today, she had to decide what she wanted her fate to be. Ben was already gone; if she died, there would be no one to tell the story about what this maniacal man had put them and others through.

Who knew how many people he had killed, tortured, and terrorized. Madyson looked up at his face. For the first time in her life, she felt hate. Randy's words angered Madyson in a way she'd never experienced. She jerked at him again, imagining her hands already around his throat. This is what her mother wanted her to avoid. This is what made her father shudder when they drove down isolated highways at night. But tonight, Madyson refused to shiver or give in.

She used her tongue to reach to the back of her throat, and foamy, watery spit landed on Randy's face. "To hell with you," Madyson said.

The saliva hit Randy like a bullet, and his neck swiveled to the side. He was in disbelief for a moment, and then his anger quickly took over. Randy pulled his fist back and punched Madyson in the eye, hitting her so hard that she fell backward onto the ground. He sprung up and began pacing the ground.

"This is the shit my daddy was talking about," he said aloud to himself. "One day, they will think they can take over. They will believe they are equal to you and challenge your authority and power as a purebred white man. We must preserve our communities," he muttered. "We must stand our ground. We must show the world that we are the only true Americans; we are the best in the world."

Randy appeared to have entered a zone of psychosis, focusing more on talking to himself in a chant-like tone. He was walking in a circle with his shotgun downward next to his leg. While lying on her side, Madyson had figured out the pattern of knots behind her arms, and she was working the rope to loosen it. She had rubbed her ankles enough to loosen the rope tied around her ankles.

Randy suddenly snapped out of his daze and turned to Madyson. "I'm going to kill you," he said. He started to pull his gun upward. Before he could get a clear aim, Madyson sprang up and jumped to her feet. The sudden move startled Randy, and he was a bit stifled. She took advantage of this, shoved him to the ground, and took off running full speed through the woods. This time she felt energy as if she were being carried on the wings of her five grandmothers. Madyson didn't feel the swamp, the mud, the sticks or logs, or any animals beneath her feet. They barely touched the ground, and she didn't feel winded as she sucked in air and propelled forward.

It took a minute for Randy to regain his composure, but he got up from the ground and began shooting at Madyson. Randy took off running behind her, firing his gun over and over again. He could barely keep up with her as she ran with the speed and lightness of a young doe.

Madyson had no idea how close or how far away Randy was. She tried not to focus on him but to focus on her pace. Her shoes were now mostly torn apart from the soles, but she didn't care. Madyson could hear the bullets firing, and when one struck the tree next to her head, she almost halted. She remembered the directions of her ancestors, her mother's face, and her last conversation with Ben; Madyson picked up speed and ran as fast and hard as she could.

CHAPTER 10

Brad pulled into the garage and put the truck in park. He thought about his visit with his mom and how his life had suddenly changed. He opened the envelope with the information about his mother's will. Brad was now the owner of his father's company and most of their land. Since Barbara felt she was not in good enough health to manage everything, she decided to start signing over the business and a portion of the property to Brad while she was alive. The money and other policies would fall into place when she died. He still had mixed feelings. He was excited to own the portion of land that wasn't far from their current property. However, he wasn't sure how his brothers would react when they learned that he had the business and most of the land. Randy had always been jealous, and if he could convince Billy to be mad, it would be a whirlwind of hell. Brad scanned the first few paragraphs of the document; everything seemed standard. The land and company had been passed to her by his father. The money was an independent policy she took out and one his father had taken out. Brad would have his attorney contact his mother's attorney on Monday morning just to make sure all paperwork was in order. Barbara had even talked to Brad about being power-of-attorney should her illness put her in a state where she could not make decisions. It was a big undertaking, and Brad told her he would think about it. He just didn't know if it was worth the hell Randy would bring.

He had promised his mother he would bring Leah and Blake to see her. He was curious about how they would respond, and honestly, whether he'd have to bribe them to go. It wouldn't be fair to make them feel forced to meet a woman who had been absent their entire life. They had learned to adapt to life with no grandparents and making them meet Barbara when she was nearly on her death bed was a big and drastic move. Still, he hoped they would agree for the sake of his mother. He would take an honest approach to the situation and hope they were feeling sympathetic.

Brad shoved the papers into the envelope and took it with him as he got out of the car and headed into the house. Grace was lying on the couch, watching television.

"Aw...this is a rare sight. You are watching television!" Brad exclaimed.

Grace had a pile of unfolded clothes at the end of the couch; she had draped one of the sheets over her legs.

"My employee told me about all of these movies on Teleflix, and I had no idea what she was talking about. I texted her and asked for a list of some of the shows and movies she tells me about. I've been binge-watching all morning. Brad, so much of life has passed me by. I have to watch more TV," she said.

Brad chuckled. "Grace, you choose always to find something to do even when everything is done. I take my movie nights with pride, and Teleflix is the best app ever. When I get time, I sneak and watch a few movies at work," he replied.

"You naughty, naughty boss," she laughed.

Brad walked over to her and leaned down to kiss her on the lips. "Well, if you consider coming home, we can sneak some movies in together," he smiled.

"I've been looking and researching. There are some great part-time work-from-home opportunities out there. Mr. Crane, you might be onto something," she said with a grin on her face.

"Yes!" he said as he did a fist pump. Brad knew he was close to convincing Grace to leave her job. Even if Grace decided to work from home, Brad figured he might be able to squeeze in a few more home-cooked meals and a little more nookie. Having the kids and his wife at home over the weekend had only increased Brad's desire for his wife to retire early.

"The more I'm home the more projects I will find for you," Grace laughed.

"And that's okay because I'm sure we can work something out," he laughed.

Grace pulled the sheet off her legs and started to fold clothes. Brad walked over and began helping her.

"On a more serious note, how was your visit with your mom?" she asked.

Brad finished folding a pair of pants and picked up a dry towel. "It was awkward at first. Then it was awkward some more. Then, she made me emotional."

"You must've found out she's been keeping up with the family," Grace said.

He looked up at his wife. "All these years. I have to be honest, I don't know how Mom could've gone all these years collecting this stuff and never said anything."

"I could tell it burdened her, Brad. Sometimes a bull will keep ramming its head into the same fence even if it hurts," she said.

"Grace, I have no idea what the hell that means," he laughed.

"I forgot you are a numbers man," she laughed. "Some people are just stubborn, even if it hurts. Now, of course, your daddy would've outright divorced your mother if she would've ever had any kind of communication with me."

Brad and Grace had finished folding the clothes, so they began putting them back into the clothes basket in neat stacks.

"Yeah, I felt sad for my mom today, but right is right and wrong is wrong," he replied.

"I am sure your father thought that family is family and black people are- well, you know," she said. "One thing you know for sure is that she never stopped thinking about you, and she always believed in you. You and your mother grew up in two different eras. You were a white man who had an education and access to a little money when you left. Where would your mother have gone if she left your father for you? Oh, that's right- back to a shotgun house in Mississippi where they probably would've called your dad and beat her to death for leaving him to defend her son who married a black girl. Yeah, that's realistic, Brad."

Brad stared at her, "I guess I never really thought of it that way."

Grace pushed the basket to the side. "I'm not saying she's right, and hell, I'm not saying that I am an advocate for your mother. She could've done more than she did, and she chose not to. I am saying that she's your mother; she messed things up, but she is trying to fix it before it's too late. I hope you will let her see the kids."

Brad took in his wife's words. He pursed his lips and gave a slight nod. "I just feel it is their decision."

Grace nodded her head. "I agree, but I hope you will use the same power of influence you have with investors and contractors when you approach this with our children."

"I guess I should try to work the BC magic. I think talking over a plate of grilled chicken and shrimp is a good place to start," Brad checked the clock. "They should be home any minute. I'm going to head to the back to clean and set up the pit."

"Sounds good. I'll start the potatoes for the potato salad after I put the clothes away," Grace followed up.

******

"Let me tell you something; you and Rashawn can slow down on the male bonding, okay?" Leah joked.

"What are you talking about?" Blake laughed.

"Um, he was barely talking to me in the store, and I even had my hair in my high ponytail that he likes. Ya'll were talking sports and making plans without me included. You will not steal my man!" she said waving her finger in the air and pretending to be upset.

"Sis, don't get mad because everybody loves the Blake Crane charm; now, he's like a bro to me. You wanted me to get to know him better and wham! I think I have a new best friend!" Blake reached down into a plastic bag that sat in front of his feet. He pulled out some snacks he had gotten from the store.

"Yeah, yeah. You just remember that if there is no more Rashawn and me, you have no best friend, so back off!" she laughed. Leah was glad to see Blake bonding with Rashawn, but she couldn't resist poking fun.

"Ooooh, straight for the heart!" Blake said.

Leah turned on the road that led to their house. The sun was almost near the center of the sky; the perfect cool breeze was blowing. The leaves were just beginning to change colors, and they were breaking way from tree branches and fluttering down to the ground.

"When the seasons are changing, it's like being in a new town. It's so freaking beautiful," Leah said.

"And the football season is so much cooler. I actually don't mind wearing my uniform anymore," Blake said.

"Yeah, you only have like four games left, but it looks like you may go to the playoffs this year. I don't know how you do it. I would never be able to play in that uniform," Leah said, shaking her head.

Blake flexed his muscles. "You just have to be the man on the field," he said; then, he kissed his muscle. He looked up just in time to see a familiar vehicle parked on the side of the road. "Hey, isn't that Uncle Randy's truck?"

Leah looked. "I don't know; I don't even pay attention to him. And that's *your* uncle Randy. I could never claim that racist pig. Maybe a damned alligator got him," she said.

They continued down the road until they arrived at the long driveway to their house. Leah turned down the rock driveway. Their father and mother were parked under the closed garage, so Leah pulled up in front of it. They got out of the car and began unloading the grocery bags. Blake grabbed the larger bags, and Leah grabbed the smaller ones.

"I hope you can justify all the stuff you bought. If not, Mom is going to take it out of your budget," Blake said.

"Um, everything I bought is for my project!" Leah objected.

"A new dress!" Blake blurted out.

"Presentation options," she rebutted quickly. "I can

tell you don't have a girlfriend yet. I have to prepare you, Blake." Leah grabbed the last two bags and headed into the side door that led to the kitchen.

Blake was getting the empty juice bottle, chip bags, and half of an eaten honey bun out of the car. His pet peeve was dirtying the car as soon as it had been cleaned. He threw the items into the trash can and looked in the center console for the wet wipes. He began wiping the seat down; he was fully focused on cleaning the seat when he heard what sounded like an animal crying. Blake looked up and around. He stepped away from the car but saw nothing. He went back to the seat and gave it one final wipe; Leah had made her way back to the car.

"What's taking so long?" she asked. "Oh, I forgot you cleaned the car yesterday, so it has to sparkle for a while."

"I'm on my way," Blake replied. He looked toward the direction of the sound again. "I heard something a minute ago; I thought there was a hurt deer or something out here."

Before he could finish his sentence, he heard it again. This time it sounded like a low cry for help.

"Did you hear that?" he said.

"Yeah, "Leah replied. "Sounds like it's behind the shed." They headed toward the shed. They heard the sound again, so they ran closer. Just on the other side of the shed was something lying on the ground. As they got closer, they could tell it was a person. A young woman who looked like a teen. She was a little older than Leah but much younger than their mom.

Blake got to her first; he kneeled beside her. One of her eyes was swollen; her nose was bleeding. There was a blueish-purple knot protruding from her forehead.

Her clothes were wet and torn, and she had no shoes on her feet. She was caked in mud, and it was apparent that she had come out of the woods. Blake tried to wake her, but she would not respond. Her hands were cold, and her face was pale.

"Go get Mom. Hurry! I don't know if she's dead or what!" Blake panicked.

"Calm down. She's not dead," Leah stated as she reached down to find the girl's pulse. "She's just unconscious, but she's pretty banged up. This is crazy, but I think she's the girl they were talking about on the news and social media. I'll be back; I'm going to get Mom." Leah stood up and ran toward the house.

Madyson rolled her head back and groaned softly. She rolled onto her side and groaned. Coughing erupted from her throat, sounding as if it were coming from the pit of her stomach. Madyson rolled onto her back again; she wanted to get up, but she felt as if she had been hit by a Mack truck. She held her eyes closed for a bit longer; she was afraid to open them. She heard voices, but she was not sure whose they were or where she was. She was glad to hear voices and even to be lying down, but she was still afraid of where she might be. She started to cry.

"It's okay. We won't hurt you," she heard a soft male voice say. "My sister went to get help." She felt a hand on her forehead. The touch calmed her, and she finally had the courage to open her eyes. She squinted her eyes open, and the bright sun barged its way in through the tiny cracks. She closed them again, slowly trying to pry them open once again.

"Don't rush yourself. You're okay now," Blake told her. Madyson closed her eyes again. She could hear footsteps coming in her direction. It sounded like more than one person.

"Oh, goodness," she heard a woman's voice. "What the hell?"

She heard the footsteps grow closer. Then, she felt the swish of air as the woman kneeled next to her beside the boy.

"Mom, we kept hearing noises, and we went to see what it was. I think she's the girl they were looking for. I, I don't know how she got here, but she's, she's in terrible shape!" Blake stammered.

Grace looked Madyson over, rechecking her pulse. Then she checked Madyson's fever and pinched the back of Madyson's hand to see if she was dehydrated.

"She has a slight fever," Grace mumbled. She sat back on her feet and stared at the girl for a minute. Grace was just as confused as her children. They lived on a piece of land that was mostly surrounded by woods. The woods eventually became the swamp, and it was hell for anybody to get through them. On the other side of the swamp was a wooded area, and the dead-end road that the state had left incomplete. How Madyson had made it through the swamp was incomprehensible to Grace, who had seen the ugliest parts of this land.

"It's okay. Calm down, sweetie. Calm down," Grace said as she stroked Madyson's head. "Let's just pick her up and get her into the house. Leah, give me that bottle of water; she is dehydrated. Go tell your dad he needs to get around here immediately," Grace commanded. She put the water bottle up to the girl's lips and tried to coach her to drink it. "You have to drink a little, okay. I know it hurts, but it will help you."

Madyson began sipping the water, taking bigger gulps as she felt the coolness of the water travel through her body. Finally, she opened her eyes and met the eyes of a beautiful, brown-faced woman with soft features to match her soft voice. Next to her was a khaki-colored boy with dark hair that was in short ringlets. His eyes were soft brown, and he had a stocky build. Madyson burst into tears again. She was finally safe.

"Okay. It's okay," Grace told her.

The boy and his mother slid their arms under her and helped her to her feet. Madyson could barely stand up, so Grace and Blake put their arms underneath hers. Grace looked up and saw her husband at the front door. Grace could already see the panic in his eyes.

"Let's get her on the porch," Grace said. "Brad, can you get some towels and a blanket to wrap her up? We have to get some of this mud off her. Leah, can you grab the first aid kit from our office and call the ambulance?" Brad ran back into the house.

Madyson was struggling to breathe, but she needed to tell them that Randy was somewhere behind her. "He, the ma-," she struggled to say.

"Sh, sh, just be quiet," Grace told her. "You're going to be okay. Let me ask you a question. Are you Madyson Johnson?"

Madyson nodded her head. "Yes, yes, I am," she mumbled.

"Your picture was on the news this morning. There was an alert out looking for you. We will call the police as soon as we get in the house," she told Madyson.

"He, he-" she struggled to say.

"Stop trying to talk," Grace told her. "You are safe now." They walked toward the house, moving slowly with Madyson. As they got near the front steps, Blake bent down to help Madyson lift her legs. Suddenly,

Grace and Blake heard rustling coming from the woods as if something were running toward them. Grace immediately thought of deer or possibly a bear that might have followed Madyson. Just as they looked behind them, a man came stumbling out of the woods, nearly falling as he ran into their yard.

"Freeze, damn it! Freeze, right now!" he yelled.

Grace jerked her head around, and her eyes enlarged at the sight of a man holding a shotgun toward them.

"Randy!" Grace yelled. "What are you doing here?"

"You let that black bitch go. I've been hunting her for days, and she's mine to do what I like with her," he yelled like a crazy man. His eyes were wild and unfocused; his voice sounded like a loud rattle. He was muddy and wet; his beard was matted to his face.

"No, Uncle Randy!" Blake said, "You can't do that. We have to take her to get help."

"I ain't the uncle of no nigger boy," he said. "And she ain't nowhere near sick the way she had me running through the swamp the past few days. It's about time she was worn down. I got her beat, and I'm taking her in. That's my hunt, and I want her now! And I'll kill every coon out here if I have to." Randy was still pointing his gun at them.

Brad had just grabbed the towels and headed toward the front door when he heard a man's raspy voice. No one came to visit them without calling, and their nearest neighbor was a quarter of a mile down the road. He opened the front door and walked onto the porch.

"Randy?!" he said, uncertain of his eyes since he had not seen his brother in so long.

Randy looked over at him. He had not seen Brad up

close in over a year.

"Well, I'll be damned. If it ain't this nigger loving son-of-a-bitch. I shoulda known you wasn't far away. You might as well come on over here with your little family. I can get rid of all ya'll unless you wanna cooperate," Randy said while aiming his gun back and forth between Brad and Madyson.

Brad knew his brother was serious. Ever since they were kids, Randy was the ominous one with a dark side. Randy was always torturing animals, talking about fighting, getting in trouble at school for pulling pranks, and bullying his classmates. If Randy said he was going to do something, he meant just that. Brad had to think of a plan quickly because he was staring down the barrel of Randy's shotgun.

******

Leah had finally found the first aid kit, and she expected her family to be on the porch by the time she got there. She had heard the door shut once, so she knew her dad had already made it outside. However, it was strangely quiet. Leah sat the kit on the sofa and paused a few steps from the front door. She slowly reached for the handle, and then she heard Randy's voice. Leah brought her hand back down. She leaned to the side of the door and looked out of the long glass window. Randy was holding everyone at gunpoint, and she realized that it was his truck they had seen on the side of the road. Leah was quite sure he had something to do with the girl's disappearance. Her family was in trouble. She peeked outside again; her dad was with her mother, brother, and Madyson. He was trying to calm Randy down. Leah left the living room and went back toward the mudroom where the side door would take her to the garage. Leah tried to move as quietly as possible, careful not to alert Randy. She entered the side door of the garage. Leah looked along the wall and spotted a long plastic trunk with a lock on it.

Damn, she thought. She had to move quickly because every minute counted. If only her parents kept guns in the house like ordinary people, but they didn't. Her mama was too worried about Leah or Blake having easy access to one. They had a security system and stun guns in the house; they kept handguns locked cases in the car, and the hunting guns were stored safely in the garage.

Leah ran back into the house and looked at the key rack. It was no way her parents would leave the keys there; it was too easy for Blake and Leah to get them. She was right; none of the keys were small enough to fit the safety lock. Leah thought for a minute. The one place her parents knew Leah and Blake would never invade was their bedroom; they were right. While her dad did not make a big deal about it, Grace would reinforce the rule of parental privacy with a punishment so strong they'd be praying for the light of day.

"Always knock before entering. If we aren't home, don't go in unless we say you can. I can smell children, especially your musty brother. So, I will know if you went into our room," she once told them. Leah and Blake were scared because they knew she meant it, but today was an exception and an emergency.

Leah opened her parents' door and looked around the room. Hiding the key in the jewelry box was too obvious. The closets were too big. She scanned the room a little longer. Her parents owned a safe, but that didn't seem logical since her dad did shoot sometimes. Her eyes fell on the nightstands. There was one on each side of the bed. Leah ran over to the side where her father usually slept and checked in the top drawer. A devotional for men and a bible. A notepad. A stack of one-hundred-dollar bills. No keys. She checked the bottom drawer. Completely empty. No keys. Though it seemed less likely, Leah ran to her mother's side of the bed. She opened the top drawer—a journal for women, a bible, three pens, and a silk headscarf. No keys. She hesitated for a minute and then decided she might as well check the bottom drawer.

"What the hell?" she muttered.

Leah found a tube of Sensual Stimulation oil, an object that felt like a giant ballpoint pen with no tip tucked into a black drawstring bag and some balls that went from small to large. "I don't want to know," she said to herself. She eventually closed her eyes and felt with her hands because she was getting distracted by the surprises. In the back, Leah felt a small box. She pulled it out and found two small keys inside. They looked like the perfect size keys to fit a gunrack lock. Leah ran downstairs and looked out of the window. She could see in Randy's eyes that he was angry. Her father was still trying to talk to him, but Randy was doing more yelling than listening. That was nothing new.

Leah looked down the driveway and saw a sheriff's car pulling up. She saw the number on the unit; she knew it was Brad's other brother. Billy had arrived, and she wasn't sure why, because he would be of no help. God had given him balls, but he had no idea how to use them. He would do more begging than asserting the law, especially when it came to Randy.

Leah ran to the garage and gently opened the door. She walked over to the gunrack and stuck one of the keys into the hole. After a few jiggles, the lock came open. Leah reached inside and grabbed the long cold steel. She grabbed one of the packages from the bottom of the gunrack and ran back into the house toward the front door.

Leah stood to the side of the door and gently twisted the knob until the door clicked open. Leah stuck the back of the gun in the crack and pushed it open. Randy had made everyone move away from the steps and now his back was to her. Leah tried to push the door open a little more, and it suddenly creaked. Randy turned and saw Leah at the door with her legs spread apart and the shotgun up to her eye.

"I don't mean any disrespect, but I suggest you drop that gun, or I'm going to blow your brains all over that police truck," Leah blurted out.

"Now Leah, ain't no use in you comin' out here with that. We already got enough problems, and I got this here under control," Billy said.

"Right, *Uncle* Billy," Leah said while not lowering her gun. She started walking toward the front of the porch and continued talking. "Just like you have everything else under control. Yeah, we know that's control then. I saw you from the window out here acting all lukewarm, as usual. Don't want to call a spade a spade because you don't want to make anybody mad. You don't want daddy mad, and you don't want Randy mad even though you know Randy is wrong. He is on my family's property, holding my family at gunpoint after he has tortured this poor woman. And what are you doing? Standing out there, begging him to do the right thing, something he's never done in his crooked life."

Billy turned red. "See, that's your damned problem, Leah. You never know when to shut your mouth! Brad talk to this gal of yourn," he yelled angrily.

Leah's mouth dropped. "Gal?" she blurted out. Billy never had the gall to speak up about anything else, but Leah had made him angry.

"Leah, that's still your uncle!" Brad interjected. He was more worried about Leah than concerned about Billy's feelings. Leah lowered the gun so that her face could be seen, but she kept it aimed from the middle of her chest.

"Sorry, Daddy, I've gotta get this off my mind," she started. "Now *Uncle* Billy, how can you talk to your niece like that? The niece who has held on to your family's little secret for the past four months. I didn't tell anybody how Bella is pregnant for one of the blackest boys your family ever met. I mean, he has it all- gold teeth, rims, and drives a Caprice Classic. Then, he dropped out of high school; you know ya'll think we all drop out of high school- "

Billy was gasping for air. He didn't know where to begin his rebuttal.

"Are you kidding me! Are ya'll really just going to nigger up the whole gotdamn family?" Randy looked at Billy and shrieked in anger.

"Well, Uncle Randy, in his defense, Bella was terrified of coming home to tell him. That's how she ended up calling me even though she wouldn't say two words to me during the years we were at the same school. So, he's just as racist as you are. He tried to get Bella to have an abortion, but she said no. She said she thought her parents didn't believe in abortions. I told her that the exception is if the baby is black, you know, like Blake and me. Then, your white family believes you can abort it, and the Lord will forgive you. Or you can be a good Christian and keep the black baby, so you can carry them around like a purse to show people that you aren't as prejudiced as we know you are. Obviously, Uncle Billy isn't a good Christian," Leah continued.

"I never told your daddy to abort-," Billy blasted.

"Oh, I know you didn't do that. You would never do that because my daddy would have kicked your ass and you know it. Let's not major in the minors, Uncle. Bella's got you a black grandbaby coming, and you've been trying to hide it. You've never been the type to stand up for anything so don't try to get mouthy today, especially when you should be thanking me. I kept the secret this whole time, but today when your brother has my daddy at gunpoint, you say I talk too much. No, you don't talk enough." This time Leah cocked the gun and put it back up to her eye.

A smile slid over Grace's face. "You know she's good for it. I taught her everything she knows, and she shoots just like her Big Mama."

Blake and Grace were still holding on to Madyson. Brad was staring at Randy, who was eyeballing him back. Everybody in Cradle Creek knew that Grace's Big Mama could fire a shot through a keyhole. It was the thing that made a lot of people back down from harassing her. Leah looked like Big Mama, talked like Big Mama, and was trained by Grace. Randy planned on killing, but he didn't plan on being killed today. His body relaxed, and he put the point of the gun down. Brad quickly grabbed it from him and took the bullets out.

Leah didn't drop her gun; she didn't trust Randy.

"Come on, ya'll," she told them. When her mama, Blake, and Madyson had made it to the porch, Leah finally dropped her gun. She knew her daddy had some unfinished business with his brothers.

"Are you going to arrest him or make me whip his ass in my front yard, Billy?" Brad said.

Billy took the handcuffs out of his back pocket and fumbled around before grabbing Randy's hands and putting them behind his back.

"Brad, why do we have to do things like this?" Billy asked. "I mean, we are brothers. Can't we talk this out?"

"I ain't got shit to say to him," Randy muttered.

"Well, there you have it. It's no use in doing something nobody wants," Brad said.

"I am damned sure ain't talking to a traitor," Randy cut in.

Brad ran his fingers through his hair. "A traitor? Because of who I married? Dad was a racist, and he was wrong. Is that the family legacy I'm supposed to uphold?"

"First off, our daddy was never wrong, you hear me? NEVER! He was right back then. He predicted the future; look at us now. Our borders are overrun with Mexicans. The damned policed can't even shoot when they feel scared, so who's supposed to protect us? The white man feels powerless. I know our sweet Bella would never lay down with a black roach, but my baby brother's too scared to holler rape for fear they'll take his job the minute one of those jabber monkeys hollers racism. Daddy predicted it all. And committed the ultimate betrayal by crossing lines with them," he said. Then, Randy spat on the ground.

"You've spent your whole life blaming your bull

crap on others. It's always something that somebody else did, never what you did! Then, you complain and complain about everything," Brad said.

"What I did? Well, let's talk about what I did. I took care of Dad and have been taking care of Mom. Billy comes around when he can, and you do nothing, of course. Guess who mom decides to leave the family business to?" Randy was fuming as he spoke.

Brad laughed and looked over at Billy. "The family left me; I didn't leave the family. My father said I wasn't welcome in his house again, even if I got a divorce. I never asked for the business and certainly never thought Mama would call me."

"Exactly! But you've always been her favorite, no matter what low-down shit you did. I bet daddy's rolling over in his grave." Randy had his fists clenched, but he wouldn't dare test Brad.

"Well, let's be honest. What would you do with the business, Randy? You ever ran a business before? No. Did either of you finish school? No. Randy, you'd have the feds investigating your ass before the first two years were up. Do you know what's so crazy about this? You were okay with taking care of Mom because you were so sure she'd give you the company. Hell, I'm sure you weren't even the one going up there most of the time. I know you," Brad blurted out.

Randy scrunched up his face and yelled, "Hell, my wife or me! It doesn't matter. We still took care of her while you were up here like a fat rat hiring all the damned Mexicans who can't even speak American!"

"You're a damned idiot," Brad said calmly. He'd had an epiphany that his brother was beyond reasoning. His hate ran so deep that there was no logic in him, and Randy was too proud of who he was. It made no sense to keep yelling and arguing with a person who had no intentions of changing.

Billy had been quiet but feeling excluded suddenly made him furious. Though he had no desire to take the family business, it made him angry that he was not considered an option by either brother. "Ya'll act like you two's the only sons. I didn't get no say-so either. I got the same treatment as Randy- a little land and a little money. What about me? Why can't I run the business?" he said.

Randy fell over in laughter, but Brad knew he was serious. "No disrespect Billy, but you don't even know how much is in your bank account. Your wife writes the checks and keeps the checkbook; half of the time, it's at the casino with her. I think you need to ask her if you can run the business; however, I'm sure she'd say yeah and bet every dollar on the roulette table," Brad said. "I didn't make the decision; Mom did. Frankly, I'm thankful. Besides, Randy will never be able to run the business anyway after today. He's on his way to prison for life."

"For chasing that hag through the woods?" Billy questioned.

"No, for running her and her friend off the road and trying to kill them. For burning a cross in my employees' yard." Brad looked at Randy and continued, "And whatever else you, Danny, and Joe have done out here, sick bastards! I got a call earlier, and they said Joe broke down at the sheriff's department and told them everything. I heard they were looking for you, but I didn't believe it. Imagine my surprise when you landed right in my yard. So, Billy comes running out here like he can save you. Both of you get your filthy asses off my property," Brad told him.

Billy was shocked. "I just came to do my job," he said.

"Bullshit, Billy," Brad said.

Billy still had Randy's hands pinned behind his back; he pointed to the police car. "I guess you'll need to come down to the sheriff's office to fill out paperwork," Billy muttered.

Blake had been watching from the door, partly for the ambulance and mostly out of concern for his dad. Just as he saw Billy about to leave, he rushed out the door and down the stairs.

"Hold up, officer. There's no need to rush. I called the department and explained the situation. They are headed out with back up. We wouldn't want Randy to suddenly disappear," he told Billy.

"See, that's the shit I'm talking about. You can't control your family. These, these- "Billy started.

"These what?" Brad asked.

"You know I wasn't thinking anything like that," he said as he waved his finger.

"Then what were you thinking, Billy? Huh?" Brad tested him.

Billy squinted his eyes and glared at his brother. "I've always been good to you, Brad. I've never treated you the same way as everybody else. I told people I was your brother with pride."

Brad glared back. "For whose benefit, Billy? What would I gain from you telling people we were brothers? But there was quite a bit for you to gain. So, don't act like you did me any favors."

"And who the hell do you think respects a man who turns his back on his family?" Billy threw the words out of his mouth like fast-paced baseballs.

Brad walked over and stood face-to-face with Billy.

"You are no different than the rest of them. Mom, Dad, all of you are a disgrace. You might not say the same things, but you go along with it. When it came to being a man and taking a stand for what is right, you chose our evil ass bloodline every time. I've spent years bearing the pain of my family's hate, trying to figure out how to deal with you all and still lead and love my family. I felt so guilty because a part of me was just trying to preserve a connection to my heritage and my family, but I've never been able to identify with you people anyway. I'm done. I don't need you; my wife and my kids are all I've ever needed. Both of you sons of bitches stay away from my family, but you tell my niece Bella if she needs anything she can come here. I know how it feels when your family is more hung up on prejudice than love."

Brad's words infuriated Randy. He couldn't take it anymore; he looked at Billy. "You ain't never been nothing but a damned wuss. You're the law, and you still can't keep things in check around here!"

Randy suddenly jerked his hands out of Billy's grip. Instead of cuffing Randy, Billy had only gripped his wrists between his fingers. Randy reached for Billy's gun and began wrestling it out of his holster. Before Randy could get it focused, the sound of a gunshot echoed through the air. For a moment, time froze, and everyone stood still.

There was a round hole through the center of the front door of Brad and Grace's home. The door opened and standing on the other side was Leah with the shotgun still up to her eye. Randy was lying on the ground with a shot through his chest, and blood was seeping into the grass. Leah lowered the gun slowly and looked at her father, whose eyes locked on with hers.

Leah slowly lowered the weapon, and Graced removed it from her hands, then laid it against the wall next to the door.

"No!" Billy wailed as he fell to the ground and covered his brother's body will his. He was weeping as Brad stood watching; Blake walked to his dad and put his arm around his back.

Leah, her mother, and Madyson walked out the door and down the steps. Police units and the ambulance were speeding up the driveway. Their lights were flashing, and rocks were flying as they pulled up in front of the house. A burgundy sedan followed the first responders.

"Those are my parents," Madyson told Grace and Leah as tears filled her eyes. Leah began to cry, too. Grace was trying to hold back. They stood in the driveway with their arms around Madyson. Madyson's parents got out of their vehicle. Karen ran to embrace her daughter. Upon seeing Madyson's face, she burst into tears, wailing almost uncontrollably. Karen cupped Madyson's face with her hands. "Look what they did to my baby. Your face! Your hair!"

Madyson grabbed her mother's hand. "Mama, it's okay. I'm still here. I'm still here."

Karen looked into Madyson's eyes as if she were lost in them for a moment. Madyson was different, still her child, but different. "Yes, you are, and that is all that matters," Karen said. She laid her head on Madyson's chest, and Madyson rubbed her mother's hair as she wept. "Oh, God," she cried. "My baby is alive."

Madyson pulled her mother back and pointed to Grace and Leah. "These are the women who saved me," she told her mother.

"Thank you," Karen said as she grabbed the hands of Grace and Leah. The four women embraced, interlocking their arms and resting on each other's shoulders. The paramedics got the bed from the truck, wheeled it over to Madyson, and directed her to lie down.

"Wait," Madyson directed them as they passed Brad and Blake, who were talking to her father. Madyson reached her hand out, and Brad and Blake reached back. "Thank you so much," Madyson said.

"No thanks necessary," Brad responded. Blake squeezed her hand. Brad and Madyson's father shook hands just before the medic headed to the back of the unit with her mother and father following behind.

Grace looked at her daughter. She no longer saw a child who didn't understand her power. She saw a young woman who listened to all the things she had been taught and loved and understood who she was. "You are strong and fearless. You are amazing and powerful. Today, you saved our family, and I am so proud of the woman you are," Grace said.

Leah smiled. "I am Big Mama's grandchild and Grace Crane's daughter." They embraced each other tightly, and a tear slid down Grace's cheek.

Trekked Discussion Questions

1. Do you think Ben was an extremist in his beliefs

and values? Why or why not?

2. What are some of the mother/ daughter relationships in the book? Discuss how these relationships play a significant role in the lives of the characters in the book.

3. Do you think Joe is truly a racist? Why or why not?

4. Why do you think Grace struggled to address her personal issues with race and her community?

5. Old Man Crane or the former Sheriff of Cradle Creek: Which type of racism seems worst-corporate concealed or overt?

6. If Ben had lived, would Madyson's experience in the woods have been the same? Why or why not?

7. How is Rashawn Blackston significant in this novel?

8. Barbara Crane, Brad's mother, attributes her actions to her responsibility and obligation as a wife. Do you agree with her actions toward her son? Why or why not?

9. In what ways are the issues women deal with present and relevant in this book?

10. Compare and contrast Madyson and Leah. How are their paths similar? How are they different?

11. Think about Blake at the beginning of the book. Think about Blake at the end of the book. How has he changed?

12. Besides racism, what are some other issues in Cradle Creek?

13. Which woman in the book is your favorite? Which woman is your least favorite? Why?

ABOUT THE AUTHOR

Jamie Mayes is a native of DeRidder, Louisiana and a citizen of Monroe, Louisiana. Jamie has a Bachelor of Arts in English with minors in Communication Studies and African American Studies from Louisiana State University in Baton Rouge, Louisiana. She has a Master of Art in Teaching from the University of Louisiana at Monroe and an Education Specialist degree in Instructional Leadership from Northcentral University.

For twelve years, Jamie was an English and Creative Writing educator in the public-school system, where she shared her passion for literature and education with her students. For the past ten years she has also traveled about sharing hope and inspiration through writing workshops and public speaking engagements. Jamie is the author of seven published books, including a cookbook co-authored with her son, Lee. Jamie believes that writing is a healing and teaching mechanism that can empower humanity. Through writing and speaking, Jamie has found her joy and ability to impact others' lives positively.

The once cocooned worm inside of me is now a beautiful butterfly that has been set free. -Jamie Mayes

www.ingramcontent.com/pod-product-compliance
Lightning Source LLC
Chambersburg PA
CBHW070858250626
47159CB00003B/1107